GOODBYE HAMILTON

It seemed the clouds that had darkened so much of Maisie's early life had really cleared away. Free at last from a disastrous marriage, she had also become a best-selling author with her very first book—all about Hamilton, the remarkable horse who existed only in her imagination, but had nonetheless proved to be a real guide, philosopher and friend. Now she was to be married again and Hamilton marked the occasion by taking a wife himself—a mare called Begonia. So the outlook was fair; but perhaps Maisie was destined never to know happiness untouched by sorrow; and certainly the next few years would bring their share of fresh troubles. Luckily Hamilton and Begonia would be there to provide support in winning through...

GOODBYE HAMILTON

CATHERINE COOKSON

CHIVERS PRESS

Library of Congress Cataloging-in-Publication Data

Cookson, Catherine.
   Goodbye Hamilton / Catherine Cookson.
      p.   cm.
   ISBN 0–7927–1595–0 (hardcover).
   ISBN 0–7927–1594–2 (softcover)
   1. Large type books.   I. Title.
[PR6053.O525G66   1993]   92–47258
823′.914—dc20   CIP

British Library Cataloguing in Publication Data available

This Large Print edition is published by Chivers Press, England, and by Chivers North America, 1993.

Published in the U.S. by arrangement with Sanford J. Greenburger Associates and in the British Commonwealth with William Heinemann Ltd on behalf of Reed International Books Ltd.

U.K. Softcover ISBN 0 7451 3470 X
U.S. Softcover ISBN 0 7927 1594 2

Copyright © Catherine Cookson 1984

Photoset, printed and bound in Great Britain by
REDWOOD PRESS LIMITED, Melksham, Wiltshire

GOODBYE HAMILTON

CHAPTER ONE

The sun was shining; it was a beautiful day; and I was going to be married for the second time. But with what a difference! The first time had been a more than quiet affair in the Registry Office, to a man who, I can truthfully say, tortured me for thirteen years, and who finally tried to prove me insane because I talked to an imaginary horse.

Well, yes, I did talk to an imaginary horse; I talked to him because I was lonely and lost. But I'm not lonely or lost any more. And strangely I haven't seen Hamilton, as I called him, since that day on the ship when Nardy declared his love for me. At times, I've felt he was still there lurking in the background, but he has never put in a real appearance.

It was eight o'clock on the morning of this very special day and I was sitting in the little study room of my house in Fellburn where I wrote *Hamilton*. I say, of my house, but it was to be mine no longer, not as a home, for I was to let my stepfather George Carter and his second wife and her children live here; I was to take up residence, as Nardy put it, in London.

Nardy's is a beautiful house; he was brought up in it, and he loved it in, strangely, the same way that I loved this house. Yet I had no reason to love this house, for I had suffered in it practically since the day I was born. Being of extreme plainness, and having a deformed arm, I was a trial to my mother, then easy prey for the man and his sister who coveted the house and what it

1

held and who could only get it by his taking me on through marriage.

Yet it was the continuous hell experienced in my childhood, my youth, and my womanhood which created that one compensation, Hamilton.

That is not quite true, however, for in George my stepfather, that big ungainly loud-voiced individual, I had a champion; and in his mother also. Oh yes, indeed in Gran, for it was her rough humour that had saved me from utter despair more than once. And then I must not forget my flesh and blood companion, Bill, my bull terrier. How I loved that ugly animal.

And there was one more very important man who came into my life at that time, the doctor, Doctor Mike Kane, brusque, bearded, and grumpy. At first, I disliked him wholeheartedly, then grew to respect and love him. And it was really he who brought Hamilton into being. After my mother had almost disfigured me with her fists, then told him I'd received my injuries through falling downstairs, he had looked at me and said, 'Come! Come! Tell me what happened; I'd always thought you had a lot of horse sense.' And that term, horse sense, he frequently applied to me. And so, you could say, it was he who created Hamilton, that beautiful stallion with the white flowing mane and tail, and the wise eyes, and his love of the ridiculous, which, after all, amounted really to the essence of my own spirit and the hunger of my soul for love and companionship...

But all my friends would be round me today, not only the old ones but the new ones too. My! My! The number of people whom Nardy had

2

brought from London had filled the main hotel in the town. Oh, and I must not forget all my neighbours in the Terrace. These people who had ignored me for years and thought I was the luckiest girl alive when Howard Stickle the assistant manager of a tailor's shop had deigned to look at me in the first place, then marry me. I knew that their opinion was that I should go down on my knees and thank God for such a break. And the odd thing about it was, they kept to that same opinion for years, right up to the day he was exposed in court as a sadist, a man who would stop at nothing to gain his ends, which were to bring into this house the woman he had been living with on the side for years, and the children he had given her. He had even gone as far as to consider murder: the stair rods hadn't become loose on their own.

But why did I stand such treatment? The simple answer is, this house. It was all I had in those days, that and my dog.

Still, that was all in the past, for on this day I was to be married to my Nardy. Nardy is an abbreviation of Leonard. It sounds silly, but I loved it, and him. Oh, yes, how I loved him.

At the thought, I put my good arm tightly around my waist and hugged myself; then sat back in the chair and closed my eyes. Was I really going to walk up the aisle of a church on the arm of George, and be married to my loved one by a minister? Yes, yes, I was.

The Reverend Hobson was a very understanding man. The two previous ministers whom we had approached hadn't been so. I was a divorced woman, and being the innocent party cut no ice. Strangely, I didn't feel a woman at all. I felt a girl, and I was a girl, because I was in love for the first time in my life; I was really happy for the first time in my life.

Of course, Father Mackin had been round. He had looked at me ruefully, raised his eyebrows and said, 'You are aware that me hands are tied?' and I had said, 'Yes, Father, and I'm sorry.' And he'd answered, 'You're not a bit sorry,' but he had smiled as he said it, and he wished me happiness ... I like him. I like Father Mackin...

'Are you comin' for your breakfast, lass? They've nearly all finished. You don't want to collapse in the aisle, do you? If you do they'll have to stick you on that horse an' get you up there, eh?' Gran's laughter filled the room and the hallway where she stood with the door in her hand, her wrinkled ageless face abeam. She stepped further into the room as I rose from the desk, and her head on one side, she said, 'We never hear of him these days, do we, your Hamilton?'

'No.' I went up to her and took her hand and as we walked from the room, I said, 'No, we don't, do we? But he's still there ready to gallop all over you, and don't you forget it.' I pulled her arm tighter into my side and we looked at each other, and our exchanged glances held feelings we couldn't put into words.

George was crossing the hall, his big face red and shining. He thumbed over his shoulder while saying, 'That lot in there—pigs, guts, hog, and artful, that's what they are. I've never seen so much grub shovelled away. You thought I could eat when I was a lad, but two of that four are

4

females.' And to this Gran answered as she now walked past him, 'Well, you took them on.'

I looked at George and shook my head, indicating that he should make no retort. Gran always got a dig in when she could about her only son's saddling himself with a woman who already had four bairns. Yet she was fond of Mary, at least they didn't quarrel. At the same time, though, she didn't look upon Mary's children as real grandchildren because they had not come through her son.

'She never lets up, does she?' George was bending down to me now, whispering, 'One of these days I'll come back at her, I will. Where's Mary?'

'She's upstairs making the beds. And you must never do that, come back at her.'

'No; I know. Anyway, lass'—his face went into a big beam—'it's come, your weddin' day.' He caught hold of both my hands now and drew me towards him. And I looked up at this man, the only person who had brought any brightness into my childhood days. I had loved him dearly. I still did.

'And gettin' a grand fellow, the best in the world. The only thing is'—his voice changed and he straightened up—'what the hell am I goin' to look like in that grey rig-out eh? Me in tails! Oh my God!' He again thumbed towards the kitchen. 'She nearly wet herself yesterday when I tried the gear on. But what'll happen when I'm goin' up that aisle with you? I tell you, she'll let you down: if she doesn't bellow she'll snigger.'

'No, she won't. And let me tell you something, Georgie: you'll look splendid in grey tails and

5

your topper.'

'Eeh! God above. That topper! It's a good job we're not leavin' by Mam's street else they'd be rollin' in the gutters. I'm tellin' you, 'cos let's face it, Maisie, I'm not built for that kind of rig-out. I'm too bulky.'

'You're not, you're just right, and you'll look the smartest man there.'

'Oh aye. Well, if you say so, Maisie. But fancy'—he screwed up his face—'being able to hire togs like that. I wonder who had that suit on last?'

'Somebody with the itch, no doubt,' I said, laughing.

'Aw! you.' He pushed me in the shoulder, and when I staggered slightly his big hand gripped my arm and pulled me forward again. Then his voice low, he said, 'There won't be much time for talkin' after this, but ... but I just want to say again, thank you, Maisie, for lettin' us stay here. I never thought in my wildest dreams I'd ever come back to this house.'

'It should have been yours really, Georgie, in the first place. You were her husband, she should have left it to you. And then that devil wouldn't have got his claws into me.'

'Well, hair goes the way the wind blows, lass, an' if things hadn't worked out as they did, although they were hell for you, I doubt if you'd be standin' here the day. Nor me either.' And his face going into a grin again, he said, 'Talkin' of wind, on me long treks I had an assistant driver. He was an educated bloke. How he come to be on the road, I don't know, he never said, but he was always spouting poetry. And he used to say,

"The wind bloweth where it listeth, and thou hearest the sound thereof, but canst not tell whence it cometh, and whither it goeth." And you can imagine what my reply was to that, can't you?'

'Yes, I can,' I said, pushing him. 'You've got a crude mind, Georgie Carter. You'd catch on to anything like that and remember it word perfect, wouldn't you!'

'Aye, I take after me mother. And I'll tell you another thing,' he now said: 'Nardy's Big Top friends, they think we're a lot of Geordie aborigines up here. I heard one of them say to his mate, "You should hear him talk, not that you'll understand him, but you should hear him." They meant me. I was talking to Jimmy Tyler in the pub last night. I'm tellin' you they think we've just been dug up, prehistoric like. By! lad, I laid it on thick just for them.'

He was laughing, he wasn't upset by it all. He now left me and bounded up the stairs. And I went on into the kitchen where his four adopted children were still at the table eating, and on my entrance their chatter subsided. They were apt to be more subdued in my presence because Auntie Maisie was someone of importance, she had written a book and it was a best-seller. And because of it, she was going to marry a gentleman, her publisher indeed, and live in London, and had let them have this house and they had to behave themselves.

I had heard them being lectured in different ways by their mother, their stepfather, and their step-grandmother, but they amounted to the same thing, they'd all be out on their necks if they didn't behave.

I smiled at them and said, 'It'll soon be time for your getting ready,' to which Betty, who was fifteen and the eldest, answered, 'It's the first time I've ever been a bridesmaid, Auntie Maisie.' Her voice and face looked serious. But when her brother John put in on a splutter, 'And never the blushing bride. That was on the television the other night, a fellow was singin' it,' Betty said, 'Oh you!' and slapped out at him. But Gran shouted, 'There's one thing I can promise you, me lad, if you don't finish that plate and scarper you'll never live to be a bridegroom.'

'Perhaps he'll turn out to be a groom to Aunt Maisie's horse.'

There was utter silence in the kitchen for a moment; then an explosion of laughter, and I looked at Gordon who was the youngest and who was blushing to the roots of his red hair, and I ruffled it, saying, 'Well, he could do just that.' And I asked him, 'What would you be?' For answer he looked at his brother and, quietly, he said, 'I'd be assistant groom to our John.'

He had a nice nature had Gordon, he'd never hurt anyone knowingly. I liked all four children but I think I favoured Betty and Gordon above John and Kitty. Then we were all brought back from a hypothetical future to the present by Gran's shouting, 'Well, you two grooms better get a brush in your hand and sweep up the muck from the horse by way of getting rid of those boxes in the backyard and tidying up the place.'

'What, this mornin'?' It was a chorus from both boys and she yelled back at them, 'Not this afternoon, or the morrow, but aye, this very mornin'. So get!'

I got, too. I left the war zone and went quickly up to my room. I looked at my bed with my beautiful blue voile dress laid on it and my cases standing at the foot of it and already packed. And for some strange reason I wanted to cry. Then going swiftly to the door, I turned the key and, throwing myself on my knees by the side of the bed, the bed in which I had never known a moment of love or happiness, I gave way to a bout of weeping. And as I knelt there, my hands holding my face, I felt a presence near me. It wasn't a human presence, and it wasn't a single presence either. Without raising my head I knew it was Hamilton and Bill standing there: Bill who had been flesh and blood, Hamilton who had been the creation of my lonely mind; they were both there and I took my hand away from my face and held it out towards them, and I felt a great peace overwhelm me and an assuredness that nothing ill would ever befall me again.

Such are the wishful illusions of the mind.

CHAPTER TWO

Doctor Mike Kane held me at arm's length. Shaking his head slowly, he said, 'This is how it should have been from the very first, Maisie, and—' his voice changing he growled at me, 'don't you contradict me when I say you look beautiful, because at this moment you do look beautiful.'

'I have no intention of contradicting you,

Doctor. But I can say in return, I don't believe you, or, let me add, beauty is in the eye of the beholder, and from under that awful bristle of yours your vision is distorted.' I put my hand up and pulled his beard. 'But under there too is the man who changed the original ugly duckling. I know it is a policy for doctors not to get involved in their patients' lives. In their illnesses ... Oh yes, they can muddle them up as much as they like: if they're not really bad when they go into the surgery they'll see all that is altered by the time they come out.' My smile had softened my words, and I went on, 'But right from the beginning you were concerned for me and, whatever else age makes me forget, I'll never forget that.'

Slowly now he bent forward and kissed me, and I was buried for a moment in the bush of his face and my throat and heart were full.

'Well'—he looked down at himself—'it'll be a pearl-grey pageant coming out of the church. Anyway, girl'—his tone had changed again—'this is likely the last private word I'll have with you for the next month or so.' And his voice suddenly rising, he cried, 'Then after, I don't want to see you ever again, except when I'm invited up to London.'

I said nothing, and he backed from me before turning and walking swiftly towards the door, there to turn again and add, 'Only one thing I'll ask. Keep that damned horse out of the proceedings.'

I laughed, then blinked my eyes rapidly, and the door closed again on the commotion in the hall and the to-and-froing down the front steps to the cars.

The door opened again and Gran came hurrying in, but then she almost stopped before continuing to walk towards me, saying, 'Oh lass, I used to think you were as plain as a pikestaff and that what you had was all inside your head, but I take it all back. An' that little blue hat ... Oh my!'

'Oh, Gran, be quiet!'

'Aye, I will, 'cos I'm near makin' a fool of meself. An' I won't come nearer you, 'cos if I do, there'll be buckets flowin', but I just want to tell you, it's ... it's as if you were me own goin' to the church this very day, 'cos I love you like I've never loved anybody else, except me lad. God bless you, lass.'

As she scurried from the room I put my hand tightly over my mouth. This was no good; I'd go up that aisle crying my eyes out.

There was the sound of cars moving away along the street. Then there were only the strange voices coming from the hall now, those of the caterers who were to serve light refreshments in the sitting-room for all the guests, that's if they were ever able to get in the house. Then Nardy and I would start on our honeymoon and our life together, and later, there was to be a dinner and dance in the hotel for the family and guests.

When the door finally opened, George stood there in all his glory. He didn't speak but came slowly towards me. There was no bright grin on his face either. Solemnly he offered me his arm and I accepting his mood, took it and went from the room and through the hall, down the steps and through the crowd of spectators, some with cameras flashing, and into the white-ribboned

11

Rolls Royce.

*   *   *

I was amazed at the size of the crowd outside the
church, but I was more amazed at the crowd
inside; I glimpsed people standing at the back.
The organ was pealing out 'Here Comes The
Bride', and I was walking by the side of my burly
stepfather and all eyes were turning in our
direction but mine could see only one man. There
he was waiting for me at the bottom of the aisle.
He looked beautiful today, too. Of course he
always looked attractive, with his kind eyes and
gentle manner and, above all, his lovely voice.

I was standing by his side now and we were
gazing at each other. I had to take my eyes from
him as I walked up the two steps to where the
minister was waiting. Betty took my bouquet,
George stood on one side of me, and Tommy
Balfour, Nardy's best friend, stood to Nardy's
side. And it was just as the minister began to
speak that my heart lost a beat and I gasped
audibly, for there, close to him, was standing the
familiar figure of my old friend in all his glory; his
coat had never shone so black, nor his tail and
mane look so purely white; his eyes were like two
stars, and his lips were well back from his teeth,
and his mouth was wide open. But that was not
all. Inwardly I cried out against what I was seeing
on the other side of the minister, for there was
standing the most beautiful cream and brown
mare. She was about half the size of Hamilton,
but if you could ever put the word wondrous to a
horse, this animal looked wondrous: her eyes were

12

as soft as those of a seal, her nose was moist, her milk-chocolate mane was floating in the air as her head moved up and down as if in answer to something Hamilton was saying, for they were looking across the minister. But it was at Hamilton I inwardly cried, Now why are you here? It's all over and done with. And what he said was, We're happy for you. You wouldn't want this day to pass without seeing me, would you? Because, don't forget, I started it all. And anyway I wanted you to meet my mate. They call her Begonia.

I closed my eyes. I mustn't laugh. I mustn't laugh; I was being married; this was a serious moment.

'Leonard Murray Leviston, wilt thou have this woman to thy wedded wife, to live together...'

'I will.'

'Maisie Rochester, wilt thou have this man to thy wedded husband, to live together after God's ordinance...'

They were still standing there, the pair of them, and I'll say this, they were behaving themselves.

'... And, forsaking all other, keep thee only unto him, so long as ye both shall live?'

Oh dear. They were nodding their heads and smiling. Yes. 'I will.'...

The main ceremony was over but the minister was still talking, telling us about the sanctity of marriage. I couldn't listen to what he was saying for I was asking myself, was there some part of me really a bit barmy? because those two animals standing there still, one on each side of the minister, were as real to me as he was, if not more real. In fact, I was thinking that at times Hamilton

13

talked more sense than this man was doing now.

By the time the minister led the way into the vestry, Hamilton and ... How on earth had I given his mate the name of *Begonia*? What a name to give a horse, *Begonia*! But anyway, they had both disappeared and things were back to normal. Nardy was looking at me so lovingly and I felt so happy; I was, as Gran would say, like fit to burst...

Outside the church, amid the headstones and the flower beds, the crowd was milling about us. I had never been kissed so much in my life, and by women too: wives of Nardy's friends, smart ladies who while smiling at me were, I'm sure, thinking, Whatever in the name of heaven can he see in her! It's because she's become famous likely, with that book...And I knew that this was the opinion of most people, because, after all, take away the frills and the make-up, there was just me left underneath, and I was well aware of what my mirror presented to me...

It was almost an hour later before we all poured out of the cars and into the house. There, the champagne corks popped and speeches were made by various men, the one causing the greatest stir coming, of course, from George, who ended his by saying in his thick Geordie accent, 'I'm her stepfather, but there's many a time, years ago, when I wished she had been a bit older and me a bit younger, and I would have changed all that,' and the only one who took this in good part seemingly was Nardy, for he clapped Georgie on the back and said, 'Well, I'm quite a bit older than you and I beat you to it.'

Gran's response came later: 'My God!' she

14

said: 'trust him to come out with something like that. The minister's wife, who had answered the call, nearly dropped it there and then an' with another three months to go by the looks of her.' Gran could be relied upon always to cap her son...

Then came the goodbyes. And for the first time since it had all begun, we were alone together, in the car making for the station, and when he looked at me with that loving look, I said to him, 'Did I act funny during the ceremony?'

'Funny?' He screwed up his face. 'What do you mean, funny?'

'Did I act as if I was startled or something?'

He shook his head, then said, 'No. But wait. Yes, I remember now: you jerked a little as if you were going to lose your balance. It was just before I put the ring on your finger, and I thought, she doesn't want it.' I leant towards him and he kissed me long and hard; then, still in his embrace, I said, 'I was startled. I saw them.'

'Them?' He drew his head slightly back from me.

'Yes. Hamilton.'

'Oho! you did?' His face broadened into a smile. 'That's a good omen. You haven't seen him for months and months; so you told me.'

'I don't know so much about a good omen. I said them, didn't I?'

'Yes, yes, you did, Mrs Leviston.'

Again he kissed me, then said, 'Explain the plural.'

'He has a mate. They call her Begonia.'

His body shook us both as he said, 'No! No! Not *Begonia*.'

I nodded at him. 'And they were standing one each side of the minister as large as life.'

'Never!'

'I'm telling you. Now why should that be? I ... I don't need him any more.'

'Oh, come on, come on. You're in for a series. I told you that. But what is she like?'

I looked away from him, through the glass panel and over the chauffeur's head and out into the swiftly passing traffic, and I said softly, 'She's beautiful: milk-chocolate brown with the most wonderful eyes in the world, and ... and he loves her.'

He pulled me round to him and, softly now, he said, 'Of course he's bound to, because she's you.'

'Oh! Nardy.'

'Oh! Maisie,' he mimicked; then, his brow touching mine, he said, softly again, 'My delightful, delightful Maisie. What have I ever done to deserve you? Never change. Tell me you'll never change.'

I turned from him, lay back against the upholstered padding and asked myself seriously, Was this happening to me, really happening to me? Had I not slipped back into the fantasy world of Hamilton and become so much lost in it that it appeared real?

My question was answered when the car drew up outside the station and the door was pulled open by Tommy Balfour who helped me out into a crowd of grey-clad figures who, like a lot of hooting schoolboys, surrounded us and accompanied us onto the platform and, when the train arrived, brought heads out of carriages as they shouted and showered us with confetti. The

16

minister had made it a strict condition that no confetti or rice would be used outside the church. And when the train began to move out and some of Nardy's friends ran along the platform by the side of the carriage giving him advice, and I saw, among them, the face of one of the older members of the publishing house, I was made to think: Why should I imagine I was odd when middle-aged and elderly men acted like schoolboys out on a spree whenever the occasion warranted.

When at last they were out of sight and we sank back into the temporary privacy of the compartment, Nardy seemed to endorse my thoughts as he said, 'And you imagine Hamilton is unusual. Did you see old Rington there skipping along like a two-year-old? I wouldn't like to see that lot after the dinner tonight. Anyway'—he put his arms about me—'we've given them an excuse to let their hair down. And you know it isn't very often our lot get the chance to do that. We're stiff-necks, at least they are, I'm not any more.' He shook his head vigorously. 'For who, I ask you, could remain a stiff-neck with Gran, Georgie, Mike, and above all, Hamilton.'

My chin went up and I put in, 'Not forgetting Begonia.'

'No, Mrs Leviston, not forgetting Begonia. Oh, Begonia; I'm dying to meet Begonia. But very likely, now that you're a settled married woman there'll be very few occasions when they will visit you, only when you are stuck for some incidents in your new book.'

'Yes I suppose so,' I said.

But why, I asked myself at this precious

moment, should I sound so unsure as to cross my fingers.

CHAPTER THREE

I had lived in London for three months and I didn't know yet whether I liked it or not. I loved my new home. The citric yellow suite and the matching curtains at the windows in the drawing-room filled it with sunlight all hours of the day. Then there was the warmth and comfort of the rose-coloured carpet that went through the eight rooms of the top flat of the house where Nardy had been born, the whole of which he had at one time owned, but which, after the deaths of his parents, had become too large for his bachelor existence.

Nardy had turned one of the rooms at the end of the corridor into a study and sitting-room for me. In it I had a desk for my typewriter and plenty of space for books. But I often found it difficult to work there, and I would find myself sitting in the corner of the comfortable couch, going over what had happened yesterday or thinking about what was going to happen tonight when we'd be doing a show or a concert or accepting the invitations of Nardy's friends.

I considered he had a lot of friends, but he maintained he had three friends and a lot of acquaintances. Heading the three friends was Tommy Balfour who had been his best man. Tommy was publicity manager in the publishing house of Houseman and Rington where Nardy

18

was editorial director. I had come to know Tommy well over the past weeks and, in a way, I felt sorry for him, because of what Nardy had told me about his mother. I'd met her only once and that was in the company of others, but I'd likely know more about her tomorrow because I was having tea with her. Then there was Alice and Andrew Freeman. Nardy had gone to school with Andrew; they were lifelong friends and I liked them, but only up to a point: I couldn't feel at home with them.

Since my marriage my appearance had worried me less and less. I had acquired something, but I can't find a name to put to it. It wasn't just confidence, for my mirror showed me the same face unfortunately as it had done all through the years, except that now it looked happy. And I was happy. I had never imagined such happiness. Every day I found something or someone to laugh at, and not least, Janet, Nardy's housekeeper, once nursemaid to him, and now maid of all work.

Mrs Janet Flood, to give her her correct title, was the first person to bring Hamilton back into my life, and of course Begonia with him.

I don't think Janet was over-happy with the situation when I first took up my position as mistress of the house, for she had seen to 'her Mr Leonard' for years. On her half-day visits she had her own method of cleaning, and she made this very evident to the new wife; and also, she had her special times for stopping and having her cuppa.

It was during one of her cuppas that I broke through the 'Good-morning, Mrs Leviston,' or

19

the 'Good-morning, Mrs Leviston, ma'am,' or simply, 'Good-morning, ma'am.' (It was as 'Mrs Leviston, ma'am' that she was usually to address me for all our subsequent years together.) But on this particular morning, knowing it was the time for her cuppa, I ventured into the kitchen and said, tentatively, 'Janet, do you mind if I join you? I feel a bit lost.'

Metaphorically speaking, it was from that moment she took me to her bosom like a long-lost daughter. And for days afterwards I regaled Nardy with titbits about her family life that he had never heard before. But it was on that first morning that Hamilton galloped around the kitchen, and he was on his own. When I told him to let up, he pulled out a chair and sat next to Janet, nodding at her every word.

But the morning she gave me a run down on her family, Hamilton got up to such antics that I had a fit of coughing to cover my mirth. She had been sympathizing with me losing my baby, then had ended, 'But God has funny ways of working, for if your child had grown up to be like that man, you would sometime or other have tried to do him in an' all.' My mouth had fallen slightly agape at this, and I was about to tell her that I hadn't intentionally tried to do my husband in, when I saw Hamilton sitting in the corner on his haunches and hugging himself with delight. Then Janet was saying, 'People long for kids but if they only knew what was in store for them, not for the kids, but for them. Eight of them I've had, as you know, and there's our Max, Billy, and Joe, all divorced, the three eldest all divorced. Then our Maggie left her husband for another man and her

20

three youngsters don't know which end of them's up, if you follow me. And what's gonna happen to young 'Arry or 'Arold, as he insists on being called, God only knows, for he's a livin' terror. Only three and a half, and he's completely out of hand. But then can you blame him, poor little fella, because his dad's new piece hates his guts. Then there's our Hilda, she's single, at least in name 'cos she's going round with this fella in a band, with his hair standin' up straight as if he'd just got an electric shock. Then there's our Greg, Rodney, and May, they're still at home, 'cos they know where they're well off. Their dad's told them more than once to get the hell ... well, to get out of it, 'cos they're livin' rent free. What they're payin' for their keep wouldn't cover one decent meal outside. But they know when they're on a good thing. They've got it both ways: Greg and Rodney have got their beer and broads outside, an' Hilda's got her so-called boy friend. I tell you, Mrs Leviston, ma'am, shed no tears about not havin' a family. I had it all taken away after May was born, 'cos he said he wouldn't mind havin' a baker's dozen. I remember the night when he said that. I came back at him, in poetry like, sayin', "If that's what you want, Henry Flood, put yourself out to stud."'

And she leant back in the chair, her face wide with laughter, her hand tight across her mouth. I too was laughing my loudest, not only at Mrs Janet Flood, but at Hamilton, who was almost standing on his head, so doubled up was he with his mirth. But Begonia wasn't laughing, she too was bending forward, simply, apparently, to find out why her mate had taken up such a ridiculous

21

position.

Begonia, I had found, hadn't a keen sense of humour. I remember putting this to Hamilton after I'd left the kitchen that morning and knowing that Janet and I had reached an understanding. And he replied, No, you're right, she hasn't as yet our sense of humour. But then she's only a two-year-old. But what she has got is a deep sense of compassion. If ever you were in trouble, you could lay your head upon her shoulder. I laughed, but noticed that he hadn't joined me; in fact, he had assumed an attitude of dignity and turned away.

But this evening I was attending the fire in the drawing-room when I heard Nardy's key in the lock, and as I scrambled to my feet and just missed knocking the tea-trolley over, I heard him say, 'Wait there a moment,' and I stopped in my tracks. He had brought someone home with him. Oh, dear, dear; this was the time of day I had come to love, when we had tea together and talked over the doings of the day. But who was it that he could say to, 'Wait there a moment.' That wasn't very polite, especially coming from Nardy, who was a gentleman of gentlemen where courtesy was concerned.

He entered the room, closed the door behind him, came quickly towards me, took me in his arms and kissed me; then, holding me at arm's length, he said, 'I've brought someone to see you.'

'Yes?' I nodded at him, then whispered, 'But why leave them out in the hall?'

'Oh, he understands.'

'He?'

'Yes. Come and sit down a minute.'

22

He led me back to the couch and, taking my hands, he said, 'I often think it must be lonely for you here during the day after Janet has gone, and if you had a companion...'

'A companion?' I put in quickly. 'What kind of a companion?'

'Oh.' He put his head on one side and squinted his eyes towards the ceiling as he said, 'A little boy.'

'*A little boy*!' The words came out of the top of my head. I didn't want any little boy ... or a little girl. I'd given up the idea of children long ago. I liked George's children, but only for short periods at a time.

'Oh, Nardy.' My voice was a whimper now. 'How old is he?' I asked, for there was flashing through my mind the thought that it must be Janet's 'Arold.

'Just on two.'

'What!' There it was again, that 'what' that had so annoyed Doctor Kane for years, but surely I could be excused and be allowed to show my amazement; and I was amazed that Nardy could plonk a two-year-old on me.

'Where ... where are his parents? I mean...'

He shook his hands up and down. 'They've had to go abroad; he's going to work in Canada, and they were going to put him into ... well, a sort of home, but when I saw him I thought immediately that you would love him.'

I withdrew my hands from his saying, 'His parents were going to put him into a sort of home? What kind of parents are they?'

'Well, as far as I can gather they are pretty high class. There's blue blood there. Look, stay there;

23

I'll let you judge for yourself.'

He hurried from the room. I heard him talking again. I sat now with my hands tight between my knees telling myself that I had been a fool to hope that this way of life could go on indefinitely.

When the door opened again I slowly raised my head, then my mouth fell into a gape, and as Nardy came towards me carrying the two-year-old in his arms I got to my feet and cried, 'Oh, you! you awful man,' for there he was holding a beautiful white poodle.

Now I have never considered poodles to be dogs. And as for my choosing a poodle after having a bull-terrier for years, well, that was chalk after cheese indeed. But this fellow I saw wasn't one of those tiny things with bows on them, or the big ones cut into fantastic shapes. Yet he was big for a poodle.

His face was within two hands' distance from me now and he began to murmur, or was it grunt? And at this Nardy said, 'He can talk. Proctor from the packing-room who owned him says he's got a language all his own. His wife was heartbroken at having to leave him.'

'What do they call him?'

'Sandy.'

'Sandy? And him pure white! Hello, Sandy.'

I wasn't prepared for the tongue that covered my face from my chin to my eyebrows, or the two feet that came out, and the next moment he had one front leg round my neck and the two back were resting on my hand as if it was a chair. It seemed such a natural position for him. His nose now was almost touching mine, and again he gave me the benefit of a free wash.

24

'Oh, Nardy, he's lovely.'

'I thought you would like him. I saw him last week but I didn't say anything just in case they pulled out from going at the last moment. Proctor's wife really was in a state. They looked upon him as their child. They'd had him since he was six weeks old. To make the break Proctor brought him to the packing-room over a week ago. That's where I really came across him. Of course everybody wanted to take him, but Proctor went into each one's background as if he were head of an adoption society. It became a bit of a joke. When I put my name forward, the first thing he asked was, "Have you ever had a dog?" And I had to be truthful and say, no, but that my wife was well acquainted with dogs. And the deed was done. Poor fellow.' He now patted Sandy's head. 'He grieved terribly at first, howled all night, the caretaker said. He used to sleep in Proctor's bedroom, sometimes on the bed. What do you think about that?'

'I like it. Oh'—I put out my free hand—'thank you, Nardy. Oh, thank you. But you know, you gave me a shock. I thought it was a boy you were bringing in.'

'A boy? A nipper? Oh, my goodness, no. I don't think I could stand a child, not now. All right for a time to have a romp with, but too much of a responsibility. No, I think we'll plump for Sandy.'

And so Sandy became, not just my companion, but our companion. Right from the beginning he was a strange dog. He did have a language of his own and an independent spirit. He didn't like closed doors, and he scratched them, or tried to rattle the knobs until the doors opened. He jumped up at all newcomers and barked in greeting. He did not like sleeping on the floor but chose the best chairs, on which he would proceed to arrange the cushions to please himself. Above all, he never seemed to be content until we were both together, when he would sit on one lap and put his head on the other. And he loved to be held in our joined arms when he would lick first one face and then the other. And he seemed as wise as Hamilton, for he came to know my moods and to act accordingly.

I had said to Hamilton, 'Well, what do you think of the new addition?' He had pursed his lips. Well, he said, he'll never be another Bill, but he's all right in his own right, so to speak. And I repeated, 'So to speak.'

*   *   *

Christmas was upon us, our first Christmas together. Looking back over the year, it had been an eventful one. I had gone through a traumatic court case; I had become the author of a best-seller; I had filled the headlines of the newspapers for a few days, at least those in the north-east end of the country; I'd had a wonderful cruise with a wonderful man; I'd had a lovely wedding; now, I was firmly settled down and life was like a fairy tale, one that I had never read or even imagined. And here we were, sitting in front of the fire, Sandy stretched between us, discussing the holidays ahead.

'I had a letter from George this morning,' I said; 'a bit longer than the "It leaves me at present" one.' I laughed. 'He says, how about us

26

going up for New Year.'

'Fine, yes. Oh, I'd love that. A New Year in the north, yes.'

'All right, I'll write and tell him.'

'You know what?' said Nardy now. 'I'd love Tommy to meet George and the family; really meet them, stay for a day or two. I get worried about him at times. That mother of his will be the finish of him. You haven't forgotten we're due there on Saturday, have you?'

'No, I haven't forgotten. But from what I've already glimpsed of her I'm not looking forward to our meeting. Anyway'—I laid my head upon his shoulder—'I might find her bark worse than her bite. I'll leave it to Hamilton to decide.' Nardy chuckled; then said, 'How's he these days anyway? It's weeks since you mentioned him.'

'Yes, it is, isn't it?' I said musingly. 'I think he's deserted me for his new love.'

'Well, you had better not let him get away altogether. Sales were down last month. Not on yours, fortunately, but we need another bestseller, so get going, woman. That horse has got to earn his keep.'

I looked around for Hamilton but he was nowhere in sight.

★   ★   ★

The following morning Nardy wakened me with a cup of tea, and, seeing him already dressed for the office, I sat bolt upright, saying, 'What time is it?'

'About twenty to nine.'

'Why did you let me sleep all this time?'

'Why not? You haven't to go out into the bleak

27

morning—and it is a bleak morning, it's sleeting—and earn your living like I have. No, you can stay at home and make a pile by just scribbling on pieces of paper.'

He had put down the cup on the bedside table and now had my face between his hands and was kissing me. I put my arms around his neck and said, 'I'll work my fingers to the bone for you until the day I die.'

A few minutes later, when he came in to say goodbye to me, he whispered, 'Janet's come. She said I'll get wringing. She's soaked through. She's a fool of a woman; she won't take the bus all the way. Practice of a lifetime, I suppose, still saving the pennies. She has no need now, but there it is, habit.' He sat on the edge of the bed for a moment, saying, 'And you know something, Mrs Leviston. I'm getting into the habit of not wanting to go to work in the morning; I'd much rather stay here with you. You know, there's not a thing to laugh about in that office.'

'And there is here?'

'Oh, yes, yes. I've just got to look at you, my dear, and I want to giggle.'

'Thank you very much, Mr Leviston, but I don't take that as a compliment.'

'You should, my dear, you should; people who can make others laugh without trying should be given special honours, say—' He thought for a moment, then he went on, 'DOB.'

'What's DOB?'

'Dispeller of Blues.'

'Oh! Nardy; if I'm capable of doing only that for you, then I'm happy.'

'You're capable of doing a lot more than that

for me, my dear.' He held me tightly for a moment, then kissed me gently, and went out.

And once more I lay back on my pillows and wondered at my good fortune. And being me, I thought, it's too good to last.

I was on the point of getting up when Janet came into the room, saying without any preamble, 'And that's where you want to stay today. I'm a bite late. That little beggar 'Arry. His dad landed him on me last night; his new piece can't put up with him. And you know something? Neither can I. He'd drive anybody up the wall. You'd think he was plugged in for the sparks seem to fly off him, he's so alive. I had to give him a beltin' before I could get out.'

'Why don't you take the bus right to the corner, Janet?'

'What! and pay double for those three stops? Oh'—she now came quickly towards me—'What is it, Mrs Leviston?'

I had suddenly felt a severe pain in my left side,' and it wasn't for the first time I'd experienced it of late. 'I keep getting a pain in my side,' I said.

'Appendix?'

'No; it's on the left side, the appendix is on the right.'

'Aye, yes, that's what they say. What can it be then? Perhaps it's wind.'

I wanted to laugh and say, Could be your cabbage, for she wasn't a good hand at cooking greens. Instead I said, 'Yes, very likely.'

'Look, you stay where you are, I'll get you a hot water bottle and some hot milk.'

By the time she had brought the hot water

bottle and the hot milk the pain had gone entirely. And after thanking her, I smiled and said, 'I'm a bit of a fraud; I can't feel anything now even when I press the part.' And I demonstrated by pressing on my nightdress.

'Could just be wind then.'

'Yes, yes, I think so.'

It was about half an hour later, I should say, when I shouted, 'Janet! Janet!' And when she rushed in she found me again doubled up, but in the middle of the bed this time.

'Oh my! Oh my! Something must be done. I'd better phone Mr Leonard.'

'No, no,' I gasped at her; 'it could be nothing.'

'You're not twisted up with pain like that for nothing. Look, who's your doctor?'

'I ... I haven't one yet.'

'Well, who's Mr Leonard's?'

I lay back on the pillow now, gasping, 'I don't know. It's silly, but I don't know.'

'I know what I'll do. There's a fellow round the corner in the terrace. He's got a plate up. Doctor somebody. Oh, what's his name? Double-barrelled I think. Morgan, Morgan, Morgan-Blythe. That's it, Morgan-Blythe. I'll get it out of the directory.'

I didn't tell her not to bother, because by now I was more than a little perturbed. I could hear her voice from the hall, shrill as it always was when she was excited or upset. It had been like that the morning she came and told me that her May had brought home the fellow with the electric hair, with the intention of letting him sleep in her room, and Henry, Mr Flood, had thrown him out, literally by the neck. During all that morning

30

her voice had been shrill.

She came back into the room, saying, 'Who do these secretaries think they are anyway, God's missises? Wanted to know what ailed me or what ailed who, or where did we live, and so on. I told her, half a dozen steps to the end of the terrace and up the street, and to get him here pronto ... or else.'

'You didn't!'

'I did. Who are they any road? Jumped up little nothin's. They're not even nurses and they play at bein' doctors.'

I said, 'I feel a fool, Janet; the pain's gone now.'

'You were no fool a minute ago. Shall I ring Mr Leonard?'

'No, no, Janet. Please, please don't. Anyway, wait until this man comes, the doctor, and see what he says.'

It was almost an hour later when the bell from the downstairs hall rang and I knew he'd now be in the lift. I waited nervously and then there he was.

He was a big man, florid, and he didn't walk into the room, he bounced. I took a dislike to him immediately.

'Well! what's all this?'

'I don't know, that's why I sent for you.'

He stared at me for a moment, before saying, 'Is it? Is it then?' Then not finding an available table near to hand on which to put his bag, he threw it on top of the bed. 'What's the trouble?'

'I ... I have a pain.'

'What kind of a pain?'

'It's very sharp. It's in my left side.' I pointed.

'How long has it been going on?'

'I've felt twinges on and off for some time but, but it hasn't had any great effect until just a while ago.'

'Well, what happened then?' He looked around for a chair, saw one at the far end of the room, brought it forward and sat down, crossed his legs, then stared at me as I said, 'I was doubled up with pain.'

'Well, we'd better have a look, hadn't we?'

He bounced to his feet now, and I pressed back the bedclothes, then made to lie down again when he said, 'Well, let's have your nightie up.'

I paused a moment while I thought, Oh, for my own dear Mike.

His hands were dead cold and my body jerked and he said, 'That hurt?'

'No, it was your hand, it was like ice.'

He gave me a sharp glance, then pressed his fingers into my right side, and while he did so I put in, 'The pain is mostly on the left.'

'Sympathetic.'

'What?'

'The pain was sympathetic.'

Now I did start as he pressed his fingers hard into my right side. He straightened up, saying now, 'Appendix.'

'What?' There I went again: it was just like the time when I first went to Doctor Kane.

'You had better have it seen to.'

'Immediately?'

'Well, that's up to you. If you've been feeling it, as you said, on and off for some time, it could go on grumbling for God knows how long. Then one day it might decide to burst. It's up to you. Could you go into hospital?'

'I could, but I don't want to, not before the holidays.'

'What's your name again?'

'Leviston, Mrs Leviston.'

He was sitting down now and, looking around him, he said, 'Nice place you have here. What's your husband?'

'He's a publisher.'

'Oh.' He turned, slanted his gaze now to the bedside table and books there, and putting his hand out, he picked up one, looked at the title and said, 'Huh! Tagore. You go in for cults?'

'Not that I know of.'

He picked up another book and made a huffing sound before he said, 'John Donne. My, my!' And as he dropped the book on to the table, he stretched his thick neck out and looked to where, on the far corner, *Hamilton* lay and, picking it up, he actually wagged it in his hand as he said, 'Your choice of reading is catholic if nothing else. They'll print anything when they print that. Barmy. Clean barmy, that woman.'

When, between tight lips, I said, 'You think so?' Hamilton sprang on to the foot of the bed. He was standing straight on his hind legs, and by the side of him stood Begonia. She too was rearing.

'You ask me if I think so. Of course I think so. Did you read the court case at the beginning of the year? That judge was as barmy as she was, telling the jury that he too had imaginary friends.' He rose to his feet now, snorting, 'Lunatics! My sympathy was with her husband. No wonder he tried to get rid of her. But I can't understand, if your taste runs to philosophers and poets, how you can stand that tripe... What's the matter with

33

you?'

He followed my gaze for I was looking at Hamilton who was now prancing round him. And I brought his head poking towards me when I answered, 'I was looking at Hamilton. At this moment he's prancing round you, and if it were possible he would take pleasure in kicking your tactless ignorant hide down the stairs.' And I grabbed the book out of his hand, turned it over and presented him with a portrait of myself.

He stared at it, then turned his head slowly and stared at me. And now, without taking his eyes from me, his hand went out to the bag at the bottom of the bed, and slowly he lifted it up. Then, still staring at me, his teeth ground together and his knobbled chin came out and his mouth opened as if he were about to speak. But apparently thinking better of it, he turned, then bounced out of the room as he had bounced in. And I drooped my head forward and the hot tears ran through my fingers.

I heard the front door bang. The next moment Janet entered the room and, seeing how I was affected, she came hurriedly to me and put her arms around me, saying, 'There now. There now. Don't upset yourself about that one. And I had to go an' pick him! He didn't stop to put his hat and coat on. You were right about your horse. I wanted to kick him downstairs meself.'

I lifted my head from her shoulder and she nodded at me, saying, 'Well, I was standin' outside; I thought I might be wanted like. Who's he to say that you're daft, or anybody else who sees things. There's my 'Arry. He saw some things I can tell you three years gone before he went for his cure, and they weren't things like a nice horse that you can talk to and can make you laugh. No, he saw black-beetles crawling over the ceiling and over the bed and over me, in their tens of thousands, he said. He tore me nightie off one night trying to get rid of them. Not satisfied with that, he banged me all over trying to kill the things. By, I'll never forget that night. It took all the strength of our Greg and Rodney and Joe. Joe was at home that time. He had left his wife, or what was she, and there they were all struggling on me new carpet. It had been a toss up atween that or a spin drier, and...'

'Oh, Janet.' I was wiping my face that had now spread into laughter, and I patted her cheek as I murmured, 'You're very good for me.'

She seemed slightly embarrassed now, for she pushed me back on the pillows, punched each side of them, pulled the coverlet up under my chin and said, 'There now. Well, a good cup of coffee is what you want.' Her face coming nearer to me now, she added, 'Should I put a drop of brandy in it?'

'No thanks, Janet, just the coffee, strong.'

'Just the coffee, strong.' She nodded, as if disappointed. Then straightening up, she said, ''Tis 'pendicitis then?'

'Sort of, I suppose. What you call a grumbling one.'

'Are you goin' into hospital?'

'*No, I'm not.* Not before the holidays anyway. And not afterwards if I can help it.'

'But you couldn't put up with a pain like that for any length of time, now could you? You mightn't have any choice.'

35

She nodded at me before turning about and leaving the room. And I thought, Yes, she's quite right. I mightn't have any choice.

I didn't get up, and so I was still in bed when Nardy rushed in at lunch-time, and my greeting to him was, 'What do you want?'

'What's all this? is my answer to that question. Did that fellow upset you?'

'He did somewhat. Anyway, Janet shouldn't have told you. And well, yes he did. He was very rude, and the fact that I won my case seemed to infuriate him.'

'Lie still,' he said. 'I'll be back shortly.'

'Where are you going?'

'I'm just slipping out for a while.'

'Nardy, please, don't take it any further. There's nothing you can do. He can simply say he wasn't insulting me.'

'Lie still, my dear.'

I lay still for a few moments, thinking that I hadn't told him I had a grumbling appendix; the complaint seemed to have been thrust into the background.

He was gone more than half an hour and when he came back he walked slowly into the room and sat on the side of the bed. Taking my hand, he said, 'I don't think our friend will express his uninvited opinion in the future, or at least for a long time. It all depends on how long he can subdue that ego you so rightly detected.'

'What did you do?'

'Oh, I just let him have it.'

'What!'

He laughed and said, 'Oh, no, my dear, not physically, in height and breadth he doubled me

36

all over. No, there's a much better way to put a man like him in his place. The mention of the Medical Council, to which I told him I was writing, had a very subduing effect on his manner. I think he's got a thing about women. Anyway, you've got a grumbling appendix and it's making itself audible: you must see about it.'

'Not until I must, and certainly not until after the holidays.'

'Well, we'll see. If that pain gets bad, Christmas and New Year will have to be postponed until such times as you can eat and be merry. Now, I'm going to knock us up some lunch.'

'Aren't you going back to the office?'

'No; I've already phoned them and told them I won't be in. Of course, the place will go to pot, me not being there during the next few hours, but that's life.'

'Big head.'

'You said it, Mrs Leviston.'

Left alone again, I asked myself why I should have let that man upset me so much. For the first time in months I was now feeling tense, afraid, for he seemed to have dragged the past into this serene new life of mine. And now it was here, I felt I should never get rid of it, not really. And this was confirmed, because for the rest of the day I saw Hamilton, and once I spoke to him, saying, 'Why can't I throw this off?' And his answer was, You should know enough by now to realize that you can never throw off the past. Everything that's happened in your life is still in it, locked away in boxes and docketed. And a fellow like him is a kind of key, and the lid's off and there you are, and the only way you can close it again is to ignore it.

'Ignore it?' I said. 'How? How can you ignore things that man said to me, and what's more, what he thinks quite a lot of other people might think?'

Oh, sure; yes, you've got a certainty there. Only fools expect everybody to love them. You should know that, an' all, by now. And the same applies to tastes in reading. Don't forget one or two reviewers were very much of the same opinion as that fellow, although not quite so strong. Nevertheless, as one pointed out, there were people who had been in asylums for years and who had never even thought of talking to a horse. This is life, Maisie. Your cocoon of love now seems the whole of life but the world is going on all round it, and you'll be brought out into the cold reality of living sometime or other. Oh, I'm not suggesting that you'll be disappointed in Nardy; no, I think you're safe for life in that quarter, but he's not the entire universe.

'You're not very comforting,' I said. I saw him turn his head away while keeping his eyes fixed on me and now he said slowly, You never took me on to be a comfort, not really; your honest judge and jury, that was more like it, wasn't it?

Yes, I suppose it was true. I watched him put out his front hoof and draw Begonia to him and turn her about, and together they walked out through the wall. And I repeated to myself: Your honest judge and jury.

CHAPTER FOUR

I had no sign of pain the following day, so we went to have tea with Tommy's mother.

Tommy lived in a surburban terraced house. It was one of these tall four-storey houses, one which still retained some of last century's elegance. And if the elegance hadn't rubbed off on to his mother, who had lived in the house since she was a child, the flavour of the last century had, for she sat in her very Victorian drawing-room, the very picture of a lady of that time. The only thing that was lacking in her attire was a lace cap. Her dress was long, almost to her ankles, and attached to it were white lace cuffs and a collar, and over all was a cashmere shawl. Her hair was grey and pulled tight back showing her ears, which were large and inclined to stick out. Her face was long, her eyes round and bright, and her mouth, when in repose, pouted slightly. Nardy said she had married late and Tommy was born when she was in her forties. Yet, even he did not know her exact age. But as Nardy pointed out, Tommy being thirty-eight, put her at one side or the other of eighty.

Well, she might have been eighty in looks and a hundred and eighty in her dress and manner, but her voice and eyes denied all this, for her voice was crisp and her eyes bright and piercing.

Tommy had greeted us at the front door after it had been opened by a woman in her sixties, whom Tommy then introduced as Bella, his mother's companion. I later learned that the companion was merely a complimentary title for poor Bella who had begun her life in an orphanage and who had for almost forty years now cooked, cleaned, and maided the mistress of the house. Bella had a round kindly face and her body was as thin as mine, for likely all the fat had been run off it early on. I'd heard about Bella and I shook her hand, saying how pleased I was to meet her, at which her face had brightened, only for it to redden as Tommy put his hand on her shoulder and said simply, 'My saviour.' I guessed now that Tommy was the reason why poor Bella had stuck to his mother all these years. To her, he was likely the son she had been deprived of.

Anyway, here I was, standing in front of the regal lady and saying politely, 'How do you do, Mrs Balfour. I'm so pleased to meet you. But I think we've brushed shoulders before, at Andrew's and...'

My voice was cut short by the voice now saying to me, 'Rubbed shoulders, did you say? You'd have to grow a bit, young woman.'

'*Mother.*'

'What?' The steely eyes were turned on Tommy.

Tommy made no answer. Then the voice said to me, 'Well, sit down and let me hear your version of it.'

She was pointing to the sofa opposite her chair and I sat down and found myself much nearer the floor. I'd heard of business men who viewed applicants placed strategically in a lower seat on the opposite side of the desk, and I felt very much in the same position at this moment as the bird-like eyes riveted on me and the voice now said, 'An imaginary horse, I can't believe it.'

'Mother, you haven't said hello to Nardy.'

'Don't be silly.' She cast her glance towards her son. 'Do I say hello to you every time you enter the room? And Nardy has surely been here often enough not to expect a hello as if he were a stranger.' On the last words she looked at me again and now said, 'Well, about this horse.'

I stared back at her. There was something already rearing in me against this woman's manner, and it took shape, for there he was standing to the side of her chair on his two back legs with his head thrust forward.

'Have you always seen things?'

'I don't quite follow you, Mrs Balfour. What do you mean by seeing things?' My cool tone seemed to take her aback for a moment and her chin, on which were showing long prominent hairs, jerked upwards. 'Well, by what you said in that book you'd imagined weird things from a child, imaginary children and dogs.'

'I didn't consider them weird; most children don't.'

'Huh! Well, I never imagined such things. Did you, Nardy?'

'No, Mrs Balfour, no, not children or dogs; but I once imagined I had a crocodile.'

I turned my gaze on my husband. That was the first I'd heard about the crocodile. And when he now turned his head slightly towards me and smiled as if apologetically, I wanted to laugh. He had never imagined seeing a crocodile. And Hamilton confirmed this by tossing his head to the side and kicking his left front leg out as if dismissing the whole idea. It was then an imp got

41

into me and I looked at Tommy and said, 'Did you ever have an imaginary playmate, Tommy? A horse or a crocodile or a dog?'

Tommy looked at me for an embarrassingly long time, it seemed. Then he looked at Nardy, and then at Bella; he didn't look at his mother as he said, 'No, I never imagined an animal, but I did imagine I had a companion. It was a little girl, and she stayed with me for a long time.' He smiled now a wry smile as he ended, 'But I could never get her to grow up.'

'Don't talk such rot.' Mrs Balfour's head was moving from side to side, and she added now, 'Bring in the tea, Bella.'

And as Bella went to obey, her mistress said, 'There's one, thank goodness, who I'm sure never had any hallucinations.'

Bella had reached the door before she turned, and her smile was tinged with bitterness as she said, 'There you are wrong, Mrs Balfour; I did have what you call an hallucination. It was about a knight on a white horse, but he was always riding the wrong way.' Her smile slipped away and she made a sound in her throat which I put down poetically to the knell tolling the death of lost hopes.

For a moment I was touched by the depth of sadness that must lie in Bella, created mostly, I should imagine, by her life spent under this old tyrant. And I asked myself, how had she come to give birth to such a nice fellow as Tommy. Nardy had told me that Tommy took after his father, who had died some twenty years ago but whom he remembered as being a quiet man with a strong sense of humour. And he must have had a

42

sense of humour and a great patience to stick this woman. Perhaps, though, she hadn't always been as she was now. But I couldn't see her any different; some women were born like her, tyrants from birth, who yet managed to cloak their inordinate desire for power until they hooked some poor fellow, such as Tommy's father.

'You could have done a great deal of harm with that book, and I've already expressed my opinion to Nardy there, haven't I?'

'Yes, you have. But you remember I didn't agree with you.'

'Besotted individuals are devoid of reason. But how on earth...' She pulled herself up short, and at this I bowed my head when I saw Hamilton do his famous kick in the back and the spiteful old lady being lifted straight from her chair on the point of his hoof before sailing out through the front window opposite, over the iron railings that skirted the patch of garden and right into the middle of the road.

'You've got a cough. People with your fleshless frame often have.'

I swallowed deeply, and while my eyelids blinked rapidly I looked at her and said, 'I don't usually cough.' Then I couldn't prevent myself from hitting back at this tactless and dominant being by smiling at her as I went on, 'Quite candidly, I was choking. You see, I have this wicked sense of humour and your last words conjured up a situation that gave me a little episode for my next book.'

'Episode, for your next book!' She was bridling now. 'What have I said that was so amusing?'

'Well, really, it wasn't what you said that made

43

it amusing, but my horse's reactions to your words, "besotted individuals are devoid of reason", by which I think you meant that Nardy could not, to put it in ordinary words, see straight, or think straight where I was concerned.'

Her mouth opened twice; her eyes widened; I watched the hairs on her chin jerk before she said, 'You mean to say you are seeing that horse in my house, and it's having reactions?'

'Mrs Balfour,' Nardy's voice broke in soothingly, 'my wife is a bit of a tease.' He cast a warning glance in my direction now. 'Of course she's not seeing the horse here; it is ... well, it is really a fictional character. We all know that, don't we, Tommy?'

There was not a little consternation in the room when Tommy didn't confirm Nardy's statement, but after a moment, during which he put his big head on one side and looked at me, he smiled and said, 'I'd give my eye teeth to see Hamilton career round this room.'

'*Tommy*!' The name vibrated like thunder over our heads, and the voice went on, '*Have you lost your senses*?'

Her son now stood up and said quietly, 'Just about, Mother,' then turned on his heel, saying, 'I'll see what Bella's doing.'

I watched the tall body sink back into the chair. The head was nodding now, and she addressed herself solely to Nardy as she said in, what for her, was a quiet voice, 'Tell me, Nardy, have you noticed anything odd about Tommy lately?'

'Odd? No. Tommy odd? No. Of all my friends and acquaintances he's the least odd. I can say that with all truth. What makes you think...?'

'He's been acting strange.' She now leant forward and beckoned Nardy towards her; and he rose from his chair and went to her, and in a whisper, with each word perfectly clear to me, she said, 'He was away all last week-end, and he wouldn't tell me where. That's the second time it's happened of late. He wasn't with you, because I rang, didn't I?'

'Yes, yes, you did.'

'Have you any idea what's going on?'

'Nothing that I know of. I haven't seen any change in him.'

I would have loved to butt in here and say, 'That isn't strictly true, dear, because only a week or so ago, you said to me, Tommy's all on edge. It's that old witch of a mother of his; she's getting on his nerves.'

'Perhaps he went to stay with a friend.'

'I know all his friends. I rang round. No one had seen him.'

'Well, did you ask him?'

'Of course I did, but he said he had been for a walk. Imagine it, not home Friday night, Saturday night, or Sunday night, and he had been for a walk. I'm worried ... I'm worried, Nardy. Look, promise me you'll try to find out what's afoot.' Her voice sank lower now: 'I think he's got a woman somewhere: some common piece has got her claws into him, and he wouldn't dare bring her back here.'

As the door opened Mrs Balfour leant back and pushed Nardy from her, and he resumed his seat, and Bella poured the tea and handed round her home-made scones and pastries which were very nice indeed, and I congratulated her on them. But

45

such praise wasn't allowed to pass, and her mistress turned from carrying on a conversation with Nardy to say, 'She has me to thank for that. She couldn't boil water when she came to me first.'

'Well, Mother, she's had forty years to learn.'

I looked at Tommy. He *was* changed. There *was* a change in him: he was standing up for himself. And so was Hamilton, for having now been joined by Begonia, he was tugging on one of Mrs Balfour's big ears while directing Begonia to pull harder on the other. And Begonia's lips were well back from her beautiful white teeth. And for the first time I recognized that she was really enjoying herself as the old lady's 'cuddy's lugs', as Gran would have termed them, stretched further and further out across the room.

I closed my eyes for a moment as I told myself I must stop this, and I took a firm hold on myself as I glanced at Nardy. He was looking rather perturbed and, as I wouldn't have him worried for anything in the world, I made myself speak to the old dragon politely: 'Do you spend Christmas at home, Mrs Balfour, or do you go away?'

'Why should I go away? What's a home for if not to spend Christmas in? Everyone makes for home at Christmas. I thought that was universally understood.'

Still endeavouring to please, I said, 'Oh, some folks, I understand, take the opportunity to turn it into a restful and entertaining holiday and book up in hotels.'

'Well,' she said, looking straight at me, 'some people are odd; that is a well-known fact too,' and I was aware of the meaning behind her words.

It was Tommy who broke in again, and what he said proved one thing conclusively, he had declared war on his mother: 'I think that's a splendid idea, Maisie,' he said; 'a knees-up, Mother Brown, would do us all good.'

That his mother was both astounded and somewhat upset was evident. And when Nardy looked at his watch and, turning to me, said, 'If you want to keep that appointment, dear, I think we'd better be making our way,' I fell in with it and said, 'Oh, yes, yes. I'd almost forgotten.' And I rose to my feet and, standing before the dragon, whose shoulder I now did come up to, I looked into those hard round eyes and, smiling, said, 'Goodbye, Mrs Balfour. You must call on us sometime when you feel able.'

She did not speak, merely inclined her head towards me.

Bella was clearing the tea things away and I said, 'Goodbye, Bella. Pop in sometime when you are free, will you?' She stopped what she was doing and she smiled at me as she said, 'I will, Mrs Leviston. Yes, I will. And thank you very much.'

I had just passed through the door into the hall when Mrs Balfour's voice came clearly to me, saying, 'What in the name of God did he see in her? an undersized giggling nincompoop.'

Nardy was in the process of getting into his coat and Tommy had my coat over one arm and my hat in his other hand. They had both heard plainly what she had said. My head drooped slightly as I walked towards them. Tommy was definitely agitated and was about to say something when Nardy, helping me on with my coat, said,

47

'We are going up to Fellburn for the New Year, what about joining us then?'

I turned, and Tommy handed my hat to me and as I looked at him I thought for an awful moment that he was about to cry; his face looked all twisted up. Then, he was saying, 'Thanks, Nardy. I'll be glad to. Yes, I'll be glad to. When may I come?'

'Come up with us; we'll be going the day before New Year's Eve. And as the office isn't opening again until the following week, we'll be staying until about the third, won't we, dear?'

I could not answer for the moment but nodded.

'But would there be enough room?'

'We'll make room,' said Nardy...

We had come by tube because the station was quite near; but now Nardy hailed a taxi, and when we were seated in it, he caught my hand and held it tightly. It was the wrong thing to do because the silent sympathy made me want to cry ... What in the name of God did he see in her, an undersized giggling nincompoop. I didn't giggle. But as to the words undersized nincompoop, that was a good description of how I'd seen myself all those years ago, a plain little nothing, loved by only two people, and knowing that their emotion had been bred out of pity. But for some time now, ever since I had won the court case and proved that I had a mind, I had felt that I was looked upon at least as an intelligent human being, still small and plain with a deformed arm, nothing about me but becoming quite good company as a conversationalist, and particularly so with those people with whom I felt at home. But that woman, she was like a demon. And that

48

was the word Nardy now used.

'She's a demon,' he said. 'How Tommy has stood by her all these years I just can't understand. But the worm is definitely turning.'

I knew he was ignoring her last remark but I couldn't let it pass, and so I said softly, 'What in the name of God did you see in me?'

He drew me closer, saying now and just as softly, 'Oh, Maisie, Maisie, you shouldn't even have to think about that. I fell, as you must know, when I witnessed your first reaction to strong drink in the Café Royal.' He now put his arm about me and hugged me to him...

Once indoors and seated before the fire with the tea-trolley to the side of the couch and Sandy at our feet, I watched him lie back, join his hands behind his head and say, 'I wonder if Tommy's got a woman. I heard years ago he was strong on one of the girls in the office, but I think she met his mother and that was that, as you can imagine.' He slanted his eyes towards me, then said, 'What a pity Bella is so much older. She's such a nice woman, Bella, and she's been slave to that individual all her life.' Then looking at the ceiling, he said, 'I would like to know where he got to last week-end.'

'Why don't you ask him?'

'Oh, I couldn't do that.' Then he added, 'Do you wish you were going up to George's for Christmas as well?'

'No. No, of course not; I want to spend it here, in our own house.'

'So do I.'

★ ★ ★

It hadn't been strictly true what I had said, that I didn't want to go up to George's for Christmas; I had a great longing to be with them all, if only for a short time. Yet, Nardy, I knew, wanted our first Christmas together to be spent in his home. And it turned out to be a lovely time.

On Christmas morning he brought our tea and toast to bed and we laughed and talked for a while. And later, when I got up to dress, I had another twinge in my side. That was the third one during the last week, but it was really nothing, just a twinge. However, I knew that the time was near when I should have to do something about this twinge, but I prayed we should get the holiday over first.

I dressed and went leisurely into the drawing-room where we were going to open our Christmas presents, but I stopped half-way up the room, for there, added to the parcels around the foot of the tree, was one extremely large one. I turned and looked at Nardy, saying, 'What's that?'

'What's what?'

'Don't be silly. That parcel. It wasn't there last night.'

'No, it wasn't.'

'I ... I didn't see you bring it in. I...'

'I didn't bring it in, Father Christmas brought it down the chimney.'

'Oh, you!' I pushed him and he said quietly, 'Go and open it.'

I opened it, and there disclosed something that delighted me on sight yet at the same time hit my conscience. And when I looked up at him, he

50

said, 'Oh, yes, yes I know what you think about animal cruelty, but those animals have been dead for years. Put it on, woman.'

I lifted up the beautiful mink coat and held it to me for a moment; my hands, going over the skins, felt they were tracing silk. I put the coat on, then hurried out into the hall where there was a long mirror. The picture it gave me was like a transformation. It was longer than my usual coats, reaching down to just below my calfs, and it had a large collar which, when I lifted it up at the back, almost formed a hood. Nardy was looking over my shoulder and there were tears in my eyes when I turned about and threw my arms around him, muttering, 'It's beautiful. It's beautiful. I never imagined wearing anything like this.'

'You suit it. It has two pockets.'

'Has it?' I fumbled excitedly for the pockets. 'For handkerchiefs,' I said.

He preened. 'Or invitation cards. At least, that's what the salesman pointed out to me.' And he bowed.

I bowed back; then tugging him back into the drawing-room, I said, 'Come and see yours. They'll seem insignificant now.'

He was delighted with his presents: a gold wristwatch, and a silk scarf with initialed handkerchiefs to match. And when I opened my smaller parcels I found in one a beautiful mauve silk negligee, in another a pair of calf gloves, and lastly, a charm bracelet, a beautiful thing in gold and platinum. Oh, I'd never known such a Christmas. And then there were Sandy's presents: a new collar and a tartan coat which, when we put it on him, he tried his best to take off, going as far

51

as to roll around on the carpet on his back, and his antics caused us to laugh and to hug him.

I look back on it as a fairy-tale Christmas. We had a jolly time at the Freemans, and the day after they came to us when a number of the staff also called in for we had arranged to go to a pantomime. And when the Dame yelled, 'Shall I beat Jack?' we yelled back with the children, 'No!' And when she went on to say, 'Yes, I will!' we all yelled, 'No, you won't!' I was back in childhood, but one I had never experienced. Later, we went to a restaurant and had a lovely meal, and enjoyed the floor show. When we returned home that night I was indeed drunk with happiness.

*　　　*　　　*

Janet, who was on holiday, popped in the morning we were due to leave for Fellburn to pick up the key. She'd always had Christmas off, I understood, to see to her family.

She came in, her face red with the cold, but this morning her stockings weren't wet for she was sporting a pair of high legged fur-lined suede boots, and proudly she showed them off, saying, 'They clubbed up and got them for me.'

Clubbed up, I thought. How many of them did it take to buy her these boots?

'What else did you get?' I asked as we sat at opposite sides of the kitchen table drinking our coffee laced with brandy.

'Oh'—she put her head to one side—'the usual, you know: a couple of aprons, three tea-towels, a tea-cosy.' Then giving a funny little laugh that wasn't really unhappy but full of understanding, she said, 'You know, you're no longer a mother after you've had eight, you're just somebody who works in the kitchen.'

'Oh, Janet.'

'Oh, yes, ma'am. Oh yes. You don't know.'

'What did your husband buy you?'

'What did he buy me? Let's think.' She put her head first to one side and then to the other while directing her gaze to the ceiling, then said, 'He brought me in a bottle of whisky.' Now closing her eyes and shaking her head, she said, 'And I don't like whisky. What I do like is a glass of sherry; but I've never been able to stand whisky. He likes it though. Ho! Ho!'

Hamilton was now at one end of the table, his forelegs crossed on it, his face almost between us both, and he was enjoying himself. Yet, when Janet said, 'You know, Mrs Leviston, ma'am, that man's never bought me a Christmas present in my life. All the years we've been together I've never had a Christmas present from him, not even a card. And some of the older ones take after him.'

It was at this Hamilton drew his head and legs back and sat down on the chair. And as I forced myself to say, 'But ... but he's likely been a good father and seen to the children,' she hesitated, then said, 'My answer to that, ma'am, is that he works when he can get it. And when the two eldest were young he made them odds and ends; he was good with his hands, woodwork like. But he's never done anything like that for years.' She stood up now, laughing. 'His main occupation in life is to see how much he can put down his gullet afore fallin' over.'

At this Hamilton couped his creels, head over heels he went. And Janet, laughing now, said, 'My mother used to say a woman in my position had three choices, the same as she'd had: the first was, to walk out and to keep on walking; the second was, to do him in; and the third was, to commit suicide.'

We were both laughing loudly now, and, as always when I laughed, Sandy joined in: he was racing round the table barking his head off.

When I said, 'Oh, Janet, it's dreadful to laugh at calamities, really,' she answered, 'Well, as I found out, Mrs Leviston, ma'am, if you didn't laugh at times, you would do one or the other of those things. Yet, you know, it's funny, Rodney, who's the only thinkin' one of the lot, says if I was to peg out tomorrow his dad wouldn't be long after me, 'cos his stay would be gone. Funny that, when you come to think of it, because there's hardly half a dozen words pass between us in the twenty-four hours. And there I've been, lying side by side with him all these years, and the only time I seem to know he's there now is when he snores.'

I didn't laugh because her words conveyed to me the sadness and futility of some people's lives. Yet, between them, she and her husband had produced eight individual people, and they in their turn were producing more. Strange, the source of the population, when you came to think about it.

Nardy came into the kitchen now, saying, 'What was all that heeing and hawing about? Have I missed something?'

'Not much, Mr Leonard,' Janet said, smiling at him; 'we're just laughin' at life, sort of. Oh, and

54

by the way'—she looked from one to the other of us now—'thanks very much for me envelope. That was very kind of you, more than kind. I'm goin' to give meself a real treat and buy a thick coat to go with these boots.'

'Well, see that you do, and don't spend it on that family of yours.'

She nodded at Nardy now, saying, 'I can assure you, Mr Leonard, I've spent me last on that lot. No, it's a coat that I'm goin' to have an' keep it for best.'

'You'll do no such thing,' said Nardy, wagging his finger at her now; 'you'll wear it in the winter, weekdays and Sundays alike. It's a wonder you haven't caught pneumonia over the years.'

'Funny that.' She looked at me now. 'I never seem to catch cold, everything else but not cold. Well, I'll away, and I'll pop over every day and see to things. And if you'll drop me a line to let me know when to expect you, I'll have the house all warm and a meal ready.'

'Thank you, Janet. I'll do that.'

After Janet had left, Nardy brought the cases from the bedroom, and I put on Sandy's coat. As I strapped it underneath his tummy I talked to him, saying, 'Oh, you are a lovely boy,' and he licked my face and made that murmuring sound that was really like a human being mumbling.

When Nardy helped me into my fur coat he pulled the collar up around my face, kissed me, then said, 'You look marvellous.'

'Oh, Nardy.' I shook my head. It never made me feel good when he paid me such compliments. The clothes might look marvellous, but I knew that I myself could never lay claim to that

55

description. Yet, a moment later when I pulled on my small hat, picked up Sandy and happened to look in the hall mirror, once again I could hardly believe what I saw. Such was the magic of clothes.

Sandy's whiteness stood out against the dark brown of the fur, and he was the one I thought looked marvellous, with his pompom head and moustaches and chin beard, and his long beautiful silken ears. There are poodles and poodles, but I've never seen one as beautiful as my Sandy.

Nardy looked at his watch, then said, 'By the time we get downstairs the taxi should be there. I hope Tommy arrives on time, that's if he's been able to make his escape.'

We needn't have worried. Tommy was at the station and was delighted to be coming with us. Nardy had booked three first-class seats and we laughed and talked during most of the journey. It was only during lunch that Tommy gave any indication of what Christmas had been like. When Nardy said, 'How did you leave your mother? Does she know you're coming north?' it was some seconds before he answered, saying as he looked from one to the other of us, 'Do me a favour, will you, my good friends? Don't mention my home to me during the next couple of days or the time, however long, I'm to spend with you. I want to forget that there is such a place as Seventeen The Crescent.'

A slightly awkward silence followed; then we resumed our ordinary chat. And back in the compartment Tommy became quite amusing and surprisingly entertaining. Apparently, he was a great reader of poetry and could quote appropriate lines to fit any topic of

56

conversation...

It was the middle of the afternoon when the train passed through Durham, and I had the strange and unusual feeling that I was home.

When we ran into Newcastle and the train ground to a halt and Nardy helped me down onto the platform, I put my head back and sniffed the air. And we all laughed as Sandy, who was in my arms, gave two short barks, and Tommy said, 'He's hooting for Newcastle.' We were at the far end of the platform and our way to the barrier was momentarily blocked by some dignitary who had just alighted and was posing for a photographer.

By the time this little business was completed the platform was almost cleared. I was walking between the two men when I saw the lady reporter, as I thought of her, look back along the platform and point. Then she was hurrying towards us. Stopping dead in front of me, she said, 'Miss Carter?'

At this point, Nardy's voice checked her, saying stiffly, 'Mrs Leviston.'

'Oh, yes, sir. I'm sorry, but I was thinking ... well, of her pseudonym, writing, the book you know.' She nodded now and, again looking at me, she said, 'Have you come back for the holiday?'

'Yes, just for a few days.'

She was walking sideways now as we moved on and she said, 'You're looking very well, Mrs Leviston. And what a lovely poodle.'

'Yes, he is, isn't he. His name is Sandy.' I could afford to be pleasant, I was so happy. I felt her eyes travelling over my coat and knew naturally she would be thinking that's what a book does for

57

you, whereas she herself was working for what she'd likely considered a mere pittance.

'Would you mind?' It was the photographer now, his camera held shoulder high. I glanced at Nardy and he smiled. I smiled too, held Sandy a little further up in my arms, bringing his face level with mine. There were a number of clicks and the photographer said, 'Thank you very much. That'll be grand. A happy New Year to you.' The journalist now added her voice to his saying, 'Yes, a happy New Year to you.' And we all answered, 'The same to you. The same to you.'

A minute or so later as Tommy helped me into the taxi and Nardy saw to the porter, I thought wryly, Such is fame, for less than a couple of years ago I could have walked down that platform and caused less stir than a stray dog, a small grey creature, indistinguishable from the nonentities of life.

When, twenty minutes later and after a number of traffic hold-ups, the taxi drew up outside the terraced house where I was born and had lived until a few months ago, the front door opened before we had time to emerge, and there was George running down the steps, the children after him, and Gran and Mary standing in the doorway.

'Oh, it's lovely to see you, lass.' I was smothered against the broad chest and enlarging stomach of George, then held at arm's length as he said, 'In the name of God! what's that you're holdin'?'

Sandy answered with a bark; he didn't like being squeezed. And, too, at that moment Gran's voice bellowed from the door, 'Let her in, you big

58

noodle; she'll be froze out there.'

I was almost carried into the hall, and here pandemonium reigned for at least five minutes, with Sandy jumping from one child to another, and the questions bouncing off my head, and hands being shaken, and Tommy being welcomed, and Gran and Mary, and the two girls Betty and Kitty oohing and aahing over my fur coat.

It seemed an age before we were settled in the sitting-room and the children shooed into the kitchen.

From the couch opposite the roaring fire I looked around the room. It was different. Still comfortable, but different, and smaller somehow. Yet it had always seemed a big room, having originally been two rooms. It was this room that had attracted Howard Stickle and his sister to the house and formed the basis of their design.

My reminiscing was swept away by Gran declaring, 'How've you done it? You're different.' Then looking at Nardy, she said, 'What've you done to her? She's not our Maisie anymore; she's a stylish piece.'

At this I preened myself and, putting on a haughty tone, I said, 'One rises in the world, Mrs Carter. Remember to whom you are talking.'

'I'll remember'—she pushed her arm out towards me—'with me foot up your a ...' She swallowed deeply; then on a choked laugh she said, 'Backside.'

Looking at Mary now, who had so far remained quiet, probably, I thought, because she was of a quiet nature and was probably, too, dominated by Gran who was inclined to rule the roost, I said,

'How do you put up with the pair of them, Mary? It must be very trying.' And I shook my head in sympathy while she smiled understandingly.

And George, taking up Gran's point, looked at his mother and, nodding, said, 'You're right, Mam, you're right; she's not the same. Got the mistress touch about her, unsettlin' our staff now, she is.'

At this, Nardy said in a serious tone, 'It is a bad habit she has acquired, George. She's done the same in my household, bringing everything down to one level.'

I sat straight-faced for a moment; then reached out my hand to where Tommy had been sitting quietly at the end of the couch and said, 'Will you be my friend, Tommy?' And he, gripping my hand, answered softly, 'For life, Maisie, for life. When you find you can't stand any more, you just come to me.'

I nearly said, 'And your mother,' and threw my head up and choked with my inward laughter.

The phone rang and Mary went to answer it. She was back within a minute or so, saying, 'It's the doctor. He wanted to know if you'd arrived. He'll be around after surgery.'

'Oh, it'll be lovely seeing him again,' I said. 'And you know what? I'm going to try and persuade him to take up a practice in London.' And laughing now at the memory, I told them of my experiences with the bouncing doctor and of his opinion of *Hamilton*'s author.

'Insolent bugger!' said George.

It was two hours later when Mike arrived. There he was at the door, those clinical but kindly eyes peering out from the bush of hair around his

60

face, his arms stretched out towards me, and I actually ran into them.

'Oh, it's good to see you.' There were tears in my eyes and tears in my voice, and I knew at this moment that he was another person that I loved, for he knew more about me than did anybody else in this room, even Nardy.

'You look marvellous.' He was holding me at arm's length. 'What have you done to yourself?'

'It's the dress. It was very expensive.'

'Nonsense.' He twisted me about, put his arm around my shoulder and led me back into the sitting-room and into the babble of voices. I cannot recall what we talked about, only that the conversation was jocular and general; and it wasn't until an hour later that Gran said to him, 'Will you stay and have a bite, Doctor?' But he rose to his feet, saying, 'No; thanks all the same, I've got to get back. Anyway, I'm on call, but I'll be seeing you all. I'll come and be your first foot.'

'That's the idea,' I said: 'a dark hairy man.'

'Watch it! horse dealer,' he said and slapped me gently on the cheek. Then arm in arm we went from the room, and in the comparative quiet of the hall, he looked at me and said, 'All right?'

'Fine. Wonderful.'

'I'm so glad. You know that, don't you?'

'Yes, Mike; yes, I know that.'—It was only on very rare occasions that I used his Christian name—'The only dim light on my horizon is that you and the family seem so far away at times.'

'You don't like living in London?'

'I don't dislike it, but I only like it because Nardy's there.'

'By the way,' he now said, his tone becoming

professional; 'referring to the story of your doctor that you described so vividly. Apart from his stinking opinion of your ability, his diagnosis was likely right, and I think I should have a look at you. Have you had any more twinges?'

'One or two, but nothing to speak of.'

'Come, come. Have you had any real pain there?'

I looked away from him for a moment and said, 'Yes, the day before yesterday. But I wanted to come up here so I didn't mention it to Nardy.'

'Well now, look'—he dug me in the chest with his finger—'the first real twinge, and I mean real twinge, you have, get on that phone.'

'Very well, *Doctor* Kane. But I'm not going to have any real twinges until this holiday is over. Above everything else, I want Tommy to enjoy himself. I must tell you about him and his mother sometime. I had an afternoon with her that really beat that doctor.'

'No.'

'Yes. I think he's ready for jumping off somewhere. She's a real case.'

The kitchen door opened now and Sandy came pelting into the hall and, with one swoop, jumped into my arms; and the doctor patted his head, saying, 'My! he is a good-looking gent, isn't he? I heard you'd an addition to the family. I like poodles. I've never understood why they call them pets because they're the most intelligent of dogs. Oh, you are a fine fellow.'

Sandy leant forward and licked the hairy chin, eliciting from Mike the retort, 'Give over, man. Give over. Sloppy individual.' Then pressing my shoulder, he added, 'I'll be away. Take care now.

I'll be seeing you soon.'

'Bye-bye.'

I opened the door and waited until he had run down the steps and was in his car; then I waved to him. When I turned into the hall again, Mary was ushering the children from upstairs kitchenwards, saying, 'Now, make the most of it, because that's your tea and supper combined. Then to your rooms with you.' And now looking towards me, she said, 'It's all ready in the dining-room, I'm bringing it in. Will you tell them?'

I told them, and we all sat down to a meal which in a way was like the children's, a combination of tea and supper, but one which we all thoroughly enjoyed.

*   *   *

New Year's Eve, the house was filled with bustle: Mary and Gran cooking, the children running errands, George stocking up with liquid refreshment, and when Tommy expressed a wish to go out shopping Nardy took him into Newcastle, and they returned with their arms full of fancy boxes of sweets, chocolates, pastries, and bunches of flowers. It was Tommy's way of saying thank you.

As was usual, for the welcoming of the New Year in the real North Country style, the dining-room table, sideboard, and every available space, was laden with food and drink. But around eleven o'clock when everybody was changing their clothes as if for a ceremony, I found myself alone in the drawing-room with Tommy. We were sitting on the couch and he was bending forward towards the roaring fire, his elbows on his knees, his joined hands hanging between them. 'You know something, Maisie?' he said quietly. 'I don't think I've ever felt so relaxed and so at home in my life as I have done since I arrived here yesterday. I know everybody is in festive mood and out to see a good time is had by all, but it isn't just that, it's ... well, I felt it when I came up for your wedding. Mainly, I suppose, it's George and Gran. They have something.' He turned his head and glanced at me, then asked, 'What is it?'

I thought for a moment before saying, 'I suppose it's because they want so little out of life, Tommy: a good fire, a cupboard full of food, a drink, a meet-up at the local at the weekend. That's their life. As long as they've got the necessities of it and a little bit extra now and again, something to look forward to, they're happy. They're free from ambition. I think that's where the happiness lies, because you know, Tommy, once you start to allow your thinking to move away from that which is necessary to carry you through the ordinary day, happiness, such as theirs, is impossible.'

'But you're happy.' He straightened himself up and faced me.

'Yes, I am, very happy, Tommy. But it's an off-shoot; it doesn't seem permanent, and I'm daily afraid of losing the feeling. I can't get it as yet to mix with the main stream of my thinking which for years was governed by fear, fear of my mother, then of Stickle. Life with Nardy has not really got through to me yet. I might as well tell you that I wake up at nights in a sweat, fearing that something will happen and I shall find myself

64

back to where I once was, consumed with fear and hate. Hate's a dreadful thing, Tommy. It eats you up.'

I was sorry I had made that last remark, for he turned from me and looked into the fire again and, his voice a mutter, he said, 'You're telling me. I've never loved my mother. I feared her, too, when I was young. The fear is still with me but in a different way. Do you know something, Maisie?' He swung round again and leaned towards me and, his voice just above a whisper, he said, 'For a long time now I've wished her dead, but of late I've been terrified of what I might do to her if I was forced to spend another full week-end with her. Do you know where I went on that missing week-end?'

I shook my head.

'I went down to Brighton. I booked an hotel room, and, like a bloody fool, I stayed mostly in it, except for a walk along the promenade. I think the proprietor expected to find I'd hanged myself or taken an overdose. He seemed glad to see me go on the Monday morning.'

'Oh, Tommy. Why didn't you come to us?'

He straightened up; gave a short, sharp laugh, and said, 'Bella told me that Mother thought I was with you and Nardy and that she was for coming round; but then, if she had, it would have proved that she wasn't as bad on her feet as she makes out to be in order to be waited on hand and foot.'

'Why haven't you married and got away?'

He lay back in the corner of the couch, saying now, 'I was in love with a girl in the office and she with me. But she was frank: she said, she just couldn't stand Mother, and in those days, it meant we would have had to live at home. It was about the time she was deciding to be a semi-invalid. And then later on, I was engaged to another girl when dear Mama had a heart attack. But when that didn't part Evelyn and me, something else did, something I never understood for years: Evelyn went off to South Africa quite suddenly; she married her cousin out there. It was like a story in a novelette: she sent the ring back in a letter, saying she was so sorry but she found it was a mistake. I saw her again about six years ago. She had come back on a holiday—her parents lived not far away—she was still married and had three children, but wasn't very happy. And she told me then why she had gone off like that: Mother had insinuated that there was some kind of lunacy on my father's side and that I had spasms every now and again.'

My eyes wide, my mouth half-open, I said, 'Never!' And he nodded slowly and said, 'But yes. I think I nearly did go a bit mad at that stage, and I confronted Mother with it. She denied, of course, the implication with regard to myself but reminded me that my Uncle Henry had epileptic fits and would disappear for short spells.'

'You should leave her, Tommy.'

'I know that.'

'Tommy.' I put out my hand and caught his as I said, 'You must take a flat and, not just a flat, a girl friend.'

His reaction to this suggestion was to place his hand on top of mine and to stare at me for a moment before saying, 'When will you be free?'

'Oh, Tommy.' I pulled my hand sharply away

66

from his and said seriously, 'There are some fine women about, lonely women, just waiting for someone like you to say, hello there. They'd jump at the chance.'

'Yes, I suppose they might.' He got to his feet now and went to the side of the fire and leant his elbow on the mantelshelf, and after a moment he said quietly, 'Yes, I suppose there's a woman somewhere who wouldn't mind linking up with me. But life plays dirty tricks on you. Something happens and you find you can't tolerate even the thought of such a thing.'

Into the silence that fell between us there penetrated the bustle in the house and a commotion in the hall; then young Gordon rushed in, waving a paper and crying, 'Auntie! Auntie! Look! You're in the paper, in the *Evening Chronicle*. Front page, look.'

He held the paper before me, and yes, there I saw this fur-clad individual holding a white poodle in her arms. She was smiling...That wasn't me, was it? But yes it was: there was Nardy at one side of me and Tommy at the other. As I took the paper from Gordon George came into the room, yelling, 'Let's have a look!'

He had a look; then put his arm around me and said, 'Film star. That's what you look like, bloody film star. And look what it says:

Mrs Leviston, better known as Maisie Carter, the successful novelist, has returned to her old home to spend New Year with her friends, Mr & Mrs George Carter. She was accompanied by her husband.

Now what d'you think of that, eh? Her friends Mr & Mrs George Carter. That'll show the lot of 'em round about. I can't wait to hear the chatter.'

Gordon now grinned at me and, his head nodding shyly, he said, 'You look smashin', like me dad said; like a film star.'

'Oh, Gordon.' I ruffled his thick hair. 'You've never seen a film star.'

'Oh, yes, I have, on the telly and at the pictures. They all wear fur coats in the winter.'

Mary, Gran and Nardy now came into the room, followed by the other children, and there was a series of 'Oohs' and 'Aahs' and 'Would you believe it,' with Gran putting the cap on it all in her inimitable way by saying, 'It doesn't look a bit like you, lass.' And when George bawled at her, 'Oh, that's you, Ma, as tactful as a billy-goat with its head down,' she bawled back at him, 'She knows I didn't mean it that way; people dressed in fur coats like that are generally empty-headed upstarts, or those no better than they should be, 'specially if they are posin' with dogs an'...'

Her voice was drowned with the laughter. Even the children were saying, 'Oh! Gran. Gran.'

And to this she responded with 'Oh, to hell with the lot of you! I want a drink; let battle begin.'

It was at this very moment that the battle inside me did begin: the pain shot through my side like a knife. I opened my mouth and gasped aloud, but it was drowned by the hubbub in the room. Dropping down quickly into a chair I lay back and gripped the arms, crying inside myself, 'No, no. Not now, not at this moment.' The pain eased a little and I looked around. Everybody was dressed in his best: the children, Mary, George, Gran, and of course, Nardy and Tommy, who always looked as if they were dressed in their best. We were all ready to greet the New Year; and this I felt sure was going to be wonderful for all of us, including Tommy. Something must happen to bring Tommy some happiness, for he had become so dear to both Nardy and me.

'Oh! Oo ... h!' My legs stiffened against the pain. Nardy was at my side now, anxiously enquiring, 'What is it?'

I gulped in my throat and said, 'Nothing, just a twinge.'

'A twinge? Come along, tell me the truth, this is no time for being heroic. You're in pain?'

I put my hand on his and gripped it tight, and I felt my nails going into his flesh as another pain racked me. When it was gone I muttered, 'It'll pass. It's just the kind of ...' I was about to say 'spasm', when I was brought double. And now, there was Tommy, and Gran, George, and Mary all about me, and I heard Nardy say, 'It's the appendix. I knew this would happen. She should have had it seen to weeks ago.'

'I'll phone the doctor.'

As George went to move away I managed to hold up my hand and cry, 'No! No! Please. It'll go.'

'Phone him.' Nardy's tone was definite, and his voice seemed to be the last clear one I heard until I saw, through a haze of pain, Mike's face hovering above me, and him saying, 'There now, it's all right. Everything's arranged; you're going to be all right.'

I remembered feeling the cold air on my face as

I was carried outside, then the floating feeling as I was lifted onto a trolley. The last I remembered was being in an enclosed room and someone lifting my arm and saying, 'You're going to sleep. You'll be all right, you're going to sleep.'

*   *   *

I was told later they had just got it in time. Another hour or so and things would have gone pretty badly with me. As it was, they had not only taken my appendix out, but also removed quite a lot of adhesions from lower down in the bowel. Two for the price of one.

Two for the price of one.

Two for the price of one.

The words were repeated as someone tapped my face and a voice said, 'Come on, my dear, your husband's tired of waiting for you to wake up.'

Slowly I opened my eyes, and there was Nardy's face above me. And as my muzzy mind said, 'Oh, my love, my love,' I opened my mouth wide and groaned. They hadn't taken it out, I knew they hadn't taken it out. This pain was awful. 'Oh, Nardy, Nardy.'

'It's all right, my dear, it's all over.'

'Oh, I can't bear this, it's dreadful.'

Someone was messing about with my arm again. I turned my head and looked at the nurse as she stuck a needle in. I looked up into her face, but it was Begonia, and I spoke her name, saying, 'Thank you, Begonia.' And the last thing I heard at this time was her voice saying, 'She called me Begonia and my name's Betty.'

70

CHAPTER FIVE

After the first two days I had a string of visitors. Everybody was very cheerful, and I had to beg George and Gran not to make me laugh. About the fourth or fifth day I noticed the change in my visitors: their merriment was forced; they didn't stay long. I said to Nardy, 'Is anything wrong at home?' And he said, 'Now what could be wrong.'

I said to Tommy, 'Something's the matter with George and Gran. What is it?'

'Nothing that I know of,' he said. 'You're a bit low; and of course you're bound to be, aren't you? After what you've gone through.'

On the seventh day I said to Nardy, 'I want to go home; I'm quite up to it.' And to this he answered brusquely, 'You're certainly not up to it, and you're certainly not coming home until the doctor gives the word. You've hardly been on your feet yet. Now look, I'm leaving tonight for home. I'll go to the office in the morning, collect some work, and I'll be back by tomorrow evening; and in the meantime, you be a good girl and do what you're told.' His voice changed as he added, 'I do miss you, dear. It isn't life when you're not there.'

How comforting were those words, how warming to my heart.

The following afternoon I had only one visitor, Mary. She said Gran had developed a cold. I looked into her face; her eyes looked slightly swollen. I said, 'Have you caught a cold too, Mary?'

71

'Yes, yes, I've got a bit of it,' she said. 'It's ...
it's gone right through the children.'

The following evening, Nardy came and
brought a message from Janet. Apparently, she
said she was missing me, and would I hurry
home. And to this I said, 'I want to hurry home.
Look, I am up.' And I went to pull myself from
the chair, but he pressed me back, saying, 'Yes, I
know you are, dear. Just give it one or two more
days. Do this for me, will you?'

'Nardy.'

'Yes, my love?'

'There's something wrong somewhere. Mary
said Gran's got a cold, and George didn't come in
last night. Is it the children? Has something
happened to one of the children?'

'No, no, they're as healthy and noisy as ever. I
left them squabbling amongst themselves in the
kitchen.'

I jerked at the chair. 'Gran's ill. Something's
happened to Gran.'

'Woman! Nothing's happened to Gran. She's
her old, loud, brash self. Well'—he paused—'not
quite that, she's ... as Mary said, she's got this
cold.'

'She's in bed?'

'No, no, she's not in bed, but ... but you know
what a cold's like, streaming eyes, runny nose.
She would have passed it onto you if she had
come.'

I went through them all in my mind. Gran,
George. *George.* I put my hand out and gripped
Nardy's. 'It's George. He wasn't in last night; he
... he ...'

'Oh, my lord! woman. I left George not half an

72

hour ago. The only thing I can tell that has happened to George in the last day or two is that his vocabulary has extended somewhat. I thought he had used every swear-word in the book, but he's added a few more.'

'Why? What's made him do that?' My tone was testy, and he spread out his hand and said, 'The bus I suppose, the passengers.'

I was puzzled. I was quick to pick up an atmosphere. There was something wrong with one of them and the rest were troubled. But who? I looked at Nardy and noticed that his face looked white and slightly drawn. I mentioned this. 'You're tired,' I said. 'You look pale.'

'Well, I've had a long day. I dashed to the office, and was held up there giving one and the other the news. They all send their love, especially Tommy. I had to make another dash for the train, laden down with manuscripts that I don't want to read. The sun was shining when I left London; when I got out at Newcastle the sleet nearly blinded me. I dumped my burden in the hall, said hello and goodbye to them all, and here I am. Of course I look pale. I'm a poor harassed man, because I've got a wife who's let her imagination run wild again. By the way, where's Hamilton?'

I smiled wryly. 'It's funny, but I haven't seen him for days. I saw Begonia once, at least I think I did, but that's all. They've deserted me.'

He shook his head. 'I don't like that. I want another book.'

'That's all you think about, books, and the money you can make out of me.'

'Yes, of course. Why do you think I married you?' And this quip he softened by putting his

73

arms around me and kissing me.

The bell went for the visitors, but he had no need to take note of it because I was alone in a side ward. Yet he looked at his watch and said, 'I think I'd better be making a move. Mary said she'd ... well, she'd have a meal ready about half-past eight, and I am a little weary and not very good company.'

I nodded, saying, 'Yes, yes, dear; and ... and get early to bed.'

We said goodbye, and as I saw the door close on him I became filled with a feeling of panic. He had never left before nine o'clock on other evenings; in fact, one night he was still here when night staff brought the milk round, and the nurse had laughingly said to him, 'We've got an empty bed next door. We could push it in, sir, if you like.' And in the same vein he had answered, 'That's a splendid idea. I'll give you a hand.' But tonight it was just turned eight o'clock and it seemed he couldn't get away quickly enough. What was the matter? Gran, George, Mary, they were all right. He himself was all right. There was nobody else, only ... Like a flash of lightning Hamilton appeared before me. He stood stiff and straight, his great eyes looking into mine. I said to him, 'Sandy.' And he moved his head twice.

I had a phone in my room. I got through to the receptionist and gave her the house number. It was Mary's voice that came to me, saying, 'Fellburn 29476.'

'Mary.'

'Is that ... is that you, Maisie?'

'Yes. Mary, where's Sandy?'

'S ... Sandy, he's'—there was a pause—'in the

74

sitting-room.'

'Mary, are you telling me the truth?'

There was a pause, and then she said, 'Yes, Maisie, I'm telling you the truth. Sandy is in the sitting-room at this minute.'

I heaved a great sigh, then said again, 'Mary.' And again, she said, 'Yes, Maisie?' And now I put it to her, 'Tell me what's wrong. There's something gone wrong, I can feel it.'

'We ... we are all right, Maisie. Everybody's all right now.'

'What do you mean, now?' There was a longer pause.

'I ... I suppose I should have told you that Gran was a bit off-colour, but she's perfectly all right now.'

'Then why couldn't somebody just say that instead of all this mystery? Has she had the doctor?'

'No, nothing like that. And she'll be in tomorrow.'

'She will?'

'Yes, yes, you'll see her for yourself.'

'Oh, that's a relief. Good-night, dear.'

'Good-night, Maisie.'

I sat down on the side of the bed. Hamilton was still with me. He had been standing by the phone. I looked at him and said ruefully, 'The quicker I get my imagination on something practical, the better.'

His expression didn't change: he neither agreed nor disagreed with me. But I nodded at him and said, 'Doctors or no doctors, I'm going home tomorrow.'

The following morning around nine o'clock

75

there was a bit of a commotion outside my door. But then there was always commotion in the corridor, comings and goings. In any case, the kitchen was almost opposite, and there was the clatter of trays and crockery for most part of the day. But this was a different commotion. The handle of the door moved and I heard the nurse say, 'She's not seeing anyone. I've told you before.'

'And I've told you before that she knows me. I ... I did a piece about her at Christmas.'

'I've got my instructions, no reporters. As for knowing her'—her voice sank—'everybody in the town knows her.'

'But I told you.'

'I don't care what you told me. Now am I to bring the sister?' The voice dropped lower again and I moved towards the door and heard the last words, 'She's had an operation. It was quite a big affair. She hasn't got to be troubled.'

'She'll be troubled enough when she finds out.'

The opening of the door nearly knocked me on my back and the nurse said, 'Now what are you up to?' To this I replied, 'What will upset me when I find out?'

'Oh, nothing, it's ... it's ... Look, Mrs Leviston; now don't agitate yourself. Come and sit down.'

'I'm not sitting down, nurse, I'm going home.'

'Oh, Mrs Leviston.'

'And stop saying, Oh, Mrs Leviston, nurse.' I caught hold of her arm. 'Nurse,' I said again quietly, 'I'm worried, and feeling like I do, I ... I won't get any better sitting in this room trying to find out what I should know, and nobody will tell me. It's been going on for days; I've sensed it.

76

And now I know that something is wrong. That reporter knows. You know. Well, I'm not going to press you to tell me, I'm going home. Would you mind, please, asking sister to come in.'

'Oh, Mrs Leviston.'

I forced a smile and said, 'Oh, nurse.'

Sister was some time in making her appearance; but before that I got on the phone again. It was young Betty who answered, and I said quietly, 'Tell Uncle Nardy I want to speak to him.'

'Yes, Auntie.'

'What is it, dear? What's the matter?'

'The matter is, whether you come to fetch me or I make the journey myself, I'm coming home this morning.'

'You're...you're not. You must see the doctor...'

'Doctor, or no doctor, Nardy, I'm coming home. Would you please bring my clothes. If you don't then I shall discharge myself, order a taxi, and get into it in my dressing-gown. I mean this.' And I banged the phone down...

Half an hour later there was Nardy, the doctor, and the sister, all saying in their different ways, 'This is very unwise of you.'

I thanked the staff; and had one little surprise when my generous tip to be distributed among them was refused. It was a rule that all such remuneration was forbidden.

You live and learn, I thought. Fancy that in this commercialized, money-grabbing age.

Nardy held my hand tightly in the taxi, but we hardly exchanged two words.

I was going up the front steps; the door opened, and there was Gran and Mary and George and

77

the four children. Tommy, I thought. Oh, Tommy! I turned to Nardy, saying, 'It's Tommy!' and the word ended on a high note, almost a squeal.

'Tommy's all right,' he answered quietly. 'He's as fit as a fiddle. At least he was when I left him yesterday except that he had threatened to do his mother in. But he laughed as he said it, so I hope he won't do anything until we get back.'

I was being held by Gran. I looked into her face. It was swollen, her eyes were red. The children weren't jolly. As usual George held me and said, 'Hello, love. Glad to see you back.'

I was relieved of my coat and hat and led like an invalid into the sitting-room. The rest followed. There was a trolley set, and on a little side-table the electric coffee-maker that I'd bought Mary for Christmas was bubbling gently away.

I had a cup of coffee; then I lay against the back of the couch and looked from one to the other and said simply, 'What is it?'

When I saw the tears well up in Gran's eyes and she bowed her head, my voice was almost a yell as I cried again, 'What's happened? What is it?' Then I was sitting bolt upright. 'Sandy! I knew it. He's gone. He's dead.'

'No, no, no.' There were hands patting my shoulders. 'No, no. He's in the kitchen.'

I relaxed and my throat had a piteous sound even to myself as I said simply, 'Please.'

Nardy now looked at George and said, 'You had better start at the beginning.'

I watched George rub his hand over his mouth and chin two or three times before he said, 'Well,

78

it was like this, Maisie. The bairns took the dog out. Yes, yes, yes'—he wagged his finger—'it's to do with the dog, but rest your mind, he's there in the kitchen. But listen. As I said, they took him out, on the same walk as you used to take Bill, through the park and into the copse. There, they took the lead off and threw the ball for him; then they chased him and he chased them, in and out of the trees. You know the game he plays. Well, as they said, there they were, the three of them, John, Kitty, and Gordon, racing round when they realized they were just racing after each other and the dog wasn't there. Now, there was nobody else in the copse, not that they could see, and after all it isn't that big, you can almost see from one end to the other of it when the trees are bare as they are now, except at the far end where the holly's entangled. And as they said an' all, coming through the park, the only people they met out with dogs was a woman with an Afghan hound, you know the one, and the fellow from the bottom of the terrace with his bull terrier, an' two young lads pushing bikes. Anyway, they couldn't find him, and it was on dark, John even climbed over the wire fence at the side of the copse, you know, the railway cutting. And he went along the line, and even under the foot-bridge, which is damned dangerous, 'cos the line curves there and the train could have been on him. Anyway, they came back here in a terrible state. We were all in a state.' He glanced from one to the other. 'It was black dark by now, but we all went out again looking, every one of us. We knocked on all the doors in the council estate but nobody had seen a white poodle. We went to the polis station and they said they would look into it. And when Mam, here, didn't take much to their casual approach about a dog being lost and did a bit of yelling, as is usual, the one behind the counter became sarcastic and said, "There's an accident, madam, on the main road to Bog's End: an oil lorry's overturned, a car's been set on fire, two people are known already to be dead, but we'll stop our enquiry if you insist and see to your dog." That's what he said, didn't he, Mam?'

Gran merely nodded and George went on, 'By! lad, I gave him the length of me tongue. Anyway, it's wonderful what a name can do. I told him who the dog belonged to, an' first thing next mornin' there was a copper on the doorstep taking particulars. And speak as you find, from then on they did everything in their power to be helpful. But there was no sign of Sandy. That night there was a big advert in the local paper offering a hundred pounds for his return. Nardy thought of that.' He nodded towards Nardy. 'And you wouldn't believe it'—a small smile touched his lips—'we had all kinds of dogs brought to the door, didn't we? Mary there'—he thumbed towards her—'she could tell you a tale about the kids that brought a poor little, distempered-white mongrel. But even now we can't laugh about anything, because it was one hell of a time. As Mam there said, knowing how you went on about Bill, what you would do when you found out about Sandy was past thinking about. Anyway, four full days passed and we were practically giving up hope when the bell rang one night. It was around ten o'clock, and I went to the door.'

He stopped and stared at me and I stared back

at him, waiting, telling myself that Sandy was in the kitchen, what more was there to know? I watched him wetting his lips; then he began again, but slower now. 'There was nobody at the front door when I opened it, but there on the step was a bundle. It was wrapped up and I didn't know what it was. But I stepped over it and looked along the street. And in the light of the last lamp I saw two figures running, one what looked like a woman, the other a child. Anyway, I stooped down and I picked up the bundle. My God! Maisie, the shock will be with me till me dyin' day. It's no good keeping it from you any more, you'll see the result of it for yourself in a minute. It ... it was Sandy I was looking at, what was left of him.'

'Don't go on ... don't go on, George. Don't go on.' Nardy had put his hand out towards George and his other arm was around me. 'She'll see soon enough for herself. Now, my dear'—he jerked me tightly to him—'he's alive and getting better every day and, given time, he'll look like himself once more. Just think of that.'

'Will I bring the basket in?' Mary's voice was small, and Nardy said, 'Yes, please, Mary.'

I didn't speak; I just waited, and a few minutes later Mary placed the basket at my feet, and I stared down on the thing lying there, which on the sight of me stumbled to its feet and spoke its welcoming sound. I thought my whole being would burst asunder in the agony of pity. This skeleton was my Sandy, because that's what he was, just a skeleton: there was no hair left on his ears, it had been hacked off close to his head; his head had been shaved and apparently with a blunt

81

razor, for the healing scars were evident; his body showed tufts of hair here and there, but in between them was revealed the bare skin, again with scars on it; the tail had no pom-pom, it was a piece of bone sticking out.

Gran was kneeling by the basket now, gently stroking one of the tufts of hair. Her face was awash, as was Mary's, and it was she who whispered brokenly, 'He's eatin' again though, and . . . and he barked this morning. He must have known you were comin'.'

George, now on his hunkers, put his finger under the chin of my poor little beast and said, 'He'll be as right as rain, won't you, laddie? Won't you?' Then looking at me, he said, 'The one who did this wants crucifying. That's the word, he wants crucifying. To tie a poor beast's mouth up with tape so he couldn't bark, or eat, or drink . . .'

'George!' Nardy's voice was firm. Then Gran said, 'Look. Look, he wants to get on your knee.'

I stared down into the hairless face. Only the eyes were recognizable, and they were looking at me and in them was a deep plea. I put out my arms and drew him upwards, and when his nose found its way into the old position under my chin I couldn't bear any more: I let out a cry that ended in a long wail, and when my tears ran onto his face he licked my cheek. Then Gran said, 'Here, give him to me. Put him in his basket.' And I gulped, I gasped, and cried, 'No, no.'

George's voice came to me now, saying, 'He'll get along like a house on fire from now on. And when you feel a bit rested, lass, you'll have to look through all the postcards and letters that were

82

sent to you in sympathy like, after the RSPCA had put his picture in the paper. Eeh! that inspector said he had never seen anything like it in his life. One thing I do know, when we can prove the maniac who did this, all I can say is, God help him.'

It was the words 'when we can prove', as if the maniac was already known to George, that brought Hamilton into view. He was standing to the side of me. His eyes looked red; there was steam coming from his nostrils and hanging in the air as if encased in frost; and he was repeating a name in my mind. And of a sudden I wanted to be sick. I pushed Sandy into Gran's arms, and as I made to rise from the couch, I felt the hands come out to help me. I thrust them aside, put my own hand over my mouth and stumbled from the room as quickly as I could...

It was some hours later when Gran and I found ourselves alone. I had gone to bed early, and here she was sitting by the bedside. Presumably she had come up to say good-night. 'Feeling better, lass?' she said.

'Yes, Gran. I'm glad to be home.' And to this she said, 'Well, the best thing I think you can do as soon as you're able to travel is to get yourself away back home, to your real home now. You've had enough of this end to last you a lifetime.'

'Gran.'

'Aye, lass.'

'Have you any idea who did this?'

She blinked her eyes rapidly, wetted her lips, then said, 'Well, you might know we've talked this over so often, you could have walked from John O'Groats to Land's End and our ideas haven't

83

changed, at least, that is George's and mine; the others are not in the picture like we are, not even Nardy. But the only one who could really wish you ill, and you know it, is Stickle. And there's something I didn't know until this business came up. He's living now not three streets away from us, in the new council estate. He must have had to sell the cottage. I made a few enquiries here and there and he's been out of work this past year, until recently. He's now driving a taxi, part-time. For Corbett's you know; they have that big garage opposite the supermarket in Bower Street that runs off the market square. I say, I made enquiries. I'm telling a lie, I got this from John. Apparently, Stickle's two lads go to the same school now and, funny, but he's chummed up with this Neil, that's the younger one. This happened after he had a fight with the older one, because ... what d'you think? The lad Ronnie, so he's called, tackled John, saying he was living in their house ... this house'—Gran now pointed down to the floor—'and this was his dad's house, Stickle's you know. That was the time John came home with a black eye, and apparently the younger lad, Neil, had a black eye an' all because he had tried to help John. It seems that the brothers don't get on. Then, now this is what made us think'—she now leant forward and caught my hand—'it was the day after the dog had been brought back that the young lad, Neil, asked John if the dog was all right, and John wanted to know how he knew about the dog. And the lad became flustered and said, it was in the papers. And of course it was in the papers ... the next night. But this was the first day back at

84

school in the afternoon. Anyway, Georgie passed this on to the polis and they went round there. It's one of these districts where you're not allowed to keep animals. There was a bit of a shed in the garden, but there was no sign of a dog having been kept in it. But, as our Georgie said, there are plenty of cupboards in the house and if a poor dog's mouth was tied up with sticky tape, as Sandy's was...'

When I closed my eyes tightly, imagining what Sandy had gone through during those three or four days, Gran said, 'I'm sorry, lass, I'm sorry. I shouldn't jabber, but I think you should be put in the picture an' know where you stand. That man'll never forgive you till the day he dies. And our Georgie swears it's him, an' that he'll get him one day. I hope to God he doesn't, lass, I do, I hope to God he doesn't, 'cos he'll do for him. He swears it must have been the wife and the young lad who brought the dog back. I understand she used to be a spritely piece, quite good looking, but they say she looks a null individual now. And Mary Pratt—you know, the Pratts who lived below us—well, her daughter's got one of the new council houses only three doors from Stickle's and from what she can gather there's hell to pay goes on there every now and again. But he still goes out dressed up like the tailor's dummy that he once was, and when anybody speaks to him butter wouldn't melt in his mouth, so it's said. Oh, he's an actor that one, and the devil's been his tutor. And, you know, he still has the sympathy of some folks. That's because you've got on and your name's countrywide now. Some folks cannot bear the thought of anybody moving upwards and being able to change their style of living.'

'Oh, Gran.' I patted her hand gently. 'I'm still myself. As for moving up...'

'I know that, lass, I know, but it's them papers. And of course, you've got to admit your mind's not like everybody else's. Now is it?'

She punched me gently. 'And there's them that wishes they had a mind like it an' could make money hand over fist...'

I again closed my eyes. This was life, ordinary life. I was back in it again.

*   *   *

The following morning, quite early, Mike popped in. He sat on the side of the bed and said, 'Well now, Mrs Hamilton-cum-Leviston-cum-Carter, how goes it?'

'Sadly I'm afraid, Doctor.'

'Yes, it couldn't be otherwise but sadly. What you've got to realize, my dear, is besides the nice people in this world, such as Nardy, and George, Gran, Mary, and me and Jane, of course, there are fiends, demons—' his teeth ground together for a moment before he went on, 'maniacs, lunatics. But it isn't the lunatics or the maniacs you've got to look out for, it's the fiends and the demons, for they are usually classed as sane. They carry around with them the appearance of normality. They do all the things that every ordinary person does, but there is in them one extra brain cell, as it were, and this brews such evil that makes the minds of us ordinary folks boggle. Howard Stickle is an example, my dear.'

There was a constriction in my throat. I felt fear

86

sweep over me, it was as if my blood had suddenly been heated to an unbearable temperature. I gasped and gripped the hands that were now holding mine, and then muttered, 'You too . . . you think?'

'Yes, I think. Who else would want to harm you? You had thirteen years experience of him.'

Yes, yes, I had thirteen years experience of him. As I nodded to myself, there was Hamilton standing by the doctor's side, towering over him. I raised my eyes and looked at him and as I did so the atmosphere was lightened slightly by the doctor exclaiming, 'Don't tell me he's standing up there again? You know how I used to go for you for looking over my head.'

'Yes, yes. And yes he is standing up there. He's confirming all you say.'

'I had a word with Gran,' he said. 'She told you last night you should get back into the big city as soon as possible, and I'm with her in that. You are too near the source of disaster here and you want to rest. You went through a pretty hectic time, you know. Do you realize that? You should have taken notice of my fellow worker in London and had it done there and then.'

'Perhaps you're right; and if I had I should have saved poor Sandy from that torture.'

'Oh, I don't know so much about that; there'd be other times. You've got to remember that: there will still be other times, as long as he lives.'

'What else can he do, except try to kill me?'

'Oh, I don't think he'll go that far, not openly anyway. That kind of individual thinks too much of his own skin, and at bottom his type are afraid of prison.'

87

I smiled wryly as I said, 'That's comforting.'

He laughed; then, standing up, he placed his hand on my head and, his voice soft, he said, 'I've heard it said that no one should be called upon to pay the price demanded of success. And you know there's something in that. Anyway, it stems back to the old saying that everything has to be paid for. But in your case, my dear, you paid even before your success. Life isn't really fair. But then it never is, is it?' His tone changing, he thumbed at himself, saying, 'Look at me. If I had my due I should be up in Harley Street raking in the shekels, and being addressed as Mister Kane, instead of having to see to a lot of barmy old girls every morning, expecting me to give them pills to keep them alive, and in the afternoon clinic handling a bunch of young ones, their stomachs sticking out a mile, some of them telling me they don't know how it happened, or that they never wanted it to happen, with here and there, oh yes, here and there, one in her forties telling me that God has answered her prayers and provided her with a miracle. Eeh, the Immaculate Conceptions I've examined. Lass, you wouldn't believe it.' He was sounding just like George, and I lay back in the pillows holding my short forearm tight against the wound of my stomach, and I was laughing while at the same time the tears were running down my face.

Dear, dear, dear, Doctor. Was there anyone like him anywhere?

*　　　*　　　*

Tommy came up on Friday night. He stayed over

the week-end and returned with us on the Monday. He and Nardy saw to the luggage. I cradled Sandy, like a baby, in my arms during all the journey. He was wrapped in a small white fleecy blanket, and no one queried but that he was a child, for he lay so quietly under the influence of a pill the vet had given him. And not until I sat in that sun-coloured drawing-room, with Sandy lying in his basket to the side of the fireplace and Nardy hovering on one side of me and our dear friend Tommy on the other, did the dreadful feeling of fear gradually slip away from me. And I promised myself it would be a long, long time before I ever visited Fellburn again ... But as the weeks went by I had a longing to see Gran and Georgie, so it was arranged that they should come down to us for the week-end. I must have been excited at the prospect, for it was only when thinking of the practicalities to cover the week-end that I remembered Tommy's mother; and quickly I turned to Nardy and said, 'Oh dear! Oh dear! Oh dear!'

'What is it now?'

'She's coming to tea on Saturday, isn't she, Mrs Balfour?'

'Yes.' And then he put his hand over his mouth and repeated my words, 'Oh dear! Oh dear! Oh dear! And George and Gran are coming on Friday.' Our foreheads touched and we repeated, together this time, 'Oh dear! Oh dear! Oh dear!'

★   ★   ★

Nardy picked them up at the station; and when they entered the hall I was smothered in George's great arms, then hugged tightly to Gran, while Sandy raced round us barking his head off in excitement. Gran picked him up and kissed him as she cried, 'He's his old self again. Thank God. Thank God.'

I took her hat and coat, then led them into the drawing-room and there they both stood speechless and gaped.

Characteristically coming from the heart, George said, 'Bugger me! but this is some place.' And Gran muttered, 'Eeh! lass, I never dreamed. You described it, but I never dreamed. It's so lovely, beautiful.'

'Never mind all the eulogies,' said Nardy; 'sit yourselves down. What do you feel like, George? A drink, something hard? ... or tea, or coffee, or what have you?'

Before George had time to answer, Gran looked at Nardy and said, 'Eeh! lad, I'd like a drop.'

'It's a drop you'll have, Gran.'

As Nardy went out of the room, I cried at them, feeling a little embarrassed but nevertheless pleased, 'Well, sit down, sit down; it's the same price.'

They sat down, but continued to look about them. Then in a voice that was slightly tinged with awe, George asked, 'D'you live in here all the time, lass?'

'Well, where else do you think we live?'

'Well, what I mean is, this room, is it just for special occasions?'

'This is our sitting-room, George; and we also eat in here most days. We usually have our tea in here and often a bite at night before the fire.'

'And does that Janet woman keep all this

clean?' Gran was nodding her head from side to side now.

'Yes, she does, Gran, and has done for years. She has a routine and gets through marvellously. I told you about her; I told you she's very like yourself.'

'What! Like me, an' livin' in a place like this half her time. Don't be daft.'

'The place has nothing to do with her character. She's as daft as you at times, I mean the way she looks at things. You'll see her in the morning. She doesn't usually come in on a Saturday, but she's ... obliging, that's what she says. "I'll oblige you, Mrs Leviston, ma'am. I'll oblige you. Happy to do so, Mrs Leviston, ma'am."'

They laughed; then George said, 'Come and sit down aside us.' He pointed to the space in the middle of the couch, and when I was seated, he went on, 'How are you really?'

'I'm fine, fine.'

They looked about the room again and Gran said, 'Could be the Ritz.'

'Aye, it could be that,' said George; then glancing sideways at me, he whispered, 'She told them in the street we're being taken to the Ritz for lunch.'

'She didn't!'

'She did.'

'Well, you're not.'

'I know that,' said Gran now; 'and I wouldn't go if I was assed.'

'Well, you're not bein' *assed*.'

Gran now leant in front of me and looked at George, saying, 'She's turned snooty.'

91

And George, smiling his big grinning smile, said, 'Oh, I knew what would happen once she come down here among the toffs. I said to you, didn't I, all southerners are snooty.'

'Well, there's a snooty one coming tonight; you can tell him what you think about southerners.'

'One of your publishers?'

I shook my head at George and said simply, 'Tommy.'

'Oh.' They both laughed. 'He's different, Tommy. He's the exception is Tommy.'

'He might be; but I've got a surprise for you, Gran: you're going to meet his mother tomorrow.'

'That stuck-up old bitch that you told me about?'

'Yes, the stuck-up old bitch that I told you about. Now she will be a match for you.'

'Well, we'll have to wait and see, won't we?'

'Yes, you will, Gran.'

Later we had a meal in the dining-room which brought forth more 'Oohs' and 'Aahs', but not as many as when Gran saw our bedroom. There, she did an unusual thing, for she sat down in the blue quilted rest chair and she cried. Her hands covering her face, she cried. And I put my arms about her and said, 'What is it? What is it, my dear? Are you all right? Have you got a pain?'

'No, no.' She pushed me roughly, muttering, 'I'm just overcome. I've never been in a place like this; and for the moment I can't imagine you livin' in it all the time. I thought your own house, back in Fellburn, was what you call ... well, the pinnacle of grandeur like, but this. Eeh! lass.' She gripped my hands now. 'I'm happy for you. I am. I am. As I said to Georgie just a little while ago

92

back there in the room, this is a sort of payment for what you'd had to go through for years. By the way, I saw him t'other day. He was openin' the door of the taxi to let a passenger out. It was near the market. And when she handed him the money he bowed to her. He looked as oily as ever, that's until he saw me. He had just closed the door when we came abreast and he was about to go round the back of the car when he stopped, and he glared at me. My God! I'm tellin' you, Maisie, that fella's full of evil. If he could have struck me down dead he would have done. You know what I thought? I wouldn't know a minute's peace if you ever came back there.'

'Don't worry, Gran, I've no intention of going back there. But you must come more often and see us.'

Little did I know at that moment that it would be she herself who would take me back there...

It was about seven o'clock when Tommy came, and there were more hearty greetings and laughter and drinks, and by half-past nine we were all very merry.

I had discovered it took only two sherries to make me merry. I would talk twenty to the dozen on those two sherries, but strangely, should I take another I would become quiet, or were I unwise enough to take a different drink, all I should want then would be to sleep.

Tommy had caused a great deal of laughter: he had told uproarious tales about his early days when he was trying to court and his mother was determined to stop him. They were uproarious, yet if I hadn't had my two sherries I would have been looking for a deeper meaning into why he should be recalling them again.

Gran, spluttering with laughter, was saying, 'And what did your ma do to the second one?'

'She sniffed at her.'

We were all laughing hilariously now.

'Sniffed at her, like this?' Georgie cleared his nostrils at one draught, and Tommy shook his head and, the tears running from his eyes, said, 'No, no, not like that, Geordie man; she did it with her whole face, like this.' He now raised his eyebrows, at the same time curling his lip upwards, the action in itself showed utter disdain, then looked down his nose, gave a slight hitch to an imaginary bust and said in a voice that was an exact imitation of his mother's, 'You dye your hair?'

We actually fell about. But then quite suddenly, his voice taking on a sad note, he caught hold of Gran's hand and said, 'With Christina Rossetti, I said goodbye to my love:

Remember me when I am gone away,
Gone far away into the silent land;
When you can no more hold me by the
    hand,
Nor I half turn to go, yet turning stay.
Remember me when no more day by day
You tell me of our future that you
    planned:
Only remember me; you understand
It will be late to counsel then or pray.
Yet if you should forget me for a while
And afterwards remember, do not grieve:
For if the darkness and corruption leave
A vestige of the thoughts that once I had,

94

Better by far you should forget and smile
Than that you should remember and be
    sad.'

We laughed no more. He had let go of Gran's
hand, and she was nodding at him now, and, her
tone quiet for her, she said, 'Aye, that was nice,
Tommy, that was nice. Not the kind I
understand, but it sounded nice.'
He was lying back on the couch, his head
turned towards me now, and I took his hand and
to my embarrassment and not a little to my
amazement, he quoted directly to me,

'When do I see thee most, beloved one?
When in the light the spirits of mine eyes
Before thy face, their altar, solemnize
The worship of that Love through thee
    made known?'

He stopped now and stared at me. I withdrew my
hand from his grasp, and he, giving a deep laugh
and turning to Gran, leaned towards her and
cried,

'Oh love, my love! if I no more should
    see
Thyself, nor on the earth the shadow of
    thee,
Nor image of thine eyes in any spring...'

'Look here! lad,' Gran's voice broke in, and it had
a flat sound to it now as she said, 'If I understood
half of what you're spoutin' I would clap. But
now you be yourself an' talk plain English.'

95

And at this, Tommy lay back into the corner of the couch and, looking up towards the ceiling, he cried, 'Dante Gabriel Rossetti. Plain English, she says, plain English.' Then suddenly bending towards Gran again, he said, 'Bugger me eyes! if you're not right, woman.'

During the latter performance I had noted that Nardy didn't laugh; and now getting to his feet, he looked down on Tommy and said, 'A cup of black coffee; then it's home for you.'

'Can't I stay here?'

The words sounded like a plea from a small boy. And I saw Nardy glance towards me, then purse his lips and say, 'You could, but I don't think the bed has been aired.'

'That won't matter. I never catch cold. May I stay?'

'Of course, of course.' Nardy's voice seemed over loud. Then he added, 'But don't forget your mother's coming to tea tomorrow. What will you do about that?'

'Go along in the morning and fetch her, and hear her say—' He now struck a pose, pulled himself up straight, joined his hands across his chest, and exclaimed, 'You've been with that woman again. Now if this doesn't stop, I'll ... yes, I'll cut you out of my will.' He dropped the pose and, nodding at us and his face unsmiling now, he said, 'That's what she said last week, that she was going to cut me out of her will. I've kept that house going for years, and now she's going to cut me out of her will. Oh, Nardy'—he put his hand up to Nardy and gripped his wrist—'I nearly hit her, I did. Honest to God, I nearly hit her.' Then he laughed, and spluttered as he said, 'Do you

96

smashing night, Maisie, a smashing night.'

I did not immediately gather up the coffee cups, but I sat down on the couch again, and there was Hamilton sitting with his two front legs resting over the end of it. And he looked at me and he repeated, A smashing night, so why aren't you laughing now?

I'm a bit worried over Tommy, I said.

Yes, Tommy. He nodded his big head and his expression was odd. I didn't know whether he was vexed or pleased. And then he said, You've got to think seriously about Tommy. He's making this his second home.

Well, what's wrong in that? He's Nardy's best friend, always has been, and he's mine now.

There are friends and friends. Nardy didn't like him spouting that poetry tonight.

Don't be silly, you're imagining things.

Huh! Huh! His big lip left his teeth and he said, That's funny coming from you.

It might be, but I'm not so vain, or mad, as to think that another ... I couldn't go on. And at that moment the door opened and Nardy entered the room, and I looked at him as he made straight for the coffee cups and gathered them up and put them on the tray.

'Is he all right?'

'For the moment.' His answer was brief.

'I'm ... I'm worried about him, Nardy.'

'You're not the only one.'

The cups stacked on the trolley, he now came and sat down beside me and, taking my hand in both of his, he looked at me for some seconds before he said quietly, 'Don't become too sorry for him, Maisie.'

99

I looked to the side, and there was Hamilton, his big head nodding slowly, and with him was Begonia, but she was shaking her head from side to side. She wasn't looking at me but at her mate, and there was a look of indignation in her whole attitude. And there was indignation in my tone as I said, 'What do you mean, Nardy, don't get too sorry for him?'

'Just what I say, don't get too sorry for him. You must have guessed how he feels about you.'

'*Oh Nardy.*' I went to pull my hand away from his, but he held on to it, saying now, 'Don't play about. You must have realized it.'

'*I don't, I didn't, I mean...*'

'What do you mean, dear?'

'Well, I felt a bit embarrassed tonight when he was spouting his love poems, but ... but he was tight.'

'Yes, he was tight tonight, but he's been solid and sober at other times when he's spouted his love poems. I'm just putting you on your guard.'

'But Nardy'—I shook my head—'How could you imagine, I mean that ... Well'—I swallowed deeply—'I think it's a miracle that you love me, but that I could ... well ...' I searched for a word, and there *he* was at the bottom of the couch, his big head wagging, giving it to me. And I brought it out on a stammer, 'A ... attract anyone else, me of all people, because ... oh Nardy, I love you so much, so very, very much, and right deep in my heart I'm so full of gratitude to you; you have given me a new way of life. And to think you would imagine that I would, or could dare...'

'I don't imagine that you would or could dare or do anything in that direction, my dearest. But you know, you are of a sympathetic nature, you hold out friendship with both hands, because, let's face it, you were deprived of it for so long, it's like a new wine to you, and ... and Tommy has drunk deeply of it lately. He's hardly ever away from this house.'

'But he's your friend. I welcomed him as your friend. You've told me you've been close for years, and he's told me that if it hadn't been for your friendship he just doesn't know how he would have got through at times. Nardy, you could be mistaken, you must be mistaken. Oh, I hope you are, because it will mean I'll have to ... well, be stiff with him.'

'There's no need to be stiff with him, my dear; I only want you to be on your guard. As Gran would say, keep your weather-eye open. I love you, my dear, I love you as I never imagined loving anyone again, and ... and I'm jealous.'

I closed my eyes. Was I Maisie Rochester who had known she would never be married, who had recognized her plainness and her overall lack of attraction, even without her deformed arm? Could this still be Maisie Rochester who for thirteen years had been married to a sadist and who had gained the love of a wonderful man and was now being told that he was jealous because another man was in love with her? No, no; it couldn't happen to her. Come off it.

'What did you say?'

'I didn't speak.'

'Yes, you did.'

I gave a small laugh. 'It was Hamilton. He said, come off it.'

'Oh'—he looked about him—'I agree with you,

101

Hamilton; false modesty on her part.'

'Oh, it wasn't that, it was just that ... that ... well, I couldn't think that these things were happening to me, or could ever happen to me, you in particular, darling.' I now took his face between my hands and said, 'Nardy, this I promise you, I shall love you till the day I die and never, never willingly cause you one moment's worry or regret.'

'Oh, my dear, my dear.' He held me gently in his arms. And as I looked over his shoulder, there they were, standing side by side and, strangely, their heads were hanging. That was odd, I thought. What had I said to make them look so sad? I had just made a vow that I would love my beloved until the day I died.

*   *   *

Mrs Balfour was sitting in very much the same position that Tommy had depicted her the previous night: she was seated in a straightbacked chair, her hands folded across her stomach. She had been seated like this for the last hour, and like a judge, or a better description would be the prosecuting counsel, she had been firing questions alternately at Gran and George. She was now looking at George. 'I understand you drive a bus,' she said.

'Yes, I drive a bus, missis.'

'Couldn't you find a better occupation than that?'

'There *is* no better occupation than that, missis. As me ma says'—he thumbed towards Gran—'it's like life: it stops and starts; people get on an' get off, some you remember an' some you don't; some are nice an' some are real bug ... nasty. You'd like to run over the nasty ones'—he grinned widely now—'but there seems to be a law against it. A pity, I think.'

Mrs Balfour pulled her chin inwards before saying now, 'You have four children to support?'

'I have that, missis.'

'But they're not your children?'

His expression changed and, gruffly now, he said, 'They're my children all right, missis, and I'm their father.'

'Oh. Oh, I was given to understand...'

'Aye, you were given to understand all right: their father scarpered and left them, and I married a woman with four bairns. But she's me wife and they are me children.'

They stared at each other for a moment, and I was about to break in when the lady turned her attention on Gran, asking abruptly now, 'Do you get on with your daughter-in-law, Mrs Carter?'

'Aye. Why shouldn't I?'

'Well'—there was a tight smile on the lady's face—'mothers don't often get on with their daughters-in-law.'

'It all depends on who the mother is an' who the daughter-in-law is. D'you think you could get on with your daughter-in-law?'

'I don't happen to have a daughter-in-law.'

'No, I know that, but say if you suddenly had.'

'What do you mean, if I suddenly had?'

'Just that.' Gran grinned at the lady now. 'Say Tommy took it into his head to get married. There would be nothin' unusual about that, now would there? He could do it any minute.'

I saw the skin tighten on the bony face, the wrinkles seemed to smooth out, the eyes narrowed and the voice came thinly through her teeth now as she said, 'I don't think there's any possibility of my son marrying, and therefore the question of my becoming a mother-in-law has no point.'

'Huh! You never know where a blister might light.'

'What did you say?'

'I said, you never know where a blister might light. I'd better translate that for you, eh? You never know what men will do, especially 'round your Tommy's age. They get a sort of itch then, if they haven't had it afore. Now there's our Georgie. He always had the itch, born with it, weren't you, lad?'

To this George replied, 'Just as you say, Ma, just as you say. But you're right.' Pressing home his mother's point, and enjoying it, he now looked at our visitor and said, 'Blisters can grow into boils, and then there's nothin' for it but a hot poultice. And the only equivalent to a hot poultice in this case is a bedmate. Come on, Ma.' He got to his feet. 'Tommy's in the kitchen supposedly nattering to Janet. I don't trust him an inch.'

· 'Nor me,' said Gran, and they both almost skipped out of the room. And when Nardy, who had been choking inwardly all this time, rose and said, 'Will you excuse me for a moment? I think it's about time we were called in to tea. It's to be a north-country one.' And he smiled at Mrs Balfour. And there I was left with her, and she stared at me hard before she spoke. 'How do you put up with that pair, Mrs Leviston?' she said.

104

'What exactly do you mean, Mrs Balfour?'

'I ... I shouldn't think that I have to explain what I mean, they are both uncouth. I have never met anyone like them before. Common isn't the word.'

'You're right, common isn't the word, Mrs Balfour, and definitely not uncouth. I think the word you're really looking for is real. They are real people, uneducated, yes, but they both have wisdom that no education could have supplied.'

'Well, well, they certainly have an advocate in you, Mrs Leviston.'

'Yes, they have, because they were the only people in my young days to give me love and bring me any kind of happiness.'

'What about your mother? I understand you were sixteen or more when she died.'

'Oh, my mother.' I nodded at her. 'My mother was not common; my mother was refined, a lady you could say, even though a pseudo one, and she was vain and cruel without any real love in her.'

'Really! I don't think it befits you to speak of the dead like that, Mrs Leviston.'

I rose to my feet, and looking at her straight in the face now, I said, 'Nor do I think it befits you to speak of the living and those who are my friends so disparagingly. Shall we go into tea?'

I saw her face working, her pale blue lips moving over one another as if she were already champing on food. Then, as I made to walk away, she said, 'A moment, Mrs Leviston. I'm'—now I recognized she had to make an effort to go on—'I'm sorry if I've upset you, but before we go in there is something private I should like to discuss with you if you can give me another

105

moment.'

I stepped back and faced her again.

'It's ... it's about Tommy. I ... I'm very worried about him.'

'Really? Why are you worried about him?'

I watched her fingers as they began to pick at the material of her dress; it was as if she was removing insects from it. 'It's ... it's concerning a woman.'

'A woman?'

'Yes. I wonder if you can ... well, help me? Do you know who she is?'

'The woman?'

'Yes, the woman.'

'No.' I shook my head. 'I know of no woman that Tommy is...well, associated with. How should I? We ... we only see him now and again.'

'That...that makes it worse.' The picking went on and she looked to the side. 'I...I understand that he often comes over here in the evenings. Bella seemed to think so. But ... but he has, for some time now, spent week-ends away from home.'

'Really?'

'Yes.' She nodded at me. 'And that suggests only one thing, you must admit.'

'I wouldn't know.'

Her voice was sharp now as she said, 'Well, you wouldn't expect a man to spend week-ends on his own, now would you?'

I could have said, Yes. In Tommy's case, yes. Instead, I said, 'Well, hardly.'

'Well, there you are then. And ... and you don't know who she is?'

'No.'

'He hasn't given you any indication, a name, a place?'

'I'm afraid not.'

'If he had told Nardy, would Nardy have confided in you?'

I thought for a moment before I let myself say, 'I'm not so sure. They have been friends for years; he...he might be honouring a trust.'

'Yes, yes, of course. May I ask you something?'

'Yes.'

'Would you ... well, I mean, would you do something for me?'

'That all depends if it's possible.'

'Oh, it's quite possible. All I'm asking is that you ... probe a little and ... and let me know ... if...'

I held up my hand. 'Please don't go on, Mrs Balfour. I have no intention of probing into your son's private affairs. And if he were to confide in me, then it would be as a friend and, as such, a confidence. Shall we go into tea now?'

The look on her face was almost vicious. She pulled herself to her feet and I opened the door for her, and with a step very firm for one supposedly crippled with arthritis, she passed through.

Seeing Tommy approaching from the direction of the kitchen with Gran on his arm, and laughing together, she called in strident tones, 'We cannot stay long. I am not feeling too well.'

'That is a pity, Mother. It would have been nice if we could have made a night of it, wouldn't it, Gran?' He now turned and looked at Gran, and she, slapping him on the back, answered, 'It would that, lad. It would that.'

Hurriedly now, I led our guest into the dining-room, fearing that she would faint before she reached there, for all the colour had drained from her face.

Immediately the meal was over, she donned her coat. She had not removed her hat at all. And when we closed the door on her and Tommy, Nardy let out a long-drawn breath, saying, 'God help him when he gets home.'

I endorsed this in my mind, and I was also glad this evening was already taken care of: seats had been booked for four at the theatre later on; and afterwards a table was reserved in one of Nardy's favourite restaurants. Tomorrow, too, had been planned. We were to show Gran and George London. And on Monday they would be returning to Fellburn.

Why should I feel guilty at the thought that I should be glad to have the house to myself again? This was something new.

I went into the kitchen to thank Janet for her big effort in making such a splendid tea.

'Oh, that's all right,' she said. 'I'm glad you enjoyed it. But she's a tartar, that one, isn't she? How in the name of God does Mr Tommy stand her!' Then leaning forward to me and whispering, she said, 'I bet she found her match in Gran, eh, ma'am?'

'She did, Janet, she did. And with George, too. But she found them very common...uncouth.'

'She said that?'

'Yes, she did.'

'Well, give me the common and uncouth any day. What do you say?'

'I say with you, Janet, yes, any day.'

I liked Janet more the longer we were together. In a way she had taken Gran's place in this new world. But strangely, I had the idea that Gran hadn't quite taken to her.

CHAPTER SIX

The weeks slid by. Nardy worked in the office, I worked on my book. He was nearly always in by half-past five. We would have tea; then talk. Some evenings, we would just sit by the fire; then go to bed and love; or we might go out to a play, or to Covent Garden Opera House. He was educating me in the world of music and art. He loved the opera, I wasn't so keen on it; my choice was the ballet. Life was good.

But there was still Tommy. He had become very quiet of late, and he wasn't dropping in so often. And even after a drink or two he had ceased to spout his poetry. Then one night came the climax.

It was a Friday evening. Autumn was setting in: the leaves in the garden opposite had turned to bronze and gold. I often sat by the window in the drawing-room looking down into the garden and thinking what a pity I never saw anyone strolling in it. All the residents in the square had keys to it, but I had yet to see anyone using one. The only human figure was that of the old gardener pottering about. I likened the garden to a jewel encased in an iron cage. Why didn't they take the railings down and let people walk among the beautiful shrubs ... and leave their orange peel,

and the beer cans, and their ice-cream cartons. I
looked to the side. Hamilton was looking out of
the window and I nodded at him, saying, 'Yes,
you're right.'

I know I am, he said. People in the main are
dirty. Some of them live like pigs. Remember Mrs
Purdy?

I remembered Mrs Purdy, a distant relative of
Nardy's we went down to Hampshire to visit. She
lived in what you would call a manor-house, and
it stank.

'Why'—I asked Hamilton—'do some women
consider housework beneath them?'

And to this he answered, Because at one time
only menials did housework and you could engage
servants by the dozen for next to nothing; but
now the servants have cars and can drive into the
country and leave their litter scattered about, so
following the example of their betters in bygone
days. But they have no servants to rake it all up
after them.

'You're being cynical.' I smiled at him, and, his
lip going up from his teeth, he smiled back and
said, You could say we are. Anyway, here's your
beloved coming.

I kissed my beloved, my beloved kissed me;
then we sat down together on the couch and I
poured out the tea that was set on the low trolley.
And then I asked the usual question, 'How's it
gone?'

'It's been an unusual day,' he said. 'I took a
new author out to lunch at the Cafe Royal.'

'Oh,' I said smiling. 'Man or woman?'

'A man. And I thought of the day I took you
there and of how different it all was, because this

fellow ... oh my God!' He closed his eyes for a moment and turned his head to the side. 'The ego of some men. You know something? This book of his is the best that has ever been written by anyone.'

'Is it so good?'

'No, it's not. I think it's quite mediocre. It's only the sex that's got it through. That's the trouble now, they think they've only to lay that on thick and they're there. And it is on thick, and the book will sell. Oh, yes, it'll sell. But there he was dictating about what would happen when it went into paperbacks and then into a film.'

'No.'

'Oh, yes, yes. And I couldn't get rid of him after lunch; I didn't get back to the office until nearly four, and then one of the clerks told me there had been two calls from Tommy's. Huh!' He laughed here. 'Likely his mother wanted to know where he was going to spend the weekend. Perhaps he had told her he was making it a long one, because he was off to Eastbourne earlier today to see an author, a man who's writing his autobiography. Aren't they all!'

It was at this point the phone rang and I stayed him, saying, 'I'll get it.'

The phone was on a table to the side of the window, and I picked it up and a voice said, 'Is that you, Mrs Leviston?'

'Yes, yes, Bella.' I recognized her voice.

'Oh, Mrs Leviston, is ... is Mr Leviston there?'

'Yes, yes, he's here, Bella. Is there anything wrong?'

'She's dead...she's dead, Mrs Leviston.'

' Wh ... at!' My voice ended on a screech that

brought Nardy to my side. I gazed at him in horror, and I put my hand over the mouthpiece as I said, 'She's dead.'

As he whispered, 'Oh, my God!' I spoke into the phone again, saying, 'What ... what happened?'

'It ... it was around three o'clock.'

She seemed to be gasping for breath now and I said, 'Where's Tommy?'

'He's here, Mrs Leviston. Will you come around?'

'Yes, yes, right away, right away.' And I banged down the phone before picking it up again to order a taxi...

Twenty minutes later we entered the house. Tommy met us in the hall. His face looked ashen. He didn't speak but after looking from one to the other of us he turned and we followed him into the dining-room. And now, sitting at the table and joining his hands together, he bowed his head over them, saying, 'I feel terrible, terrible.'

'What happened?' Nardy was standing by him, his hand on his shoulder. And now he raised his head and looked up at Nardy and muttered, 'You know I...I went down to Eastbourne. Well, Bella phoned the office and they gave her the address; but I'd left by then, and when I got back, there she was.'

Now Nardy had him by the shoulder shaking him and saying, 'Well, what happened?'

'I don't know, except what Bella said. About two o'clock she had a sort of seizure and ... and she rang for the doctor for her. And when he came, he said it was a heart attack and he would get her into hospital. But as he was examining her

112

she just ... well, she went.'

Both Nardy and I groped for chairs and sat down, and as if of one mind we both put our elbows on the table and held our heads in our hands for a moment. The relief was making me sick, as I'm sure it was Nardy.

Tommy was shaking his head. 'I...I feel awful, man, dreadful. The times...oh, the times—' he now wagged his head slowly from shoulder to shoulder, his eyes screwed up tight as he went on, 'I've wanted her dead. I've prayed I'd come home and find her dead. I've prayed she would have a heart attack. And then, only this morning, she said, "Where are you going?" and I said, "I'm going down to Eastbourne for the week-end. What are you going to make out of that, Mother?" I had no intention of staying away for the week-end, not now, not any more, for it didn't do any good. But ... but that must have finished her.'

'No. No, of course it didn't.' Nardy's voice was harsh now. 'She must have had a bad heart for years.'

'Well, that was something I didn't know. But, oh God! Nardy, I feel weighed down.' He now looked at me, saying, 'I should feel free—shouldn't I, Maisie?—like you did after you got rid of Stickle, but I don't. I feel ... well, I feel trapped inside myself. I'll never get over this feeling of guilt, because instead of hating her, I should have tried to understand her needs of me, and ... and shown her some love, but I didn't. I didn't.'

I rose now and went round and put a hand on his shoulder as I said, 'She didn't show you any, not real love. You mustn't blame yourself for that.'

'I think I'll blame myself till the day I die. When I saw her lying there she looked so ... so helpless, and so very, very old, pityingly vulnerable. Oh, my God!' He again drooped his head on to his hands, and I said, 'Believe me, Tommy, this feeling will pass. I had something similar when my mother went. It will pass, I tell you, it will pass. Anyway, I think the best thing you can do, and Bella too, is to come and sleep at our place for the next day or two. When will they take her away?'

'In the morning.'

'Well, then, both of you ...'

'No, no. Thanks all the same, Maisie. I've got to stay here, at last until she is finally put away. Then I'll know what I'm going to do. This ... this house has been a drag on me for years. I'll ... I'll likely sell it, and ... and settle Bella some place. And then we'll see. Thanks for coming.' He looked from one to the other; then getting to his feet, he squared his shoulders and said, 'You two have borne the brunt of my moaning for a long time now. I'm sorry I burdened you with it. I must have been a proper pain in the neck at times. Well, it's all over. The only person I'll have to moan about now is myself and my conscience.' He held up his hands as Nardy was about to say something, and he went on, 'It's no use. I know myself too well, Nardy. I'm a coward. If I hadn't been I would have made a break years ago, before things got on top of me. It wouldn't have upset her half as much then. But then again'—he shrugged his shoulders—'I couldn't have done

114

that as I was her only support. That's been part of the trouble. You see, when my father died he was almost bankrupt: she hadn't a penny after he went, and she liked this house. And, of course, I had to have a home. So, what was more natural than that I should keep it going. And that's been part of the resentment. You see, I felt trapped from the beginning: were I to marry I couldn't run two homes, my wife would have to come here.' He smiled now, a wan sad smile, 'You get the picture? At least you've had it for a long time now. But don't worry.' He held out his hands to both of us. 'I'll be all right. I've been blessed in one way, I've got you two, and always will have, I hope.'

CHAPTER SEVEN

It was the day of the funeral, a Wednesday; she had been buried on the Tuesday. Apart from the heads of the office and Nardy and myself and Bella, there were no other mourners at the funeral.

Nardy had returned to the office. Tommy was to see the solicitor with regard to his mother's will. That's how things stood, until six o'clock that evening.

We had finished tea and I'd washed up and I was about to go and change because we were going to the opera when the lift bell rang. Nardy and I were both in the hall. He went and opened the door and in walked Tommy. Or did he race in? or jump in? I'm not quite sure. There was the strangest look upon his face. Was it full of glee, or was it devilish? His large grey eyes looked almost black and, spreading his arms out towards us both in an exaggerated dramatic way, he said, 'My friends. My friends.' Then noticing the look on Nardy's face, he dropped his arms to his sides and, his voice changing, he said, 'I'm not drunk, I'm solid and sober, but you see before you, dear friends, a man so full of hate that he'll have to live ten lifetimes before it's burnt out of him.'

'What's the matter with you? What's happened?' Nardy's voice was terse.

'May I sit down and have a drink *now*?'

I turned to go to the drawing-room and Tommy followed me. Nardy went into the dining-room to get the drink. When I sat down, Tommy, bending over me, said slowly, 'You've got your Hamilton, Maisie, I've got the devil.'

'Oh! Tommy. Tommy, what is it? What on earth's happened?'

Nardy was entering the room with a tray, and Tommy called, 'Make it neat, Nardy, and a double.'

He threw off his whisky in two gulps; then sat down on the couch and drew in a long shuddering breath before looking up at us and saying, 'You also see before you a rich man.'

We exchanged a glance, Nardy and I, both thinking the same thing, he had become deranged in some way. And he, picking up our thoughts, said, 'Sit down, Nardy, sit down. You'll need to sit before I'm finished. And I'm not barmy, I haven't gone round the bend. But it wouldn't surprise me at all if I did. I've been with my solicitor all afternoon'—he nodded at Nardy—

116

'and I expected him to say, "Well, Mr Balfour, there's little to talk about. Your mother's will is very straightforward. The house was in her name, as you know, and of the thousand pounds that her aunt left her, she has, as you know, taken the interest every year. But apart from that, I don't think there's anything further to discuss." That's what I expected him to say. But what did he do? He invited me to sit down. He smiled at me, and then said, "Your mother was a very strange lady, Mr Balfour." I could have been flippant and said, you're telling me, but I remained mute, until he said, "Right from the beginning she wanted this matter kept strictly private. No one was to know anything about it until she died. Then I'm afraid, if you had been married—" he then poked his head towards me and said, "You are not married, are you?" And to this I replied, "No, I am not married, sir." And so he went on, "Well then, the estate won't go to the animals so I can say now that everything appears to be straightforward, seeing that you have no brothers or sisters to make their claim on the estate."'

Tommy stopped here, wetted his lips, then again exchanged a glance with us both and said, 'I repeated, "Estate?" and the dear old fellow nodded and said with emphasis, "Yes, estate." At this I smiled and said, "A terrace house and a few pounds." And then you know what he said?'

We waited while he stared at us, swallowed deeply, then put his hand to his throat and stroked it as if trying to push his Adam's apple down his gullet. And then he went on, 'He said, "I wouldn't consider seventy-five thousand pounds and four considerable properties to come

117

under the heading of a few pounds." And he smiled as he said it; and I stared at him, and I couldn't speak for a time, then I said, "What?" And he repeated, "Seventy-five thousand pounds. And there are the four properties, here in London, let as offices at present, but worth not less than one hundred thousand pounds each."'

We were both speechless. We continued to gaze at him and he at us, until he went on, 'It was fifteen years ago that her aunt died. She lived in Devon. I'd only met her once. I was a young fellow at the time, in my twenties, and I thought Mother and she could be sisters, they were so alike. Well, when she died, Mother went down to see to her affairs. She had always, I think, imagined her to be slightly hard up. And thinking about it now, she very likely got the idea of the games she played with me from her dear aunt, for the solicitor tells me that she was surprised to be left the four houses and amazed at the sum of money, which then was about fifty thousand pounds, apparently the aunt had played with stocks and shares. What Mother had expected, so I understand, was the cottage and the furniture, which then would have been worth about fifteen hundred pounds. I remember she stayed down there for four or five weeks, and it was such a nice respite for Bella and, of course, for me too. Oh, yes, me too. Then when she returned ...' He stopped and, wetting his lips, he looked from side to side; then pointing to a chair, he said, 'I can see her as if she were there now, sitting in the chair with her arms folded across her stomach, telling me that the aunt had left her the little house and that she had sold it and she was richer by a thousand pounds. But she had put it in the bank and had decided each year that the interest would buy her a winter or a summer outfit, and in that way it would ease my purse. Those were the very words she used, ease my purse.'

He was silent now. We were all silent. We just couldn't take it in. That dreadful woman to hang on to him all these years, to plead poverty so he wouldn't leave her.

He now asked quietly, 'Can you believe it?'

'No. No.' Nardy's voice was small. 'It's diabolical.'

'Yes, that's the word, diabolical, because every month it's taken nearly all my pay cheque to keep things going: Bella had to be paid, as small as her wage was, she had to be paid. Poor Bella. What she's gone through too.'

His head dropped back on his shoulders now and he said, 'I've always wanted a car, but I've told myself again and again I'd never be able to afford one. Yet, all these years I could have had a car, couldn't I?' He looked at me now and said, 'Couldn't I, Maisie? I could have had a car . . . two cars, three cars. And I could have taken her out and about. Can you see the reasoning in it? Oh!' He closed his eyes tight and clenched his fists now and shook them in front of his face as he said, 'Why am I asking such a bloody silly question? Of course, anybody can see the reasoning of it: with a car I'd be able to drive away, wouldn't I, with a girl beside me? And with money like that I would have had half a dozen, no, a dozen suits and shirts to match. Aye, shirts to match instead of Bella having to turn the cuffs, which she has done for years.' His head was

119

wagging now. 'Yes, Bella's turned the cuffs of my shirts for years.'

He got abruptly to his feet and in silence we watched him stamping up and down behind the couch. Twice he went the length of the room and we didn't move. And then he stopped and, leaning over the couch towards us, he cried, 'I wish I had killed her. I do, I wish I had killed her. I would willingly spend the next ten years in a cell for the pleasure of having killed her.'

'*Stop it! Stop it!*' Nardy was on his feet now. 'That's no way to talk. You would have never killed her.'

'Oh, you don't know, Nardy. What do you know about it, really? You only saw the rehearsals, you didn't see the real acts. You didn't have to sit with her night after night and listen to her. If I wanted to read, she wanted to know why I didn't talk, and if I talked she would always slap me down as if I was a little boy, saying, "Don't talk such tommy-rot. Poetry!" she used to say. "No real man reads poetry." When I pointed out Keats, Browning, Byron, and the rest, her answer was, "They weren't real men, they were perverts." It's many a long day since I talked poetry in that house. You know what she did once? She turfed nearly all the books out of my room and gave them to somebody who was collecting for a jumble sale, among them an early edition of Keats, and an edition of Shelley's poems arranged by Stopford Brooke.' He pointed his finger into Nardy's chest, saying, 'Macmillan published it. And then there was...'

'All right, all right. I know about that, you told me. But now it's over. Come and sit down and

120

listen to me. As you said, you're rich, and you've still got a long life before you.'

'What, at thirty-nine?'

'Yes, at thirty-nine. Don't be ridiculous. Sit down there.' Nardy pushed him back onto the couch. 'Now, the main thing for you to do is to come back to work, at least for a few weeks, if not for good. In the meantime, buy that car, learn to drive, get yourself out and about. You once said to me, how wonderful it would be to do a world tour. Well, do your world tour. But first give yourself time to think.'

'Oh, I've given myself time to think. I've walked for miles before I came here. You know that? When I went back and told Bella, she couldn't believe it. She just couldn't. In fact, she thought I was crazy, like you two did.' He gave a wry smile now. 'In fact, I'm asking myself, am I not crazy? Anyway, crazy or not, I'm selling that house, and I can't think of the thousands that'll bring in these days. Huh!' He laughed. 'Talking in thousands now when for years I've taken the tube because I couldn't afford to run to taxis. Anyway, Bella's got a hankering after Brighton. She's spent her one week's holiday a year there for some time past, and so I'm going to buy a flat and she can move into it. It will be a place for me to go at the week-ends when I'm at a loose end. Anyway, I'm giving her ten thousand. If anybody's earned it for a lifetime's work, she has.'

'That's good of you.'

He looked at Nardy, saying now in a bitter tone, 'No, it isn't. I'm doing it mainly to get one back on her; she'd go stark staring mad if she thought that Bella was getting a cut off her cake.'

'You're not doing it to spite her.' I spoke for the first time. 'Well, you're telling yourself you are, but you are really doing it out of the goodness of your heart.'

'Maisie'—he slowly shook his head—'there's no goodness in my heart at the present moment. I disliked her. I loathed her at times, but I knew nothing about hate, real hate like that which is in me now. I tell you, I could...'

'No more of that!' Nardy was shouting at him. 'And get it out of your mind; in fact, make yourself laugh about it.'

'*What!*'

For a moment I thought Tommy was going to go for Nardy physically, for he bent towards him and his voice was a yell as he cried, 'Laugh at what I've gone through since I was a lad? Laugh?' He now thumbed towards me, saying, 'Maisie wouldn't tell me to laugh, Nardy, for she knows what it is to live with a sadist.'

I got to my feet and went towards him and, taking his hand, I said, 'Yes, I do, I do, Tommy; but I also know that the sadist wins if you let hate of him corrode you. I went mad for a time under such treatment. And just lately, when Sandy there'—I pointed to where the dog was lying curled up in his favourite place, hugging the fire—'was tortured, and I felt there was only one person who would have done it, there was in me for a time the feeling that if I came near Stickle I would make sure I had a knife in my hand, and I would tear the flesh from him bit by bit as he had done from that poor little beast. Then I knew that the only sane thing to do was to put distance between the perpetrator of evil and myself. Well now, Tommy, there's a great deal of distance between your perpetrator and yourself, and, as Nardy said, you have a long life before you. Get that car, then do a world tour, then get married.'

He was staring down into my face and he repeated, 'Get the car, do a world tour, then get married. Thank you, Maisie, I'll think about it. But now, I'll make myself scarce because I've just remembered this is the big night at the opera. You've had tickets for it some time.'

'Oh, that doesn't matter; you stay where you are and I'll make a...'

'You'll do no such thing. I'm off.' He stood up and buttoned his coat. Then laughing a laugh that was threaded with bitterness, he said, 'You see the beginnings of the new man. But I'll tell you what you can do, at the week-end you can come and help me choose the car.'

'We'll do that, we'll do it with pleasure.' Nardy was walking up the room with him. I didn't follow, and at the door Tommy turned and said, 'Be seeing you, Maisie.'

'Yes, Tommy, yes.'

I stood where I was until I heard the outer door close, and then Nardy came back into the room. And when he reached me, we looked at each other for a moment but didn't speak. I stooped down and picked Sandy up into my arms and he snuggled his head into my neck. And it was then I said, 'She would have left it all to the animals, and she wouldn't even let him have a dog, or a cat when he was a boy. She was a fiend.'

'She was that all right. But you know something, dear?'

'What?'

123

'I feel more worried about him now than I was before, because he will go on hating her.'

'Time will tell,' I said. Then looking at the clock, I added, 'We'd be late, wouldn't we?' And he nodded and said, 'Yes, we'd be late. But what does it matter? I don't think I could enjoy even the singing of angels at this moment.' Then reaching out his arm, he said, 'Come and sit down and let us thank the gods that we are what we are and we have each other.'

And as I sat down, still holding Sandy, I added, 'And Sandy.'

'Yes, of course, Sandy.'

'And Hamilton.'

'Oh, yes, Hamilton.'

'And Begonia.'

He smiled but he didn't laugh.

Tommy had come into a fortune, but it seemed to have put a damper on all merriment.

*   *   *

Tommy got his car. He took driving lessons, a crash course, and passed first time. He sold the terraced house, bought the flat in Brighton, and Bella, hardly able to believe that this was happening to her, went to live there, and found herself a part-time job in relieving a nurse who was looking after an invalid, a woman, the antithesis of her previous mistress. She kept her week-ends free so that she could be in the flat and see to Tommy, should he care to come down. So life for her had fallen into what she termed, a fairy-tale pattern.

Tommy said he wouldn't dream of leaving

Houseman's, but he intended to ask for an extended leave in order that he could realize his dream of doing a world tour. He had it all mapped out.

CHAPTER EIGHT

It was again a week before Christmas, and both Nardy and I were in a dilemma. Gran had been unwell for some time. It had started with a cold. It had developed into pneumonia, and Mary kept saying that Gran wished she could see me. Remembering the events of last New Year, I was afraid to go back to Fellburn. So we talked it over and we came to the decision that we would go up for just a couple of days and see Gran, and if she was on the mend we would come straight back.

Also there was another tangent we had to sort out. Tommy had bought a host of presents for the children, all kinds of things. He seemed bent on spending. Shortly after he had come into the money, he had presented me with a diamond brooch and matching earrings, and Nardy with a magnificent pair of gold cufflinks. More than once Nardy had warned him that the rate at which his money was going would soon see him back to where he had been. But Tommy had laughed and said in an airy fashion, 'Why, since I sold one of those houses to the advertising firm, I'm not even making a hole in the interest on the money. And who've I got to spend it on but my friends? And as charming as dear Housey is and our friend Rington, do you know they never once invited me to dinner at their homes ... Oh yes, you were, you were'—he had nodded to Nardy—'but never me. No, my friends are few, but they're of the best quality.'

He could say the nicest things, could Tommy. But here we were, and Nardy was saying, 'Well, as he was coming to us for the holidays the best thing for it is to let him come up with us. But I'm not going in that car; he's a madman behind that wheel. You'd think he'd been driving in Le Mans races for years. No, let him go up his way and we'll go by train as usual.'

And so it was arranged.

I phoned Mary and told her we'd be up the next day, but not to expect us to stay very long, especially not over Christmas. And also to prepare for an invasion by Tommy.

So, once again we were getting off the train in Newcastle station, and I was carrying Sandy in my arms and was dressed in my fur coat and hat, but fortunately there were no photographers and journalists there today. Our luggage was light, only two cases, one filled with presents, the other with our night clothes and toiletries.

We had to stand for a few minutes in a queue for a taxi. Then one drew up. The driver turned his head towards us and the constriction in my throat, at the sight of him, caused me to grip Sandy so close that he yelped. And in the same instant, Nardy, who had bent down towards the driver, clutched my arm, pulled me back onto the pavement, and almost dragged me along to where the next cab was approaching. He himself was gasping as he gave this driver our address. Then when we were seated, he gripped my hand,

126

saying, 'It's all right. It's all right. Stop shivering; nothing can happen. He wouldn't dare attempt anything. There's nothing he can do. And we'll get back home as soon as possible. Now stop it, stop shivering.' But I couldn't stop shivering. And for the first time in weeks I saw Hamilton. He was crouched on the opposite seat, and seemingly filled with the same fear that was coursing through me. When Nardy said, 'We will go back tonight, we'll get the midnight train,' Hamilton immediately made a great obeisance with his head. And when I could force myself to speak, I said, 'We must wait and see how she is.'

When we reached the house the children swarmed over us, and Mary greeted us warmly. George wasn't in. She said he was along with his mother. And yes, Gran was pretty low. What was the matter? Wasn't I well?

The children were scattered back to the kitchen with Sandy while we went into the old sitting-room where Mary had tea ready, and I said simply, 'We ... we came face to face with Stickle. We almost got into his cab.'

'Oh my! Oh, my goodness! No wonder you're looking white. Still, I'm sure he knows you're on to him. He wouldn't dare start anything.'

'He'd better not,' Nardy said grimly. Then he asked, 'Do you hear anything of him?'

'Yes, now and again. His lad seems determined to pal up with our Gordon.'

'Does the boy mention his father?'

'No, never, Gordon says; but there're signs that the man has been at him now and again, for Gordon once said Neil had a split lip; and another time he said he couldn't hold his pen. Anyway,

127

don't you worry, nothing's going to happen. He wouldn't dare.'

'That man would dare anything, Mary. Oh, the look on his face when he recognized me. For a split second there was that oily smile of the yes, sir, yes, madam, look, the tailor's shop smile. And then that awful look of hate enveloped it.'

As I warmed myself at the fire I thought about hate. It was a dreadful thing, hate. Look how it had changed Tommy. Thinking back, I realized that all my life I had been in touch with hate. I recalled the trunk in the attic upstairs in this very house, and it was still there, and my mother's wedding-gown was still in it, meticulously slashed to a hundred and one pieces. I remembered the night I first saw it and glimpsed a little the rage that must have consumed her to make her cut that gown into ribbons and then lay it out piece by piece to fit its original shape before doubling it in half and putting it in the trunk.

Once hate becomes alive it is difficult to kill. I had tried with regard to Stickle, but there it was, churning in me now, yet almost obliterated by my fear.

Nardy pulled at my arm and brought me out of my reverie, saying, 'Come on, let's get along to Gran's while there's still some light.'

There was more bustle. I went into the kitchen where the children were going mad with Sandy and, picking him up, I said, 'I'm putting him in our bedroom. Now, please, don't let him out no matter how much noise he makes. Play with him up there, but you won't, will you, let him out?'

Mary, coming behind me, said, 'I'll see to that now. Don't worry. Do you want me to call a taxi?'

'No, we'll walk.' I looked at Nardy, and repeated, 'We'll walk, yes?' He nodded, and a few minutes later we set out.

Our entry into Gran's street didn't go unnoticed, and people called to me, saying, 'Why, hello there, Maisie. How are you? By! you're lookin' bonny.'

It was the usual greeting when people meant to be kind.

George opened the door to us, and I was once more lost in his bear-hugging embrace. But there was no great laughter issuing from his lips today and after he had shaken hands firmly with Nardy I said to him, 'How is she?' And he pursed his wide lips and wrinkled his nose before saying, 'She hasn't been too good, Maisie, not too good. But she's turned the corner now. It's funny to see her lying there without a bellow in her. Just thought lately, if anything were to happen to her, life would lose its spring, at least for me, because I haven't been meself since she took to that bed.'

'That's natural.' I patted his arm. 'Anyway, here, take my coat, and'—I stabbed my finger at him—'don't leave it lying on the couch for the cat to curl up on.' I was aiming to be cheerful because I could see that there was a great change in him. And yes, I thought, the spring would go out of all our lives if anything happened to Gran, Gran whom I had loved first because she, like her son, was common, and through her I had imagined that everything nice in this world must be common.

We went upstairs and I opened the bedroom door and I saw her expression change. But, oh dear me, how she had altered. She did look ill,

129

really ill.

When I bent over and kissed her she lifted one weak hand and patted my cheek. I had to keep the tears from my voice as I said, 'I can't leave you for a minute, can I? Why can't you look after yourself? I'm tired of trailing after you.' It was the same way in which she would have greeted me had our positions been reversed. And she smiled, a pale, wan smile; then her mouth dropped in at the corner and her voice came as a croak when she said, 'It's because you went away.'

'Well, here I am back, and I want you out of that bed.'

'I'll be all right...The bucket.'

I looked round the room for the bucket, and she lifted her hand wearily again and smiled as she said, 'The bucket was hanging—' she drew in a deep breath, then went on, 'on the knob of the bed...the bucket, but I wouldn't kick it.'

'Oh. Oh, Gran.' It was too much. The tears spilled over from my eyes, and I turned away and Nardy took my place and I heard her say, 'Ah, lad, lad.' Then, after a moment when I turned to the bed again, she looked at me and said, 'Sandy?'

'He's back in the house. They're all looking after him.'

'That fella?' She was again aiming to smile.

I glanced at Nardy, then looked at her again and said, 'Which fellow, dear?'

She closed her eyes and showed a slight return of her impatience before she brought out, 'Ham ... il ... ton.'

'Oh, him. Oh, he's here all right.' I looked towards the bottom of the bed. 'He's standing there with his girl friend Begonia.'

130

Her smile widened and she made a sound like, 'Aha.'

'He's going to make an honest woman of her, they're going to be married.'

I put my hand out and squeezed Nardy's as I saw the bedclothes shake. She was laughing inside. And when Nardy, bending towards her, said, 'Tommy's riding down on her,' she made a croaking sound. Then as suddenly, her expression changed, and, turning away from the bed, I said quickly, 'We're tiring her.' It was partly an excuse for myself to get out of the room for I felt that I would howl audibly.

A minute later, down in the passage, George was opening the door to the doctor, and once again I was enveloped in a bear hug, and it could have been a bear because his face was more hairy than ever. Yet, I noticed when he held me at arm's length that it was mostly grey now. He, too, seemed to have changed so very much in a year. Yet, his voice was as I remembered it, and his compliments were as caustic as ever. 'You haven't altered much,' he said. 'I thought they went in for high living up in London; you're getting scraggier.'

'I'm in the fashion,' I replied.

Taking off his hat and coat now, he said, 'You've seen her?'

'Yes.'

'She's had a rough passage.'

'Is she all right now? I mean, is she over it?'

'I should think so. She'll have to go steady ... How long are you staying?'

'Well'—I hesitated, then looked at Nardy 'only for a couple of days.'

'Not for the holidays?'

'Not ... not this time.'

He didn't ask the reason why but just nodded his head; then going towards the stairs, he said, 'I'll be seeing you; I'll call in at the house after surgery.'

In the kitchen I said to George, 'Can I help you?' and he replied, 'Aye, yes. Get yourself back to the house and have something to eat. Once the meal's over, Mary'll come and relieve me. Go on, now.'

I wanted to protest, but Nardy put in, 'Do as George says.'

So we went back to the house and had a meal. Then, just as she was about to leave for Gran's, Mary said, 'What with one thing and another I haven't been able to do much turning around regarding beds. But John is sleeping up in the attic because Betty wanted a room to herself. You know what they're like. But there's another single up there. Do you think Tommy would mind...?'

'Not a bit of it,' Nardy put in now; 'he'll be in his element. He'll think he's camping out with the boys.'

'Oh, there's only John sleeps there; I don't let Gordon go up, because there would be skull and hair flyin'. Those two...funny, but they're at each other's throats most of the time, yet, let anyone else go for either of them and there they are like close buddies.'

Just as she finished speaking there came the sound of screeching brakes outside the front door, and Nardy said, 'He's arrived.'

We opened the door and there, grabbing up parcels from the boot, was Tommy. As I stood

132

with the others waiting for him to bounce up the steps I thought, Of all that could happen in a year! for Tommy, of all others, seemed to have changed out of all recognition.

As soon as he entered the house the children's squeals and high laughter filled the place and his greeting to Nardy, Mary and me was lost under it.

Some short time later I opened the sitting-room door and there was Tommy sitting on the hearthrug, Sandy lying across his knees, and John, Kitty and Gordon squatting near him; only Betty was standing. But they all turned as Nardy and I entered the room, and Tommy, rising to his feet and for the first time, mentioned Gran, saying, 'How did you find her?' He seemed to have forgotten that Gran was our main reason for being here.

'Pretty bad, but doctor says she's turned the corner,' I said.

'Good, good.' He nodded. Then, looking at Nardy and his expression changing, he almost cried, 'Five hours, twenty-three minutes, with only one stop! How about that, laddie?'

'You're a maniac.'

'I never went over sixty ... Well, just now and then to pass something. You could have saved your railway fare.'

'I've got a whole neck, that's something to be thankful for.'

Tommy, now casting his eyes over the children and nodding towards Nardy, said, 'He's old, crotchety.'

'So am I. Come on you lot!' It was George coming into the room. 'Scram!'

'Aw, Dad, you're back.' It was a chorus from

133

the three younger ones, and he replied, 'Never mind, Aw Dad, you're back. I'll give you two seconds to get off your hunkers before I skelp your lugs for you.'

Rising to her feet, Kitty looked at John and Gordon, and, the three of them nodding together, said, 'Promises, promises.'

With raised hand, George advanced on them crying, 'I'll carry out me promises on your bare backsides if you don't get.' And laughing, they ran from the room.

In this moment I felt happy for George: here he was with his four adopted children and loving them as he had once loved me when I was small; and I could sense that his affection was returned fourfold.

After George had marshalled them out of the room and we were left alone with Tommy, we both looked at him as he sat on the couch, his long legs sprawled out. And when he didn't speak, I said, 'Tired?'

'No, not really.' He looked, first to the right and then to the left. 'Somehow it's all changed,' he said; 'I suppose it's because Gran isn't here.'

I didn't answer, for a moment thinking that he was right. But then, Gran didn't live here. Yet she had been here when he last visited. However, I realized he was right, for, to me, even were Gran here, the house wasn't the same, which was natural for it was occupied by a family now, and their different way of life had changed the atmosphere.

Nardy was saying to Tommy, 'When are you starting on your run around the world?' And Tommy answered, 'Oh, sometime in March.'

Then he looked at me and said, 'Can you imagine longing for something all your life, then when you get it you don't want it.'

'Not really,' I said as I thought, I've wanted to be loved all my life, and now I'm being loved I want to go on being loved. I have never wanted it to lessen, this feeling that has existed between Nardy and me, because I know he has been and is happy. That I had the power to make him happy always appears to me a miracle and not a small one.

Tommy was still looking at me as he said, 'I don't want to go on the damn tour. I realize now that I would much rather take her ladyship'—this was the name he had given to his car—'and run around the country, and perhaps take her over to France.'

'Oh, you'll enjoy it once you get going. And what an experience to do a world tour. I wouldn't mind it myself, would you, Nardy?'

Nardy shrugged his shoulders and pursed his lips before answering, 'I hate flying and I cannot see myself being months on a boat. Rough weather and I don't agree, do we?' And he smiled at me as he recalled our cruise together before we were married.

Tommy now straightened himself up abruptly on the couch and, bending forward, placed his elbows on his knees, and with his hands dangling between them he looked down at them as he said quietly, 'I've had a kind of funny feeling on me of late that something was about to happen. It's made me wonder about the damned tour. Keeps niggling at me. I'm not given to that kind of thinking. It worries me.'

135

Nardy rose hastily to his feet, saying, 'Which all goes to prove, laddie, that you're in need of a holiday. Now come on, let's go along to Gran's again.'

As we walked down the room, I thought it was strange that Tommy should be troubled by premonitions, for he wasn't really the type. But then a little of his fear rubbed off on to me as my thoughts ran ahead. Enough! Enough! He can't do anything. He wouldn't dare.

Then as we entered the hall I saw Hamilton in the far distance. He looked solemn, sad, and his outline wasn't clear. Begonia was with him, and I watched him turn her about while she still looked over her shoulder at me with those compassionate eyes of hers, and I thought, Gran is going to die.

CHAPTER NINE

The following day, I spent the morning and all afternoon with Gran, and she definitely seemed stronger. As George said, she had turned the corner at a gallop since I had come. At one stage in the afternoon when we had the room to ourselves, she held my hand and she said, 'I'm goin' to make it now, lass. I thought me number was up, and that's why I trailed you all the way here. I'm sorry.'

'Oh, stop your jabbering.' I used her tone. 'I've been wanting to come for months, but ... but you know why I didn't.'

'Aye. Aye, lass.' She moved her head slowly. 'He's still about.' She drew in a long breath, then

136

said, 'I heard at the club that he'd been taken on full-time with Morgans Motors, the taxis, you know. But he's not liked among the fellas, plays the big "I am" too much.' Then after a moment, she said something that brought the fear of him galloping back. 'It must rankle enough to drive him mad,' she said, 'to know how you've got on, being famous like and married to a gentleman, and your name in the papers through your books. It was in last week again, saying you had done another best-seller.' Once more she gasped, then ended, 'By! it must burn him up.'...

My staying with Gran all day had afforded Mary a break, but Tommy had now brought her in the car. She was to stay the night. Apparently he had had the children out nearly all afternoon and they'd had a rare time.

Before leaving, I told Gran I'd be round in the morning first thing and that the last thing I was going to do before we got the train was to slip in to see the doctor.

I made her laugh: 'I've a good mind to go to the surgery and wait me turn,' I said. 'You can imagine what he'd say when I walked in, can't you? And what's more, I'd likely meet my old friend there, you know, the one who used to greet me with, "You here again? It's your nerves."' At this, she caught my hand and said, 'You know something, lass? Love must agree with you, 'cos you could end up being quite canny-lookin'!'

'Go on with you!' I flapped my hand at her. 'I thought all you've had was pneumonia, not softening of the brain.'

Nardy hadn't come with Tommy. Being a good cook, he was seeing to the meal tonight. And so,

137

for the first time I found myself alone in the car with Tommy, and he, with his hand on the starter turned to me and put my thoughts into words, saying, 'You know, it's the first time you've sat there.'

'Don't be silly,' I said; 'I've been in this scary thing a number of times.'

'Not sitting there in the passenger seat.' He started the car and almost in the one motion turned quickly out from the kerb, and I said, 'Oh, Tommy, for goodness sake, drive carefully.'

'You're safe with me, madam.'

'I don't know so much.'

'No?' He glanced at me. I made no answer to this, but loudly I said, 'Look, there are traffic lights ahead.'

His laughter filled the car and his only answer was, 'Oh, Maisie.'

At one point I glanced at the window and then turned sharply to him as I said, 'We're going through the market place.'

'Yes, I know.'

'But why? This is the long way round.'

'Oh, I didn't know it was the longer way round. I just thought it was another route. The children showed me.'

'Tommy.'

'Yes, Maisie?'

'Please drive a little slower, and go straight home.'

'Anything for you, Maisie.'

It was as we were nearing the terrace that he said, 'Let's elope, Maisie. What about it, eh? Let's go straight on.'

This should have come over as something

funny, but it didn't, and Nardy's words came back to me: Don't get too fond of Tommy. And now my voice took on the tone of a jocular reply as I said, 'I'll elope you! if you don't pull this contraption up slowly and not jerk my stomach into my mouth. Whoever taught you to drive wants to take lessons.'

A minute later he was helping me out of the car, and there was laughter on his face as, bowing towards me, he said, 'That'll be one pound seventy-five pence, ma'am.'

I went to push him, but he caught hold of my hand, and like that he ran me up the steps and pushed open the door, to enter the hall hand in hand and to see Nardy crossing it. He had on a white apron and he was carrying a dish. He looked at us, and it was some seconds before he said, 'You're back then.'

'Only just,' I said. 'He's as mad as a hatter.' I now jerked my head back towards Tommy. 'He shouldn't be allowed on the road.'

'How did you find Gran?' I was walking into the dining-room with Nardy now, and I answered, 'Oh, much better, really much better.' He placed the dish in the middle of the table, then turned towards me, and swiftly I put my arms about him and said, 'I love you. The more I see of other men, the more I love you.'

'That's comforting.'

My arms still about him and aiming to take that look out of his eyes, I went on, 'You know what Gran said, she said that love suited me, so much—' I gave an embarrassed laugh before finishing, 'I would one day end up being quite canny-looking.'

'You've always been canny-looking to me, much more, beautiful. It's got nothing to do with how you look, it's the whole of you.'

We were in as tight an embrace as my shortened arm would allow when a voice from the doorway said, 'Oh. Oh, I'm sorry.'

We turned to see Tommy standing there, and I, purposely making my voice airy, said, 'Oh, that's all right, Tommy. There's nothing to be sorry over. I was merely telling my husband how much I loved him and, as Gran would say, how I'm the luckiest lass in the lane.' And I smiled at Nardy, who was now taking off his apron, then walked past Tommy who was still standing in the doorway, and as he looked down on me I noticed the pain in his eyes.

It was ridiculous. Here I was in this house where I had spent an agonizing childhood, a torture-filled marriage, and now there were two men who ... loved me. I could hardly make the claim to myself when I knew I had been the most fortunate of creatures in finding Nardy, but now that Tommy, too, should have an affection for me seemed beyond belief. As I was constantly reminding myself, I was still me, and no matter what they said, I was a plain woman.

★　　★　　★

If it hadn't been for the children's chatter and George's usual raw remarks dinner would have been a very strained affair.

After it was over and the dishes washed and the breakfast set for the next morning, we had a game of Monopoly in the kitchen with the children.

140

It was close on ten when they went to bed, and after a drink in the sitting-room, Tommy admitted to being tired and he, too, said goodnight. Then Nardy took Sandy out to do his last little bit of business, and when he returned he laughed as he said, 'He got it over quickly because it's enough to freeze you out there.' I said good-night to George and as usual his good-night made me breathless. He then shook Nardy's hand as if for a long farewell, as he was wont to do each night, and we went up to bed, Sandy bouncing before us and straight into a blanket-lined basket.

It was as we were lying enfolded in each other's arms that Nardy said to me, 'What happened in the car?'

'Happened in the car? What do you mean?'

'Well, you came bouncing in together like two children who had been up to mischief.'

'Oh, Nardy, that was Tommy, Tommy's way. He ... when I got out of the car, he said, "That will be one pound seventy-five pence, ma'am," and as I went to push him he caught my hand and ran me in. Nardy, Nardy'—I took his face between my hands—'all this should be the other way about. It's I who should be afraid of your being interested in anybody else. Don't you see?'

'Not really, dear, because big fellows like Tommy always arouse the mother instinct in women. They start by being sorry for them.'

'Well, I have no mother instinct except towards you. Oh, good gracious me!' I now flounced from him, making the bed bounce, and, my tone changing, I said, 'I can't believe this.' Then rising on my elbow I looked down on him and said, 'Mr Leviston, stop this nonsense at once. I want to hear no more of it, ever.'

In answer, he smiled gently, saying, 'Lie down, Mrs Leviston, I want to put my arms around you. But before you do, would you mind switching off the light? Thank you.'

In the darkness we lay close, laughing now and loving before we both fell into a deep sleep...

Sandy was inclined to night sickness, especially should he have been given titbits of anything fishy. At home I could control his titbits, but it was impossible to stop the children taking pieces off their plates and holding them in their fingers and wagging them under the table. It was a kind of a game to see which one of them could attract him first.

Sandy was a very intelligent animal. Whenever he was about to be sick he would endeavour to wake us, not by barking but by a series of sounds that was very akin to muffled language, and was always accompanied by a paw scratching not too gently on whatever part of your anatomy he could reach.

I was usually the one whom he managed to waken first. And I was aware that his talking was penetrating my sleep. Yet in this state I must be dreaming because I couldn't feel a paw scratching my arm or my neck.

Gradually I came out of sleep and into the awareness that he wasn't just talking, but was whining. I leant over the side of the bed and put my hand towards his basket. It was empty. I next groped for the light and switched it on, and there I saw him standing by the door. And when I said, 'What is it, dear?' He didn't move far from it but began to bark.

Most poodles have a yapping bark but not our boy. He has a hard shrill bark that one would have credited would come only from a larger animal.

I got out of bed and tiptoed towards the door, whispering now, 'What is it? What is it, dear?' Yet, as I stood bending over him I was conscious of something strange, and when my mind put into my sleepy brain a name that I could attach to this oddness, I became suddenly wide awake, and at the same instant pulled open the door, only to scream, 'Oh, my God!' and bang it closed again. I now stood bent double, half-choked with smoke; then I was screaming, 'Nardy! Nardy!'

'What is it?' He was sitting up.

'Fire! Fire!'

'What? No!'

I threw his dressing-gown at him and got into mine; then I grabbed up Sandy and once again I was at the door. But Nardy pulled me back, saying, 'Stay where you are.' He pulled open the door, then turned his back towards the hallway and coughed before thrusting me further into the room yelling, 'Stay there! Shut the door!' And then he was gone.

Presently, I heard cries and muffled screams coming from the landing. I rushed now to the window and, pulling it open, I put my head out into the frost-filled night and screamed, 'Fire! Fire!'

This bedroom window was at the back of the house and, looking down, I could see the whole of the yard and part of the garden illuminated with a warm red glow.

In panic now, and still clutching Sandy who

had his forelegs tight around my throat, I rushed across the room and opened the door, only to see, through the smoke, that the same red glow was coming from the direction of the stairs.

The next thing I knew I was knocked to the floor. Automatically, I let go of Sandy, but his legs clutched my neck and he seemed to dangle from me, assisting the smoke to choke me as someone pulled me forward.

Now I knew we were in the bathroom and that there were others packed there. As a wet towel was thrown over my head I managed to gasp, 'Nardy!' And George's voice, like a far distant croak, came at me, saying, 'He's here. Now do as I say. Follow me, right down. Come on. Betty is behind you, then Gordon, then Kitty with Nardy.'

I didn't ask where John and Tommy were. George seemed to be in charge; they must be all right.

Just before George pulled me forward out of the bathroom I managed to open the top of my dressing-gown and stick Sandy's back legs down inside of it to where he had the support of the cord around my waist. But his forelegs were still round my neck.

We were now on our hands and knees crawling towards the landing. Then I knew a moment of real terror when I saw not only the bannisters of the stairs blazing but also the carpet itself. But I was being pulled upright as in turn was Betty, and then we seemed to be all dancing from one flaming tread to another until we reached the great blaze of the hall. Here it seemed that all hell was let loose and everything more that was to happen happened at once. Water sprayed onto us;

my face was speared with stinging jets; hands were reaching out and pulling us towards the door. At the same time there was a crash behind us and I turned to see the lower part of the stairs fall inwards and Nardy and Kitty, whom he seemed to be holding in his arms, disappear from view. Yet, not entirely. Nardy's head was sticking upwards above the tread of the stairs, but Kitty must have fallen through into the cupboard below. In this instant, I remembered Howard Stickle saying that there was dry rot in the stairs. This was when he had loosened all the stair rods in an effort to finish me off that way.

As I gave a muffled scream someone lifted me bodily and carried me outside and into the cold night and a great bustle of noise. And when I was stood on my feet I strained to go back towards the house, but the fireman's arms were tight around me. Then Betty and Gordon were clinging to me, and Sandy was whining like a child.

When I heard a voice above the melee shouting, 'Get them into the ambulance,' I cried, 'No! No!' And now I almost tore Sandy's legs from my neck and pulled him up from the dressing-gown and thrust him into Betty's arms; then I clawed at the man who tried to restrain me, crying now, 'My husband! My husband!' And his voice came as soft as a woman's, saying, 'There now. There now. Look, they're coming out.' And there was George on one side of Nardy and the fireman on the other and behind them another fireman, and, lying across his arms, was Kitty.

I flew to Nardy and was about to put my arms around him when George, his face ashen and his hair singed to his scalp, said quietly 'Leave him

145

be, Maisie. Leave him be.'

Something in his voice made me step back and my tortured gaze went over my husband's body. His face looked all right, but then I saw that the lower part of his dressing-gown was a charred mass and his pyjamas seemed to be sticking to his skin.

As for Kitty, her body was quite inert and what must have been her nylon nightdress was like a black veil from her neck downwards.

As one in a nightmare, I watched them both being laid on stretchers and put into the ambulance, and as the door closed on them I rushed to get in, but was held back by George. For a moment I was standing pressed close to him. He had only one arm around me and for the first time I noticed that the other was hanging limp by his side. He now pulled his arm from me and clasped his brow, and his voice sounded almost a whimper as, his head jerking upwards, he cried, 'Oh Christ! I thought they were out. I yelled up the stairs. I thought they were out.'

I, too, now gazed upwards in horror to where, hanging out of the fanlight in the roof of the attic, was the figure of John. There was a great commotion all about us. I had been unaware until then of all the people huddled in groups with coats over their nightwear. But as the turntable ladder passed the top of the now blazing windows and swung close to the jagged hole in the roof, everyone became quiet. We watched the fireman put his arms out towards John, but the boy appeared too terrified to grasp the man's hand; then it seemed that he was tossed from the window, and he was clutched in the fireman's

146

arms. Hastily now the ladder was pulled away and the man descended. And now George was holding John in one arm and trying to still his loud crying. Then once again the ladder was being hoisted towards the roof; but there was no one now at the gap to take the fireman's outstretched hand. And I cried inside myself, Oh no! No! Tommy! Please! Please! Don't give up.

The next minute we could see the fireman lean forward from the ladder, to which he was attached by some form of lead, and grip the sides of the fanlight window and then disappear from view, and in doing so he lifted the silence from the crowd in the sound of a concerted moan, and a voice near me said feelingly, 'Silly bugger. Stupid bugger. Fanlights are hell to get out of.'

Then suddenly the moan changed into a drawn out 'O ... oh!' as the fireman's head reappeared through the gap. Then silence again as the man obviously struggled to help Tommy upwards. He seemed to straddle the intervening distance between the window and the ladder with his feet while pulling Tommy's bulky figure forward.

When they both became still I realized the fireman was giving himself and Tommy time to breathe.

The ladder swung away from the roof and billowing smoke. And within a minute or so the two men had reached the street. The fireman was still on his feet, although he stood bent over while he coughed the smoke from his lungs. But not so Tommy, for his tall body had concertinaed: his head was sunk deep in his shoulders, and his knees were pulled upwards. Once again a stretcher was brought, and the next minute he, too, was whisked away in an ambulance.

Of a sudden I thought I was going to faint. It was only George's voice that checked me and beat me to it, for he said quietly, 'Maisie, look after them, will you?' And thrusting John into my arms, he himself toppled over on to the road, and as if from a distance I heard an ambulance man saying, 'No wonder, look at that hand.'

I looked at the hand that one of the men was laying gently across George's chest. It was black and it looked as if the fingers were burnt to the bone, and two of them were hanging at a funny angle.

There came a blankness in my mind. I don't remember Mary arriving; I only heard her say, 'Oh my God!' before she got into the ambulance with George. I then recall myself being bundled into an ambulance with the children, and we were all crying...

What followed in those early hours is confusion. At one point I must have fainted; but by daylight the following morning the children and I were back at Gran's.

It was sometime later in the morning when the doctor appeared. 'You all right?' he said.

I couldn't say yes, I just moved my head, then I muttered, 'I'm...I'm about to go to the hospital.'

'I've just come from there.' He looked to where the children were standing and he went towards them, saying now, 'It's all right, it's all right.'

'Dad and Tommy?' It was John asking the question, and the doctor said, 'Your dad's fine. It's just his hand. And Tommy, he'll be home shortly.'

It was Betty who now said, 'And Kitty,

Doctor?' And at this he paused before answering, 'She'll be fine.' Then he put his hand on my elbow and, pushing me towards the door, said, 'Get into the car. I'll be with you in a minute. I'm just going to have a word with Gran. How's she taken it?'

'Not very well. It hasn't done her any good.'

'No, I shouldn't think it has.'

It was a full ten minutes later when he himself got into the car, and we had gone some little distance when he growled, 'By God! somebody'll pay for this.'

It was then I gave voice and put a name to the feeling that had been raging behind a shield in my mind since I had stood in the road and watched the flames coming out of every window in my old home.

'*Stickle.*'

'*Who else*? It seems it must have been set off in three different places, so I'm told. The sitting-room window was open. If there's any justice he'll do a long stretch for this.'

The sitting-room window! I thought back to the time when he had mislaid his key and I happened to be at Gran's, and he had got in by the sitting-room window. He had said afterwards that a different sneck should be put on it as anybody could get in by slipping a knife underneath it as he had done. I had done nothing about it because at that time if a burglar had got into the house he wouldn't have frightened me half as much as my then husband had done.

As I whimpered, 'He's determined to get me,' there appeared on the front of the windscreen, as if he were seated on the bonnet of the car, the

149

face of Hamilton. He looked like a wild horse might: his eyes were blazing; there was smoke coming out of his nostrils; his lips were right back from his teeth. And as I stared at him I knew that some part of me was in rebellion, while yet another was sick with fear.

When he turned and galloped away into the darkness I said, 'Nardy. How bad is he?'

'His legs are no pretty sight. They had put him under when I left. But ... but the child, Kitty, she's in a bad way.'

There was a catch in my throat as I said, 'Really bad? I mean...'

'Yes, really bad. Her slippers must have had plastic soles and her nightie was made of that inflammable material. Damn and blast it! Like Nardy, her legs got it. But it was the smoke almost did for her; and Tommy had a bellyful of it, too. But what I've heard he owes his life to a fireman who must have risked his own neck to get him out of the attic. And Tommy had risked his own to push the boy out. God! why didn't you poison that fellow when you had the chance.'

Yes, why hadn't I? But such a thing had never crossed my mind; until I tried to finish him off by raining his own collection of bottles on him.

In the hospital a nurse led me towards a bed; not the same one I had last seen Nardy in; this one was covered with a plastic cage.

I looked down on him. His face was lint-white; his arms were lying stretched down by his sides. There was some sort of shield over the lower part of his body. As I whispered his name the nurse said, 'He's asleep, dear. He'll be like that for a while.' And so I sat down and kept my eyes on

150

that beloved face...

A short time elapsed, then Mike came to my side, saying, 'Come away now.' Then he added, 'George is out too.'

I followed his pointing finger and I saw a face in the bed opposite. I could hardly recognize George; I had forgotten that his hair had been burnt off. One arm was stretched out and covered with bandages.

I now looked around for Kitty, and when I couldn't see her, I said, 'Where is she ... Kitty?'

'In another ward.' Mike nodded at me, and the nurse put in, 'She's in intensive care.'

Intensive care. What did that mean? Near death? Oh no! Oh no! Mary would go mad, George would go mad, and all through me. It was only me that Stickle wanted to get rid of. Or was it? Or was it everyone that was living in the house he had coveted for years?...

'Here, drink this. Drink it up.'

I didn't recall being taken from the ward and seated in an anteroom. But, looking up into Mike's face, I said, 'I'll kill him.' And he answered soberly, 'Well, if you don't, somebody will or should.'

CHAPTER TEN

The next three days are hazy in my mind. The only thing that stands out clearly is, later that first day, sitting by Nardy's bed and, when he opened his eyes and whispered my name, I could not even speak his. Although the nurse had said he was heavily sedated and was, as yet, in no pain, nevertheless, the pain seemed to be expressed in every line of his face.

George had had two fingers amputated; but, fortunately, so the nurse had said earlier, the working part of his hand had been saved. But they were still fighting for Kitty's life.

I had been to the bank and made arrangements about money, and had then bought clothes for myself and the children. But wherever I went I was escorted by a plain-clothes policeman, while a uniformed one was on duty outside Gran's house because we were being continually harassed by reporters.

It was now known that the fire must have been started deliberately; but what I couldn't understand was that Stickle apparently wasn't the culprit.

After Mike had spoken to the police, they had gone to Stickle's house, only to find him in bed and hardly able to move with back trouble. And confirmation had come from his own doctor who had said he had been called in two days beforehand. Moreover, I learned that they were troubled in another way for the younger boy had gone missing. This I read in the local paper.

Who then had done this ghastly thing? Paraffin or petrol rags must have been pushed through the letter box, whilst the kitchen window had been forced and oil-soaked rags thrown in there as well. The perpetrator must have actually got into the sitting-room and soaked the couch with oil.

Now that suspicion had lifted from Stickle I was presented with the thought that perhaps some of George's workmates had it in for him, reasoning that when an ordinary man like George prospers it can arouse jealousy among his associates: George now lived in a very nice house, or had done; moreover, he had a car and had been able to take his family, including his mother, on a fortnight's holiday. Could the devil who had done this be one of George's associates? I put this question to Mike, and he said, 'Could be. Could be. But I would have bet my bottom dollar it was the work of Stickle. The dog business last year, too. Yet old Howell says he attended him the second day you were here, in fact the very afternoon before the fire. He said the man was in dire pain, and he's still not up. And what's more, apparently he's very worried about his boy who went missing that same night and hasn't been seen since... Could it have been his boy?'

We looked at each other.

I was again sitting beside Nardy who was still in a very painful and critical condition, but he could talk a little. And I almost burst into tears when he turned his eyes on me, saying, 'Maisie, smile. Come on, do.'

'Oh, Nardy.'

'Go on, smile. I'm all right, so smile.'

My eyes misted. I smiled; then he said, 'That's better.' After a moment he asked, 'How is Kitty really?'

'She's ... she's holding her own. George is with her nearly all the time, and Mary.'

'Gran?'

My smile widened as I answered, 'It's amazing, but she's got her fighting spirit back again. And her voice. She's sitting up and letting everybody

153

know it. The shock had the opposite effect on her to what was expected.'

'Tommy?'

'He's all right,' I said. 'He went back yesterday, you know.'

'Yes, I know.' He moved his head. 'But he didn't look ... he didn't look right.'

No, Tommy didn't look right. He had suffered no physical injury, only taken in a lot of smoke, but he was oddly quiet as if he were still under shock. If I hadn't been so worried about Nardy and Kitty I should have been more worried about Tommy. But Kitty was fighting for her life, and my dear, dear beloved Nardy had just missed losing his, and there lay before him weeks of pain and treatment before he would be himself again, if ever.

I sat with my beloved until he went to sleep. Then I went along the corridor to where Kitty lay in the intensive care unit. I looked through the door and saw George sitting there, his bandaged hand lying across his chest, his face turned towards the cot, and I knew I mustn't go in, my emotions were too near the surface. If not the sight of that child, then the look on his face would be too much for me. I went out into the sleet-driven night, and was fortunate to see a taxi at the gate letting down some passengers. Within a few minutes I was at Gran's, and the minute I entered the house I knew there was something further wrong. Mary was there and she was seeing to Gordon, dabbing at his eye.

'What is it? What's happened?'

She looked up at me from where she was kneeling on the mat before the fire, Gordon in

154

front of her, and she said, 'It's that Stickle boy, the older one, he collared him and punched him. He imagines Gordon knows where the young one is, the one that is lost, he even said he was hiding him here. Can you imagine it?'

I bent down towards Gordon and asked quietly, 'What did he actually say to you, Gordon?'

'He ... he said that if I didn't tell him where Neil was, it would be all the worse for him when they did find him, his father would skin him alive because Neil was a liar.'

'Why did he say that?'

'I ... I don't know, Auntie, except that he thought Neil had told me something and it was a lie.'

When I sat down on the couch Hamilton appeared to the side of the fireplace and was throwing his head from side to side. But I actually shook mine at him as I dismissed the thought that Stickle could have set fire to the house: he had been attended by a doctor, hadn't he, who had verified not only that his back was bad but also that he was practically unable to move on the night of the fire.

However, even as I now silently protested, Hamilton's head kept bouncing up and down until his mane streaked out from behind him as if driven there by a strong wind.

'What is it, Maisie?' Mary was holding my hand, and I closed my eyes for a moment, saying, 'Nothing, nothing, Mary; I was just thinking.'

'You look tired.'

'I'm certainly not the only one'—I smiled weakly at her—'you must be worn out.'

'Oh, I don't mind being worn out. I wouldn't

155

mind anything as long as I felt that Kitty was ...'
She stopped and closed her eyes tightly, and
Betty, suddenly bursting into tears, flung her arms
around her, crying, 'Oh, Mam, Mam,' and in
broken tones, Mary soothed her, saying, 'She'll be
all right. Don't worry, dear, she'll be all right.
They're doing everything possible, and your dad's
with her.' Mary now turned her head and looked
down at me saying, 'It's odd, isn't it? but the
nurses say she cries if, when she wakes up, he's
not sitting there. I've never known a man who
loves children so much.'

I too, had never known a man who loved
children so much.

'Well now. Well now.' Mary's voice became
brisk. 'Let's have something to eat. Come on,
Betty; you see to the table. And by the way'—she
looked at me again—'we've got to do something,
Maisie, about where you ought to sleep. That
couch'—she thumbed to where I was
sitting—'would break anybody's back. But in the
meantime, will you go upstairs and sit with Gran
for a bit and we'll call you down as soon as the
meal's ready. She'll want to know how Nardy is.
And tell her ... tell her that Kitty's all right. You
know what to say.'

As I rose from the couch I thought it was
strange how Mary had somehow come into her
own in this crisis. She was no longer in the
background. She had the whole situation in hand.

As I made towards the stairs there came a
knock on the door, and John said, 'I'll see who it
is, Mam.' But Mary caught his arm and
whispered, 'If it's one of them reporters, tell them
there's nothing to say.'

I was about to go up the stairs when John opened the door, and there, in the dim light, I saw the figure of a policeman and another plain-clothes man standing by his side. Going quickly towards them now, I recognized the policeman who had been on duty outside up till yesterday, and he said, 'Good-evening, Mrs Leviston. I ... I wonder if you'd come down to the station with us? There has ... well, there has been some developments.'

'Yes, yes, of course.' I paused, then looked to where Mary was coming along the passage and I called to her, 'I'm to go to the station, Mary; something seems to have come up.'

Within a couple of minutes or so I had my hat and coat on again and was seated in the back of the police car. As it started up I leant forward and said, 'What is it? I mean, is it some news from the hospital?' There was a tremble in my voice, and the policeman turned his head towards me, saying, 'No, not ... not that, Mrs Leviston.' He hesitated, then said, 'It'll be explained to you by the sergeant.'

I sat back and remained quiet. But when I actually entered the station I felt a shiver pass through my body: the last time prior to entering this room I had left a cell and was about to appear at the magistrates' court.

'Will you come this way, please?' Another policeman was leading me along a passage. He opened a door and there, rising from a table was a sergeant, together with a woman officer and a person I imagined to be a plain-clothes officer. But sitting at the other side of the table was a boy, who looked to be eleven or twelve years old. He

157

was thin and had a white peaked face and eyes that held a deep fear. Before anyone spoke I knew that this was Stickle's son, the one who had gone missing. On the table before him was an empty tea-cup and a plate with biscuits on it.

'Will you please take a seat, Mrs Leviston?' It was the sergeant speaking.

As I sat down I kept my eyes fixed on the boy, and his were tight on me, and I saw he was afraid of me.

The sergeant was speaking again. 'This is Neil, Mrs Leviston. I think you should hear what he's got to say.' He now looked at the boy and said, 'You tell Mrs Leviston what you told us. And don't worry, your father or no one else is going to touch you ever again. And Mrs Leviston will not be angry with you, will you, Mrs Leviston?'

I said, 'No, no,' and waited.

The boy had his hands in front of him on the table and began to nip his fingerends one after the other as if he were pulling off a tight glove. Then his head jerked backwards and he gulped in his throat, and again the sergeant said to him, 'It's all right now, it's all right. You have my word for it: I said no one will lay a hand on you in future, and I meant it. Now go on; tell Mrs Leviston all you know.'

The boy brought his head forward and he stared at me for some seconds before, his voice coming like a croak out of a dry throat, he said, 'My da set fire to your house.'

I remained perfectly still. Although Hamilton was going mad at the other end of the room, galloping backwards and forwards in the restricted space, I did not look towards him but kept my gaze fixed on the boy.

'He ... he said his back was bad. They sent me to bed early on. My mam had ... had gone to Middlesbrough. My grandad had died, she had gone to the funeral. Da said his back was bad and he couldn't get out of bed and Ronnie went and phoned for the doctor.' The boy gulped again, looked at the sergeant, and when the sergeant nodded at him, he turned his gaze once more on me and said, 'I ... I went to watch the football match, but it was too cold and I came home and went in the back way and sat in the kitchen near the stove to warm me hands, and ... and then I ... well'—he looked upwards—'heard the chain being pulled, and I knew it wasn't our Ronnie because I had passed him in the yard, he said he was going for a message on his bike. I went to the bottom of the stairs and I heard me da's bedroom door closing. And I thought it was funny because I knew he had told the doctor he couldn't go to the lav, and the doctor had told our Ronnie that he could get a loan of one of them bedpans from the Red Cross.' He sniffed now; then rubbed his nose with the side of his forefinger before going on, 'Later on like, I had a bad head. I often get bad headaches an' me mam gives me a pill. She keeps them in her room, and I asked our Ronnie if I could have one, and he went into the bedroom and he brought a pill down. But it wasn't like one of the ones me mam gives me, these were just round hard ones, this was one of those long ones with powder inside. It was like one of her sleeping pills, but he said it was all right, it was for headaches and to go and take it. So I went into the back an' got a cup of water, but I don't know

159

why, but I didn't take the pill, I pushed it down the sink. Then after I had gone to bed, our Ronnie bent over me and I made on I was asleep and ... anyway...'

He started to pull on his fingers again and once more he looked at the sergeant, and once more the sergeant nodded at him; and then he began again: 'I heard our Ronnie come into the room again, and I knew he was putting his coat on. Then I heard me da's door open; then the stairs creaked and I knew they had both gone down. Our bedroom window looks on to the yard and we are near the end of the block and there's a lamp there and it gives a little bit of light, and I saw them comin' out of the shed. Me da was dressed and he was carrying a case and he went out of the back door. But our Ronnie didn't, so ... so I got back into bed again quick.'

He stopped again and looked down at his hands which had become still on the table, and the sergeant asked quietly, 'Can't you recall what time it was?'

'No 'cos I think I went to sleep for a little bit before our Ronnie came back into the room and took his coat off. But I don't know how long.'

'Do you think it would be after twelve o'clock?'

'I don't know.'

'It doesn't matter. Go on.'

And he went on.

'I became sort of frightened, I don't know why. I kept wishing me mam was back and I wished we had never come back. We had left the house afore an' gone to live in Middlesbrough with me granda. Then he was taken to the hospital and his council house was given to somebody else, so we

160

came back. And ... and—' He was gulping now, and the policeman bent towards him and said, 'Would you like another cup of tea?'

The boy shook his head, then, speaking more quickly now, he said, 'I heard them coming up the stairs. But they didn't go into the bedroom. There's a chair on the landing that you can stand on and get into the loft, and I heard the hatch being pushed back. An' then after that I heard the bath being run. It was then the door opened and I knew that our Ronnie was standing over me. I...'

The boy was staring at me now with pleading in his eyes and, his voice still coming in a rush and as if he was appealing to me for understanding, he said, 'I nearly screamed like I do in a nightmare, and I think I would have but he went away, and ... and they were a long time in the bathroom. Then ... then he came to bed, and he was soon asleep. And I must have gone to sleep. But it was the next morning when I went down into the yard to get some coal for the fire, Mrs Dixon from next door, she came to the fence and asked me how me da was. And when I said he was gettin' better she laughed and said he would be when he hears his lady wife's house was burnt down last night. That's what she said, his lady wife. And then she said something about him gettin' his own back.'

I watched the boy now close his eyes and draw in a long shuddering breath before he added, 'I was sick. I ... I went in the lav and I was sick. Then I went into the shed. He always keeps two petrol cans in there, full, in case it's his turn on nights and he needs more petrol. One of them was empty and he hadn't been on night call for a long time. And our paraffin can was empty an' all.

161

It ... it was then I knew I had to find me mam, and I got on a bus for Middlesbrough. But I got off half-way 'cos I knew if I'd found her she'd take me back there, an' me da would knock the daylights out of me, an' our Ronnie would an' all. So... so I just kept on.'

He stopped, and there was silence in that bare room. Hamilton had ceased his prancing. He was standing behind the boy, and I said to him, Strange, isn't it, that a man like Stickle can have a son like this who holds no part of him. He was likely all his mother. I put my hand out and laid it on his joined fingers that had formed into a tight fist, and I said, quietly, 'Thank you for telling me. And don't worry; as the sergeant says, no one will hurt you in the future.'

I rose from the table and went out, and the sergeant followed me.

He led me into an office and, after offering me a chair, he sat down at his desk and said, 'Now we've got to prove the boy's words, and I've no doubt in my mind that we shall. Also what the boy didn't tell you is that it was his father who tortured your dog, and it was him and his mother who brought it back. They really meant to take it and bury it, but they thought that with attention it might still live. Apparently the man struck them both when he knew what they had done. It was after that she left him. It's amazing'—he shook his head—'to look at him, and I remember him well when he was in court before, you would think that butter wouldn't melt in his mouth. Well, let's hope, for his sake, that the child doesn't die, for I understand she's in a bad way. And your husband too.'

'What do you do next?'

'Well, our next step, I think, is to get a search warrant for the house. Of course, he'll be in bed with his bad back, but it's under the roof we must look to find that case.'

'When will you make the search, do you think?'

'Within the next hour, I hope. We shall contact the boy's mother again. After the boy went missing we contacted her in Middlesbrough. She felt that the boy would make for there. We asked her to keep in touch, but we haven't heard from her since yesterday morning. The boy himself was found just outside the town in an old disused barn. He must have been lying there for a couple of days. The two policemen who found him, or really it was their dog who smelt him out, said he was ravenous.'

'What will happen to the boy?'

'Oh well, we'll arrange to keep him away from that house, while Stickle is still there anyway. Then there is the elder son to be dealt with. He's obviously had a hand in it too. Now I'll get one of the men to run you back home, Mrs Leviston.'

As I rose to my feet I said to him, 'No matter what time of the night it is, would you get word to me about what you find ... in the roof, and also let me know that he's in custody?'

'I'll do that. Yes, I'll do that, Mrs Leviston.'

When I arrived back at Gran's I took Mary aside and I told her briefly what had transpired. She gaped at me open-mouthed.

'My God! My God!' she said; then putting her hand to her mouth, she muttered, 'If my Kitty were to die he could be brought up for murder, but things being what they are, they would bring

163

it in as manslaughter. But it would be murder, wouldn't it?' Her voice suddenly rose, 'Murder!'

I took her by the shoulders, saying, 'Sh! Sh! Gran'll hear you.'

She became still within my hold and, looking into my face, she said, 'Strange, isn't it, Maisie, that all this has come out of kindness, your kindness. If you hadn't given us that house to live in, this wouldn't have happened to us.'

I knew she didn't mean to stab me in the heart but her words had done just that. In this moment I felt responsible for Kitty, and Nardy, and George, George who might find it difficult to drive a bus again.

As I turned away she said, 'I didn't mean to upset you, Maisie. Don't take me wrong.'

Then she rushed past me as she heard George's key turn in the front door, and a moment later, when he entered the kitchen, I could see by his face he was relieved. And when they all gathered round him and, his voice thick, he said, 'She'll make it,' Mary dropped her head towards him and he put his good arm around her and Betty, and he looked at the two boys and me, then he said, 'What d'you think?'

We remained silent. Then he went on, 'She was awake, really awake and she said, "Hello, Popeye."'

At this the boys sniffed, then giggled.

And George went on, 'And I looked down on her and said, "Hello Olive Oil."'

His chin knobbled as he made an effort to keep back his tears. Then, almost roughly, he pushed Mary from him, saying, 'Stop your bubblin', woman, and get me something to eat; I'm as hungry as a horse.' And on this, for the first time in days, he laughed as he turned to me, saying, 'You'd better look out for yours. How is he anyway? Still kickin' his heels up?'

My smile was tentative as I replied, 'He's up and down, you could say.' Then I added, 'May I see you a minute?' I walked towards the kitchen again and he followed me.

Quietly, I told him what had transpired at the police station; and during the telling he gripped the top of his head with one hand while staring down at the other bandaged one, and then, from between his teeth, he said, 'If he gets off with this I'll swing for the bugger. I will, Maisie. I tell you I will.'

*　　*　　*

I didn't hear anything from the police until the following morning at eight o'clock. It was from the sergeant himself, who was accompanied by a plain-clothes man.

Only Mary and I were up, and in the kitchen, without any preamble, the sergeant said, 'We've got him. Of course, he raised a fuss, couldn't get out of bed.' He gave a tight smile as he added, 'We helped him up. That was after we had examined the loft. There was a case there that reeked of petrol. There were two empty bottles in it; one had definitely held petrol, the other paraffin. One was rolled in part of a towel, likely to make sure they wouldn't jingle as he carried the case. I can see why he had it up in the attic because if he had put it in the dustbin, the smell might have aroused the dustman's curiosity, for

165

he would be more likely to open the case. Then his son, the elder one, who's a bit of a bully-boy, almost gave him away by shouting, 'It was me da's house anyway.' We took him along, too, and, like all bullies, he broke down after a time and confirmed his younger brother's statement.'

'His wife?' I asked.

'Oh, she was there all the time, and strangely she never said one word. We interviewed her, but it was plain she knew nothing whatever about it. As her young son said, she was at her father's funeral the day it happened.'

It was Mary who asked now, 'When will he be tried?' And the sergeant said, 'Oh, I couldn't put a date to that yet. But don't worry, I can't see him getting bail. I can't see anybody coming forward to stand for him if it was asked for.'

Later that day, as I sat beside Nardy, I broke the news to him, and surprisingly he said, 'There was never a doubt in my mind but it was him. A man like that would have worked out every detail. I ... I knew he had from the first. But anyway, my dear, you're safe now.'

I held his hand and looked down into his grey face as I asked, 'How's the pain?'

'Bearable. They're very good. Oh, so very good. But ... but I wish we were home, at least, for your sake. It must be very crowded at Gran's.'

'Oh, I don't mind, dear.'

'Why don't you go into an hotel in the city for the time being?'

'Oh, I couldn't do that, it would upset them. Don't worry about me. My goodness! I'm the least of your worries.'

We became silent for a while, and then, as if

making conversation, he said, 'How's the weather? I can't see anything from here.'

'Oh, it's grey, and damp, and cold, yet you forget about it when you come into the hospital; all the wards look gay.'

'Yes'—he moved his head slowly—'they always say that hospitals are the happiest places at Christmas. The nurses are so cheerful. That one over there at the desk, she's always got a smile. She calls me, laddie.'

I looked towards where the nurse was standing, and then looking down on him again, I said, 'She's very pretty. Now don't you pay her too much attention.'

As he closed his eyes for a moment, I thought of the trite things one says in place of words that are spurting upwards from the painful emotion tearing at your innards: chatting about the weather, the Christmas decorations, and the pretty nurses. I felt of a sudden I was quite alone: Nardy was there, but he wasn't still with me; I was back in the days when I had only Bill my bull terrier, George and Gran on one side, and the doctor as a bulwark against insanity.

That reminded me. I must call in at the evening surgery when on my way home and tell him the latest news.

'Have you heard from Tommy?'

'Yes,' I said, 'I heard from him yesterday. He's coming up at New Year. He said he was writing to you. You haven't had a letter yet?'

He smiled weakly, then he asked, 'Did you give Janet her Christmas box before we left?'

'Yes, yes.' My throat was full, and I was, in a way, grateful to the Scottish nurse who appeared

167

at the bedside with a glass in one hand and a spatula in the other with pills on it, saying, 'Now then, laddie, open your mouth and close your eyes and see what God'll send you.'

It was a long time since I had heard those words. Gran used to say them to me as she popped a sweet into my mouth. 'Open your mouth and close your eyes and see what God'll send you.' It was too much. I heard myself laughing, and the nurse turned to me and said, 'Is that a new one to you?'

I put my hand over my mouth for, standing by the bedside between me and the nurse, was Begonia. She put up a front leg on to my arm, saying, I'd go now; they'll be wanting to do his treatment, that's why they've given him the pills.

When I put my lips gently on Nardy's, they trembled, and his hand came onto the back of my head and held my face close to his for a moment. Then, his kind eyes looking into mine, he said, 'Don't worry; we'll get through. The main thing is, Kitty's making it. Go on now. Go and see your prehistoric bushman, he'll do you good.'

I could say nothing, not one word, not even a goodbye. I walked out of the hospital. It was dark now, and I was grateful for it, for the tears were streaming down my face.

The doctor held his surgery from five till half-past six. It was almost half-past when I got off the bus, hurried up the street, and pushed the door open into that room that I knew so well. There was only one patient left waiting to be seen, and who should it be but *You again*, the woman who always greeted me with those words, 'You here again? It's your nerves, I suppose?' And yes,

I was greeted by those very words.

Half-rising from the seat, and a smile on her thin face, the woman said, 'You here again?' Only this time she didn't add, 'It's your nerves?' at least not in that way. What she did say was, 'I heard your house was burnt down. As I said to our Susie, you are an unlucky sod. First you had a pig of a man, then that to happen. It's enough to give anybody nerves. And you wrote a funny book, didn't you, about things you imagined seeing when you were in a breakdown?'

I reared, Hamilton reared, and Begonia stood on her dignity. 'Yes,' I said, 'I wrote a funny book, but it...it wasn't because I was in a breakdown.'

'No?'

'No.'

'Oh, I thought it was. Our Susie read it. She said it was like what fellows see when they've got the DTs. White elephants going up the wall, and ants crawling all over them.'

I was back in the old life, sitting here on a Monday morning, waiting my turn, looking around at all the weary faces, and, should I be unfortunate, seated next to this particular woman listening to her complaints, which always began: 'It's the neck of me bladder, you know. He can do nothin' about it.' And sometimes she would add, 'I don't know why I come.' But here she was, still coming.

Miss Price, one of the secretaries, was standing in front of me now, surprise on her face, and her manner and voice so changed from the old days as she said, 'Oh, Mrs Leviston, shall I tell the doctor you're here?'

169

'No, don't bother, Miss Price, I can wait.'

At that moment his door opened and the patient came out and my 'neck of the bladder' acquaintance rose, nodded at me, saying, 'Be seein' you then'—she seemed sure of this—then went into the surgery.

'How are you, Mrs Leviston? I was so sorry to hear about the trouble. Were you injured in any way?'

'No, no, Miss Price; fortunately not.'

She bent nearer to me now, a prim smile on her face as she said, 'I've read your book. I think it's very funny. I bought a second one for my mother's Christmas box. I wonder if you'd autograph it for me sometime, Mrs Leviston?'

'Yes, certainly, I'd be pleased to.'

Life was funny, wasn't it. This particular secretary never, as I remember, gave me a civil word all the years I was Mrs Stickle and a regular customer here. To her I was just one of those nerve-ridden individuals who wasted the doctor's time. Odd how a little bit of fame could alter a person's attitude towards you. I hadn't liked Miss Price then and I didn't like her now.

A few minutes later the lady with the weak bladder came out of the surgery and she waved to me and I waved back. Then I went in and was greeted immediately with, 'What the devil are you doing here?'

'I've come for a bottle and a note.'

'How long have you been sitting out there?' He thumbed towards the door.

'Not long.'

'Why didn't you go to the house and see Jane?' His head jerked in the other direction now, and to this I replied, 'I wanted to see you alone for a few minutes. Did you know that it was Stickle?'

'Yes. Well, I knew it all along,' he said, nodding his head the while; then he added, 'Sit yourself down...Yes, I was along at the station this morning; I heard it all. God! I hope he gets his deserts. If ever there was a fiend on this earth, he's it. How are you feeling?'

I sighed before I answered, 'I just don't know,' but then contradicted myself by adding quickly, 'Yes, I do. I feel I've gone back years, and it was confirmed a few minutes ago when I met up with your last patient. We always seemed to come on the same day; she reminded me.'

He gave a laugh now. 'Oh, you mean Water Lily.'

'Water Lily?' I felt my stomach shake. 'Is that what you call her?'

'Yes. She's had trouble with her inner tubes for years. They're all right now, but she won't have it. It's nerves with her really.'

When the high laughter erupted from me he rose quickly and came round the desk, saying, 'Now, now, what is it?'

The tears were running down my face. I was laughing and crying at the same time, and he put his arms around me and held me for a moment until the paroxysm passed.

Wiping my face, I looked at him and said, 'Nerves? You saying she's got nerves? For years she's accused me of visiting you simply because I had nerves. She hadn't nerves, it was the neck of her bladder. It was always the neck of her bladder.'

We were both laughing now. 'Come round and

171

have a drink,' he said. 'I've got one call out tonight so far, then we'll have a bite.'

'No thanks, they'll be expecting me back.'

He shook his bushy head, then said, 'It must be a tight squeeze round there, and you haven't been used to tight squeezes this last year or so living in your lap of luxury up in the wicked city. Come and spend a couple of days with us in the New Year; I'm sure Nardy would be happy to know you're having a change.'

'Yes, yes, he would. I'll try to arrange it without hurting feelings.'

'Do that.'

He stared at me now; then placing his hands on my shoulders, he said, 'You know it's going to be a long job with Nardy, don't you?'

'I've...I've sort of guessed that.'

'They'll make a good job of his legs in the end, but it's going to take time. You can't replace large areas of skin all at once.'

'No, I suppose not.'

'Anyway'—he grinned at me now—'he's going to be all right. And the child too. Oh, it was touch and go with her, and I'm afraid she's in for a long spell an' all. It'll be worse for her in the long run being a girl, because she'll be scarred up to her chest. Still, she's alive. And George'll get by; he's got the main part of his hand, and that's something. And Tommy? Have you heard anything from him?'

'Yes, I had a letter, but he didn't say how he was feeling.'

'The smoke nearly finished him off. If it hadn't been for that fireman he certainly would have been a goner. And the experience has left its mark

172

on him. I had a talk with him before he left. All his bounce had gone, hadn't it? He was always so cheery.'

'Yes.' I nodded.

'Sure you won't come in and have a drink?'

'No thanks, Mike, not tonight, but I'll likely take you up on your other invitation.'

'Good. Good.'

He was leading me towards the door when he stopped and said, 'You know, Maisie, it's funny to see you back in this room again. I often think of the old days and they're not all that far away. And you know something? I can tell you now, I got to look forward to your coming; there was something about you that was different.' He leant his hairy face down to me as he added, 'I didn't know it was because you were accompanied by a blooming great horse.' He chuckled now, then said, 'How is he by the way?'

'Oh,' I replied, 'I don't see him so often, not since he took a wife.'

'*Never! A wife? Never!*'

'Oh, yes. Why shouldn't he? I took a husband.'

'Well, yes, there's something in that. Freud would be able to supply the answer there. Or would it be Jung? What do you call her?'

'Begonia.'

'Be ... go ... nia.' His face was twisted up so much in disbelief that the hair seemed to have taken over so that even his eyes were invisible for a moment.

'It's a nice name.'

'For a horse?'

'She's a mare ... naturally, and she's definitely a lady, smallish, cream chocolate coloured, with

173

lovely soft eyes.'

I was swung round and pushed in the back and through the door into the waiting room and past a surprised Miss Price. And then I was in the street and he was saying, in no soft voice, 'I refuse to certify you, you'll have to get somebody else. But it will have to be done.' And I went on my way really laughing for once and wondering what Miss Price would be making of that.

The lonely feeling had gone. Strange how that man could bring comfort to me, reassurance and the will to persevere. I asked myself again: What would I have done without his help all those dreary years?

My mood was changing, telling me that I should be thankful that Nardy had escaped with his life, that Kitty was getting better, that Tommy was alive, and there was still George. And this is what decided me to go into the church. It was only two streets out of my way.

When I entered I could see that the confessions were over, and there were only three people altogether there, a mother and small child kneeling before the crib, and a woman lighting some candles.

I knelt down at the end of a row facing the side altar in the very place where I had knelt once before and startled poor Father Mackin when in a sort of confession I told him there was a horse dressed in bridal white galloping up the aisle. Poor man. I could recall the look on his face.

I sat back in the pew; I hadn't said a prayer. I was now looking towards the high altar, but no words of thanksgiving entered my mind. But I wasn't surprised when I saw my two friends

174

kneeling side by side on the actual altar steps. Hamilton's coat was gleaming like the back of a seal. His white mane was hanging gently downwards and touching that of Begonia. She always wore hers to the left. Her cream skin seemed to ripple softly in the candlelight. In another moment I may have dropped off to sleep, such was the feeling of peace, but a voice aroused me, saying quietly, 'Well! well! 'tis you.'

'Yes. Yes, Father, 'tis me.' I went to rise from the pew but his hand on my shoulder pressed me back; and then he sat down beside me, asking softly now, 'How are you?'

'Not too bad, Father.'

'What a thing to happen. God forgive him. It was in the evening paper. The man's mad; but I doubt if he'll do you any more damage after this ... How is your husband, and the child?'

'They both seem to be getting along nicely.'

'That's good. That's good. I'm due to visit tomorrow; I'll look in on them.' He sighed now, then said, 'The things that happen. And you were so settled in your new life, and your book selling like wildfire.' He smiled now. 'By the way'—he leant towards me—'does he still keep you company? You know ... you know who.'

'Oh, yes, Father.' I nodded solemnly at him. 'In fact'—I pointed towards the altar—'they've both been kneeling there.'

He turned his head and looked towards the altar as if he were expecting to see them; then looking at me again, he whispered, 'Both? Another one?'

'Yes. Oh, you wouldn't know because that book isn't out yet, but he's married.'

He pulled his scraggy chin into his neck, turned his head slightly to the side while keeping his eyes on me and said, 'You're joking?'

'No, no, Father, I'm not.'

'He's married?' He sounded like Mike in his disbelief.

'Yes, and very happily.'

'Glory be to God! You're still seeing things then?'

'Oh yes, Father.' I now saw his cassock shake, then his voice rumbled in his throat, and again he was leaning towards me, asking now, 'Is she *in* or is she *out*?'

'Oh, I'm sorry to say, Father, I think she's out.'

'Oh, she would be. Connected with you, she would be.' His lips were tight together now, yet the rest of his face was smiling, and the words were whispered as he said, 'What denomination?'

'Presbyterian, I think, Father.'

'Oh, my God!' Then, his voice altering, he asked, 'But how d'you know?'

'I ... I think it's the look on her face.'

'Oh, do they look different, the Presbyterians?'

I thought for a moment, then whispered 'Yes, I think they do, Father.'

'Ah'—he straightened up—'you're still a queer girl, marriage hasn't altered you. You know something? I remember the day you told me that the big fellow, Hamilton, was just behind me.'

'Father—' It was I who now leant towards him and said very softly and slowly, 'he's there again now.'

I watched his head move swiftly from side to side, and then he said, 'No kiddin'?'

'No kiddin', Father. They're both there. She's

to your right hand and says she's very glad to make your acquaintance; she'd heard a lot about you.'

'Really?' His eyebrows were moving up into peaks. And now he asked in a stage whisper, 'And his nibs? What has he got to say?'

I paused a moment, and then I said gently, 'He seems to think you're wasted in this job, Father. He thinks you would have made it on the stage, been a wow, in fact.'

I watched the smile spread over his face and he nodded at me as he whispered, 'He's nearer the truth than he knows—do you know that? 'cos that was what I wanted to be in me mad youth. I saw meself holding audiences spellbound. Then the dear Lord took a hand and said He had an audience already made for me. But you know something?' He paused; then his lips twisting into a wry smile, he said, 'I've never yet been able to have a spellbound one. There's an old fellow sits there Sunday after Sunday'—he pointed to the middle aisle—'and as soon as I open me mouth he closes his eyes. I tell you, the minute I start he goes to sleep. And I kid meself the fellow works night-shift, because me pride won't let me accept that what I've got to say would put anybody to sleep, not week after week, anyway.'

'Oh! Father.' My stomach was shaking. 'I think God made a mistake in dragging you in.'

'No, no.' He shook his head vigorously. 'No, no; He never makes a mistake. He knew what He was doing: I was so puffed up with self-importance. In those days I thought I was funny, I wanted to make the world laugh, and pride is a great sin and He saved me from that.

177

Anyway—' his grin widening and his whispering becoming almost inaudible, he went on, 'He's allowing me a little compensation in me old age because we're starting an amateur theatrical group along at the club and they've asked me to direct. What d'you think of that for kindness? Of course, I've only got another two years to go. You know, I'm nearly on me time.'

I looked at him gently, saying, 'Well, you don't look it, Father; and you'll be greatly missed.'

'Oh, I look it all right: the mirror never lies, and this'—he tapped his ear now—'I'm having to have a hearing aid. I can see me father getting on his hind legs in his grave because there he was, ninety-three when he died, and he had half of his own teeth left, his eyes were as good as a pair of binoculars, and his hearing ... oh, he could hear your thoughts, could me father. And now look at me: false teeth I've had for the last twenty years, glasses for even longer, and now a hearing aid; the next thing will be a wheelchair. Anyway'—he looked at his watch—'I've got to see a couple in the vestry, they'll be here any minute now, I'll have to be away. But how long are you staying in town?'

'That depends, Father, on how soon my husband can be moved.'

'Then we may be bumping into each other again?'

'Yes, Father.'

'Would ... would you like to kneel with me and say a bit prayer?'

'Yes, Father.' So, side by side we knelt down, and now I did pray: I said, 'Thank you, God, for two kind men, for the doctor and this dear old

178

priest, who have brought me back on to an even keel.'

The hand came on my shoulder, the voice said quietly, 'Good-night and God bless you.'

'Good-night, Father.'

'Pop in anytime you feel the need.'

'I will, Father.'

He stepped out of the pew, then stepped back again, and there was a deep twinkle in his eye as he put his head close to mine, saying, 'I hope your friends haven't left their visiting card on the altar steps.'

And to this I answered quietly and soberly, 'No, Father, I'm sure they haven't, they're both house-trained.'

He pushed me gently; then I watched him walk towards the vestry before I rose from my knees and went out of the church and into the dark street. But my spirit was light, and I felt I had the strength to face the future, which in the weeks ahead would be a pain-filled testing time for Nardy, not forgetting the same painful experience that would have to be endured by Kitty, and for myself, the facing of Howard Stickle once again across a court-room.

CHAPTER ELEVEN

It was the second week in February, a Tuesday, eleven o'clock in the morning, and I was back in that court-room as if I'd never left it, the only difference being, Stickle's and my places were reversed. It was the second day of the hearing. As on that first occasion two years ago, it seemed that Stickle might even get the better of me. For yesterday his doctor had stood in the witness-box and confirmed that the man had had a bad back and to his mind was in extreme pain. No, he said, he hadn't examined him for the simple reason that the man was unable to turn on to his side; nor had he visited him the following day—there was an influenza epidemic and he had extra calls to make.

When questioned by Mr Collins—yes, it was the same counsel who had defended me but was now appearing for the prosecution—he had hummed and ha'ed and then admitted that he had not thought the man's condition warranted a further visit from him on that particular day.

When I had left the court last night I felt that the doctor's statement could or might, in a way, leave the case open to doubt, in spite of what the younger boy had said and the older boy had admitted. For Stickle's defending counsel had claimed that the older boy had been bullied into making a statement and the younger one was a highly strung emotional child with a strong imagination and given to drawing attention to himself, and endeavoured to substantiate this supposition by stating that the accused had admitted having very little love for the younger boy, and that he had thrashed him on occasions for his lying; and further, that any disharmony in the house between him and his second wife had been caused by her defence of the boy.

When I said to Mr Pearson, my solicitor, that there seemed to be a possibility that Stickle would wangle out of this through his defending counsel, he said to me, as he had done once before, 'Wait and see. Remember Mr Collins.'

Yes, I remembered Mr Collins. He seemed to be a slow starter.

The court-room was packed to capacity. I was sitting next to Mr Pearson; on his right sat Tommy, on my left sat George; behind us sat Mike and the veterinary surgeon. Behind them was Gran, Mary, Betty, and Father Mackin.

Mr Collins was now referring to the incident of the dog, and as his words revived the horror of my first sight of Sandy, I was for turning and glaring at the man in the box. It was only the fact that he had never taken his eyes off me all yesterday, nor yet this morning, that prevented me from doing so. When he had entered the dock yesterday morning, a policeman on each side of him, I knew that his well-brushed appearance, his sleeked hair, his long pale face, would have elicited in many minds in the court-room disbelief that such a man was capable of torturing a dog, let alone setting fire to a house in the hope it would kill one in particular of its inhabitants. But in the witness-box his mien altered somewhat when Mr Collins asked, 'Do you deny this?'

'Yes. I do.' The words came from deep within Stickle's throat. 'It ... it was Neil that did it. He's ... he's like that with animals. A bit wrong in the head.'

'You say your son is wrong in the head? Mental?'

From under my shaded gaze I saw Stickle wag his head from side to side before he muttered, 'Not quite mental, but he's been recommended to see a psychiatrist by the school doctor.'

'Yes, I understand that too, but I suggest this was because of your treatment of him.'

'That's a lie!' It was almost a bellow.

'Everything's a lie in your estimation, Mr Stickle. You seem to be the only honest person in this court. Well, we'll leave the case of the dog and come to what, but for the grace of God, one might say, could be making you stand now facing not only a charge of arson, with intent to cause grievous bodily harm, but also a charge of murder on two counts. Two of the victims of your hate, a man and a child, are still in hospital and it is only by a miracle, I understand, that the child is still alive. As for Mr Leviston, it will be a long, long time before he is able to walk.'

'I didn't do it. I was in bed. I couldn't move.'

'Oh, you couldn't move? Well, the police have given evidence that once they got you out of bed and on your feet, you moved with some defiance; you even resisted arrest.'

'It was the shock.'

'Oh, then'—Mr Collins smiled—'if that's the case we must recommend to the Medical Council that all people with bad backs should be given a shock, and the employers in the country will be so grateful for the reduction in absenteeism for there will be a swarm of men returning to work.' Then, his mood altering like lightning, he went on quickly, 'I suggest, Mr Stickle, you had nothing more wrong with your back than I have. What you did was premeditated: you knew how to get into your former home; you knew that your former wife was there. Your insane hate of her prompted you to plan carefully, but not carefully enough: you took an ordinary attache-case,

182

stuffed it with rags, filled two bottles, one with petrol and one with paraffin and went out into the night; and your presence on the street would cause no local comment because you were a taxi driver and on night call. And had you been stopped ... well, you were on your way to your employer's garage to pick up a car. You reached the house, you quietly forced open the windows and it only took a matter of minutes to soak those rags and throw them into the room, and push the rest through the letter-box. You knew there were other people in that house besides your first wife, and you hated them too because they were living in the house that you had coveted, then plotted and planned to possess...'

'Objection, my Lord.'

'Objection overruled.'

I now had my head up, my eyes wide, and I saw Stickle glance towards the judge. He too was the same man who had presided over the earlier case. Mr Collins was going on. 'Being frustrated in that, you could not bear the thought of your down-trodden former wife not only rising to fame through her literary efforts, and marrying a gentleman of no small means, but also that she dared to come back to this town and stay in the house that you and your son had openly declared should be yours. It was too much to bear; you must put her out of the way for good and all...'

'Objection, my Lord.'

The judge now warned Mr Collins in a half-hearted tone that he must not allow his feelings to cloud his judgement.

'Yes, my Lord.' Mr Collins inclined his head towards the bench, then returned to the attack.

'You are a conceited man, Mr Stickle. And to put it into common phraseology, a two-faced one. Oh, definitely that I would say, for your demeanour suggests mildness, but all the while it is covering up a raging ferocity of hate, which has spread to cover all those connected with your first wife. You are a Jekyll and Hyde, Mr Stickle. Years ago your sister preyed on a young lonely girl in order to secure, for you, an excellent home...'

'*You leave my sister out of this*!'

Stickle's attitude had undergone such a change that it brought a stir in the court. Gone was the meek, placid-looking man. Someone had dared to say a disparaging word about the only person that, I'm sure, he had ever loved.

'Mr Stickle, please.'

'Don't you "Mr Stickle, please" me, stick to the point. You've been doing it all along. My sister was worth a thousand of her, and she didn't do any pushing. That's the one that did the pushing.' His finger was now pointing at me, his eyes spurting hate. 'She was man mad, she would have taken anybody. She looked nothing, she was nothing. A barmy cripple.'

The judge's hammer rapped on the bench. When it did not subdue the high murmur in the court, it rapped louder. The jurors had their heads bent towards each other and the voice of the judge rang out, 'I shall have this court cleared unless I have silence. And I must warn the accused to control himself.'

He had silence and in it, my breath seeming to stick in my throat, I stared at Stickle. He was gripping the sides of the witness-box and bending

184

over it; there was saliva running out of the corner of his mouth. I could see the beads of sweat on his brow and it was just as Mr Collins was about to resume that Stickle's voice, addressed to me only, yelled, 'Yes, I did it, and I'd do it again. Just give me the chance and I'll get you yet. By God! I will. I'll get-you-yet.' The last words were spaced, then were followed by, 'You crippled, undersized, barmy sod, you!'

My head drooped onto my chest. I was dimly aware of the bustle that ensued, of the policemen hauling Stickle back into the dock, of the judge's hammer banging loudly on the bench again, of Mr Collins and the defending counsel standing below the judge, talking earnestly, of George's arm around my shoulder, of Tommy taking the vacant seat and holding my hand. I heard my own voice as if from a long distance whimpering, 'I want to go home.'

'Stay put. Stay put. It won't be long now.' It was Mike's voice from behind.

I saw the legs moving away from below the judge's bench. I heard the bustle slowly subside, and a silence again came on the court. But all the while I kept my head down, my mind yelling at me, You undersized, crippled, barmy sod, you! I was aware now of Gran's voice repeating, 'Oh, lass. Oh, lass,' and somebody saying, 'Sh! Sh!'

The judge was speaking. It came to me he had been speaking for some time. My mind seemed to have gone blank. I became aware of his words now: 'When you were last in this court, I can recall being surprised, nay, amazed, that a man of your appearance and demeanour could stand proved of subjecting your wife to mental cruelty,

185

sadistic mental cruelty, for thirteen years. I can still allow myself some surprise that, and I have confirmation here'—he now looked down at the desk and picked up a paper—'to the effect that you have been examined by two psychiatrists who find that your mental state is normal. So therefore I must come to the conclusion already stated by the prosecuting counsel that you are of a Jekyll and Hyde nature and part of that nature can deceive onlookers into imagining that they are dealing with a very ordinary person, a quiet-natured, even refined man. Yet, I'm sure that there are those who from time to time must have questioned this quiet nature, when it was known that your former wife left you, that your younger son appeared at school with facial disfigurement and bodily bruising which was supposed to have come from fighting with his brother. Yet, people can still be forgiven for still seeing you as this ordinary man. But Howard Stickle, it has been proved in this court today that you are anything but an ordinary man. The setting fire to your previous home with the intention of at least injuring if not killing your former wife, and without a thought of the other occupants of that house, four of them children. That act was an act of viciousness beyond ordinary conception. You, Howard Stickle, have admitted your guilt. It is now up to the jury to decide whether your admission comes from a sane or unbalanced individual.' There were more words but they were forming a fuzz in my mind. Someone handed me a glass of water. I sipped at it. A voice said, 'Do you want to go outside?' I shook my head.

A short time elapsed. There was a buzz of voices about me. I felt I was going to collapse because there, holding me up on one side was Hamilton and on the other, Begonia, and they were saying, Hang on, hang on. It won't be long. It can't be long. Then a voice broke in on theirs, saying, 'Here they come.'

'Do you find the prisoner guilty, or not guilty?'

'Guilty on all charges.'

The glass was at my mouth again. I took another sip of water, then I was looking upwards. My head didn't seem to belong to my body, it wanted to roll from side to side, it seemed so heavy. I was looking at the judge and he was addressing Stickle. I felt a great sigh escape from the bottom of my stomach, spiral up through my chest, my throat, and out of my mouth at his words: 'I sentence you to twelve years imprisonment. To my mind it is a just sentence for the acts you have perpetrated. I see you as a cruel, calculating, and wicked man, and for the safety of your former wife and those connected with her, it is wise to see that you are put in a position where you can offer them no further harm. And let us hope by the time your sentence expires you will have rid yourself of the fearful hate that has consumed you and brought you to the position you are in today.'

He had hardly finished speaking when a scream vibrated through the court, and Stickle, held now on each side by the two policemen, was glaring in my direction as he yelled, 'What's twelve years? I have a son, he'll see to you, you bloody, barmy...'

His voice could still be heard as he was dragged

down the steps to the cells below.

It was too much. As Hamilton put his foreleg around me I let myself go...

I came to in what, I suppose, was one of the offices at the back of the court. I kept my eyes closed for some time and was aware of low voices murmuring. I wasn't interested in anything they were saying until I heard someone say, 'The boy. His case will come up tomorrow. He'll likely be sent to a special home. Sergeant Green says that since he broke down and spilled the beans he's been different again. It was the father's influence, I think, that brought out the worst in him. He's expressed a wish to go home to his mother, but I don't think she's very anxious to have him. That's another one the verdict will have pleased because by all accounts she, too, has gone through the hoop with that fellow.'

'She wasn't in court?'

'No.'

'Mind, I didn't think he would get that, twelve years. I imagined the old boy would give him five or perhaps seven at the most, but twelve! Of course, he would remember that last time he was in court when butter wouldn't melt in his mouth. And then, it was arson, and you can get life for that.'

'Are you all right, lass?' It was Gran's voice. 'Come on, sit up and have this cup of tea. It's all over. You're all right now. Come on.'

There were hands under my shoulders, and I was brought upright on the leather couch. The room seemed full of men. I turned my head and looked at the man who had helped me up. It was Mike, and he repeated Gran's words, 'It's over

188

now, lass,' he said.

I made no movement, not even to blink, I just stared at him, for Stickle's hate was still ringing in my ears and his words, 'What's twelve years?' And I shuddered as I thought that the verdict might have taken a different turn had not the counsel brought up his sister May's name. Strange, May had been the instigator of all that had happened, because, yes, she had manoeuvred me into marriage with Howard because of her one desire to give him the security of a good house and a wife with a bit of money. But it was the mention of her name that had condemned him. Strange, strange...

*　　*　　*

There was no celebration after this case as there had been after the previous one, when we had all gone back to the house, and the drink had flowed, and Nardy had sung. He had sung to me, telling me of his love before he had actually voiced it. And we had all sung. It had been a wonderful night. But this time there was no drink except tea, and we sat crowded in Gran's kitchen, just the family and Tommy: the rest had gone their ways. I kept saying, 'I must go to the hospital. I must tell Nardy.' And one after the other they said, 'There's plenty of time. Rest yourself. 'Tisn't every day you pass out.' This hadn't even raised a titter.

Mary had made a scratch meal, but I couldn't eat anything, neither could Tommy. And after a short while George said, 'You won't be satisfied until you go, will you? So I think you'd better get

189

yourself away.' He looked at Tommy and Tommy said, 'Yes, you're right, George.'

And so I was sitting alone in the car again with Tommy. He had come up yesterday especially for the case, but prior to that I hadn't seen him for a month. I knew he wrote to Nardy, and I felt peeved at times that he didn't come up at the week-end to see him. But Nardy had made excuses for him, saying that he was seeing to his work as well as his own, as they hadn't taken on anyone else. But I still thought he could have made the journey for his life now seemed to be spent racing around in this car.

We drew up in the car park next to the hospital and as he took out the keys and was about to get out, I put my hand on his sleeve and said, 'What is it, Tommy?'

'What do you mean, what is it, Maisie?'

'Aren't you well?'

'Yes, I'm well, that's as well ... as the doctor would say, as can be expected. We've all been through a difficult time. Perhaps you remember.'

This wasn't the Tommy I knew, and I said, harshly, 'Tommy, please don't take that attitude with me.' And at this he lay back in the seat and drooped his head forward for a moment before he said, 'I'm sorry, Maisie, but, I don't feel myself these days.' He gave a shaky laugh now and glanced at me as he went on, 'I don't read poetry any more: I don't spout it to myself as I'm getting dressed; I don't quote it at people on every possible occasion. The hate of my mother and her duplicity over all those years to keep me tied to her apron strings has deepened tenfold. And that's only the beginning of it.'

190

I had my hand on his now, saying softly, 'You are the same Tommy. This is all the result of shock. We are all undergoing it in one way or another, and we are all, yes, we are all worried about you, and especially is Nardy. You are his best friend. He thinks the world of you.' I didn't know whether this was absolutely true now but I was making myself say it.

He withdrew his hand from mine and, bringing himself upright in the seat, he said, 'Nardy. I . . . I want you to break something to him, because I'll find it difficult to tell him, but I'm leaving the firm, really leaving, not just taking the sabbatical to do the tour.'

'What!' The question came from high in my head. 'I . . . I understand that you are for promotion when Mr Rington goes at the end of the year.'

'Yes, I understand that too, but it's come too late. Anyway, I've told God the Father'—this was Tommy's nickname for Mr Houseman—'and all being well, I'll be off permanently at Easter, that's if they can find a replacement.' He now showed a bit of his old self when he dug his thumb into his chest, saying, 'Of course it will be difficult to find anyone to replace me.' Then he went on, 'June, at the latest.'

My voice was very small when I said, 'What are you going to do?'

'Oh'—his reply was airy—'I've got it all planned out. I'm not just going to do a world tour, I'm going to discover the world. I'm going to travel. I'm sick of London. I'm sick of the whole country. Everything's changed. Oh, this is not a new thought. You see, I used to set my judgement by the House of Houseman, and the people who worked there. In the main, we were all ... well, sort of gentlemen, you know what I mean, at least on the surface. Our attitude to one another, our manners. We still opened doors for secretaries; we still bid each other good morning; and bloody was about as far as we went in language, at least while on the premises. But all that's changed.'

I looked through the windscreen at the flashing lights of cars coming and going in the darkening twilight, and after a moment I said, 'That to me is a poor excuse for opting out, which is only another name for running away.'

'Perhaps you're right. Perhaps the main trouble is I'm immature, I need to grow up. But I'll have to get going, won't I?'

His hand on the door handle again, he asked, 'When do you think you'll be coming home, back to town?'

'I don't really know but I'm going to see the doctor to find out when it will be safe for Nardy to be moved. The graftings could surely be done in London.'

'And when will you be up again?' I asked him.

'Likely at the week-end.' He was smiling at me now. 'By the way, Hamilton hasn't got a spare friend he could let me have? I need someone to talk at at times.'

I smiled back at him as I replied, 'I'll see what I can do. But there's one thing you must remember, Tommy, you must never talk at a horse, you must talk to him.'

'OK I'll remember that.'

We parted smiling, but I didn't see Hamilton galloping before me, nor yet Begonia. But halfway up the hospital corridor my step slowed, and it came to me that Tommy was desperately lonely, and I said to myself: He should be married. Yes, he should get married. And I earnestly hoped that he would...

Nardy looked much brighter. He put both hands out towards me in greeting, and he was the first to speak, saying, 'I know all about it.'

'You can't. I've just come from there. Well, I mean, I went back with Gran and them, but...'

'Sister was off duty. She was in the court. She came back bursting with it.'

Of a sudden I was grateful to the sister, for I would have found it painful, even to describe in a little Stickle's intense hate of me. The fact that I could arouse such hate in a human being both worried and frightened me.

Nardy was saying, 'It's all over. He's been put where he won't trouble you for a long time, and he'll likely find plenty inside to work out his hate on. Oh, my dear, you look so tired.'

'I'm not tired. I don't do anything to make me tired, but—' I paused, then drew one of his hands tight against my breast as I added, 'I'd love to be home. Wouldn't you?'

'Two minds but a single thought. I saw the specialist yesterday. He says two or three weeks. Let them have another go at me. They're all so very good, marvellous, and I'm feeling better every day.' He asked now, 'Has Tommy gone down to see Kitty?'

I shook my head, 'No, no, he hasn't; he's going straight back to town.'

'Without coming in?' There was a hurt note in his voice and his expression was a puzzled one.

193

'He purposely didn't come in,' I said, 'because he had something to tell you and he couldn't bring himself to it.'

He waited, staring straight at me, and when I said, 'He's leaving the firm,' he made a small noise in his throat, then said, 'No!' and added, 'Well, I'm not really surprised.'

'He's in a very odd mental state, has been since that night,' I said. 'I can't get to the bottom of it. He told me just a little while ago that he doesn't read poetry any more, nor spout it, and that he is disillusioned with the firm and the country and everything.'

Nardy turned his head and looked towards the man in the opposite bed who was in an even worse state than himself, having being scalded when a boiler burst, and he said, quietly, 'But that isn't like Tommy.' And looking at me again, he asked quietly, 'Is that all you gathered?'

'What do you mean, dear, is that all I gathered?'

'Well, he didn't confide in you personally about anything?'

'No, no, not at all.'

'He's been avoiding me.'

'Oh, no.'

'Oh, yes. Do you know that the last time he was here he didn't stay five minutes, and I know that he made two visits to Kitty. I wouldn't have known he had been in again only one of the nurses told me what great fun he had caused in her ward. He had them all singing K ... K ... Katie. Beautiful Katie. And then George and Mary came on the scene and it ended up more like a party.'

All of a sudden his head jerked upwards and he said, 'Well, if that's the way he wants it, let him have it.'

'Oh, but Nardy, he thinks the world of you.'

There I was again saying something I was doubting in my own mind. And Nardy said, his tone serious now, 'What does that really mean, Maisie, when somebody thinks the world of you? If they think the world of you like I do of you, and you of me, they want to see the person they think the world of as often as possible. Friendship, you know, can be as strong as love.' Then his mood changing, he made an effort to lean towards me as he said, 'Come along, don't look like that. You see the man over there, the second from the end? He's got a pet phrase: There's nowt so funny as folk. His family come in and they talk round his bed and he never opens his mouth until they go, and then he looks down the ward, his face one big grin, and he says, 'There's nowt so funny as folk.' His wife brings him sweets; she talks all the time. His grandchildren come in and eat the sweets. His daughter brings him fruit, and his son-in-law practically goes through that. He's got a grandson who comes in in full motorbike kit, stands at the bottom of the bed and shouts as if his grandfather was sailing up the Tyne, "Hello, codger!"'

I was smiling now, even laughing, and I said, 'You'll have to write a book about your experiences here.'

'No, I'll just tell them to you, and you put it in. By the way, where's Hamilton?' He turned his head slowly and looked about him, then added, 'And his dear wife?'

My voice was quiet as I replied, 'Strangely, I

haven't seen either of them for some time except for a moment or two in the court.'

'Oh, come now, come, you've got to get hold of him again. Put a halter on him; he's our jam on the bread.' He gripped my hand now and in a whisper he said, 'Bring Hamilton back. You're always happier when he's about; you're more yourself.'

I didn't answer. I just looked at my dear, dear husband who was telling me that I appeared much more sane when I conjured up a horse and his mate and gave them life form.

I noted that he hadn't alluded to Stickle's last throw at me: You crippled, undersized, barmy sod, you! But then perhaps the sister had been thoughtful.

CHAPTER TWELVE

I didn't write to Janet to tell her that I would be going down because I knew she would scurry around cleaning places that didn't need cleaning. So when I put my key in the door and stepped into the hall I was amazed to hear a childish voice coming from the direction of the kitchen.

I had got the first train down this morning with the intention of getting the business done with regard to Nardy's future treatment. I had a letter from the hospital doctor which was to be given to the doctor with whom I had made an appointment over the phone. I pushed from my mind the suspicion that the hospital doctor had written this letter with some reluctance. Anyway I was aiming to return north tonight, because somehow I couldn't let a day pass without seeing Nardy. So here I was, at a quarter to one, and evidently Janet was still here and she had a child with her, likely the grandchild she had spoken of.

Not to startle her, I called loudly, 'Janet! It's me.'

A very surprised woman looked at me from the kitchen door at the far end of the hall, and as she did so she thrust her foot backwards and I heard a small shrill voice say, 'Oh, gag!' or something that sounded like that.

'I didn't expect you.' Janet reached out and pulled the kitchen door closed after her, then came towards me, saying, 'Are you all right? What's happened? Why are you...?'

I held up my hand now, flapping it at her, saying, 'I've just popped down, Janet. I'm ... I'm seeing a doctor this afternoon about Nardy. I want to bring him home as soon as possible.'

Whatever she was going to say next was stilled as she turned her face to the side to where a small boy was emerging from the kitchen. He was bent over, rubbing his shins, and he said, 'You bloody well kicked me, Gag.'

I watched Janet close her eyes for a moment, then, stretching out a hand, grab the little fellow and thrust him back into the kitchen; and, before closing the door on him, she growled, 'You stay put. Don't move. Do you hear?'

Then as I took my hat and coat off she came up to me again, saying, 'Sorry, ma'am, Mrs Leviston. It's a long story. But I'll get you a cup of tea first.' She was definitely flustered.

'Don't bother with tea, Janet. Let's go and sit

197

down and have a sherry, I'm needing it, and by the look of you'—I smiled now—'so are you.'

I went into the drawing-room, but stopped just within the doorway. I hadn't forgotten what this room looked like, but on the sight of it, at this moment, it appeared like heaven, all gold and blue. Turning to Janet, I said, 'Oh, it looks wonderful. You've got no idea how wonderful it is just to see it again.' And I put my hand out to her and patted her arm as I added, 'It's just as if I had left it yesterday. Go on, bring the sherry in.'

A few minutes later I was seated on the couch and Janet was perched on the edge of the chair opposite me. I had briefly given her my news concerning Nardy and Kitty, and the rest of the family, and she tut-tutted here and there, the while shaking her head. Yet, all the time I knew that what she had to tell me of her own troubles seemed naturally much more important at the moment. And, to bring the matter up, I said, 'Who is our visitor? Where does he come in?'

She sighed now and seemed to slip further back onto the chair before she said, 'He's me grandson, ma'am, you know, the one I told you about, one of our Maggie's lot. Oh, I've had a time of it, I can tell you. I told you, ma'am, she went off and left the three of them with Jimmy, that's their dad, but she saw them every weekend. They were like Yo-yos: first with their dad and his new fancy piece, and then with our Maggie and her bit. Anyway, ma'am, to cut a long story short, our Maggie scarpered.' She nodded her head at me now. 'Yes, she did it again from the fellow she left Jimmy for, she went off with another one. And where to? As far as I can gather, Australia. And

198

Jimmy's piece finding them on her hands all the time wouldn't have it, and she threatens to walk out on him, and Jimmy's at his wits end an' for putting the lot of them into care. But my Harry got on his hind legs and said they had to come home, I had to take them; and there was I with Greg, Rodney and May still clinging to me skirt tails. And Max, who I told you was divorced, well he's out of work and he landed. Well, I can tell you, ma'am, I nearly went round the bend. But I was just saved by Hilda. You know, she's single but she's got a boy friend, and she's got a bit of a flat, and they're a couple, dyed hair, the lot. But I must say she turned up trumps and said she'd take Doris and Gloria—Doris is eight and Gloria's nine—for a time. But there was no way she would have young 'Arry'—Janet now thumbed towards the drawing-room door—'because he's a holy terror. But in a way it's understandable, for he's been passed from dog to devil and he's listened to so much he doesn't know right from wrong, I mean with regard to talkin' like. Well, as you've just heard, ma'am, it comes out as often as God Bless You with him. Anyway, for the last few weeks he's been mostly with his grandad, his dad's father, and that man should be locked up. Well, he is for a time because he's now been put in a home. So there you are, ma'am. It was either staying at home to look after him, because nobody else will take the responsibility of him, or bringin' him along of me.'

'Well, don't let that worry you, Janet. If you don't mind bringing him, I certainly won't mind his being here, and I'm sure neither will Nardy.'

'Oh, you don't know what you're sayin',

ma'am. He never stops talkin' and askin' questions. But I wouldn't care if it's in ordinary English. Oh! I'm ashamed to me boots at times. And I wouldn't take him in a bus, not to save me life.'

'*You don't walk all this way with him?*'

'I do, ma'am.' She made a deep obeisance with her head. 'You haven't heard him. He's got one tone, and that's loud. And if people don't look at him when he starts, they look at me and they tut-tut-tut. Mind, at times I feel like turning on them I do; I'd like to hear their language when they're behind their own doors. And the trouble is he picks up everything so quickly. He's bright, more than bright for his age, and he comes out with things like an old man at times. But of course, that's his grandad. And I don't get any help from the lads at home: they encourage him; they think it's funny. Yet, ask one of them to stay in and look after him an' they leave greased lightning standing.'

'Come on, Janet.' I rose to my feet. 'Let me go and meet the culprit properly.' I smiled widely at her, but she did not return the smile.

'You'll have to be prepared, ma'am, an' not be shocked,' she said.

'It will take a lot of language to shock me, Janet.' My tone and face were serious now. 'I had a husband once who, from almost the day we were married, sprayed me every night with the most vile language, and I mean vile language, not just swearing.'

'That a fact, ma'am?'

'Yes, it's a fact, Janet. And that man got his deserts a few days ago, twelve years.'

200

'Yes, yes, I know that, I read it. But to think he treated you like that. For meself, I don't mind swearin', but I can't stand dirt.'

I understood what she meant only too well: I couldn't stand dirt either.

When I entered the kitchen and really looked at Harold Stoddart for the first time, a sort of gurgle spiralled up from my stomach and stuck somewhere at the top of my breast bone. He was what you call, podgy. He had round dark eyes in a round face, topped by a mass of fair hair. But this combination didn't make him look like a cherub, anything but.

'Hello there,' I said.

He made no reply, just fixed those dark round eyes on me, until Janet said, 'Say hello to the lady, young 'Arry.'

The eyes were turned from me and took on a glare as he looked at his grandmother and said, 'I've told you, Gag, 'tain't 'Arry, 'tis 'Arold.' Then looking at me again, he stated, 'I'm 'Arold, like 'Ark the 'Arold Angels Sing, that 'Arold.'

'That's not Harold,' I now stated, holding the young man's eye; 'That's Hark The Herald Angels Sing.'

'Same.'

'No, it isn't.'

'Bloody well is.'

''*Arry*.'

'Well 'tis.'

'You behave yourself, d'you hear?' Janet was bending over him. 'Or you know what you'll get.'

'Smacked arse.' The round face went into a wide grin now. Then he almost fell on that same part of his anatomy as Janet's hand slapped him lightly across the ear. And now the small face twisted up, the lips trembled as he said, 'Oh, Gag, that 'urt.'

It was obvious, however, that there was no resentment in the child's statement; but Janet, for her part, was visibly disturbed. And I came to her rescue by saying, 'Can you knock me up a poached egg or something quickly, Janet? I've got an appointment with the doctor at half-past two. But in the meantime this young man and I will go into the drawing-room and have a talk.'

As Janet groaned I held out my hand, and to my surprise it was instantly taken. Together, we walked across the hall and entered the drawing-room. But immediately we crossed the threshold my young companion said, 'She won't let me in 'ere, Gag won't.'

'Well, I can understand that.'

'What? What d'yer say?'

'I said, I can understand your grandmother not letting you come into this room because there's a lot of ornaments that you could easily knock over. Come and sit down.' I led him to the couch. And when he went to climb on it I said, 'No, not with your feet, sit down.' And I lifted him up and plonked him on the edge of the couch, his feet sticking out before him.

I did not sit down by his side, but took the chair that Janet had vacated earlier, so that we were facing each other. And I was about to speak when my young visitor said, 'This your 'ouse?'

'Yes, this is my house.'

'All on it?'

'Yes, all on ... of it.'

He now let his gaze range round the room as

far as his head could see over the end of the couch. Then he made an exclamation, I don't know whether of condemnation or admiration: 'Bloody hell!' he said.

'*Harold*!'

'Yes?'

'Do you know that you are swearing?'

The round eyes gazed fixedly into mine. Then he said, 'What d'yer mean?'

'I mean that you were using bad words.'

'What bad words?'

'Those that you've just said, when you were looking around this room and you were surprised by the colours and the size of it.'

His eyes were screwed up, and I saw that he was thinking. And now, when that loud, toneless voice said, 'You mean bloody hell?' I managed to say calmly, 'Yes, that's what I mean. Those are swear-words.'

'Swear-words?'

'Yes, swear-words, not nice, not for little boys to use.'

'Uncle Max uses 'em, an' Uncle Greg, an' Grandad Stodd, he uses 'em all the time ... swear-words.'

'Well, they are grown up, you are just a little boy.'

'I ain't. I'm four-an'-'alf, comin' up five ... You the woman wots got a norse?'

I swallowed deeply now, closed my eyes for a second, and knew what I would see when I opened them, and there he was, hanging over the back of the couch, his whole big black sleek body shaking with laughter, while Begonia stood at the head of the couch gazing solemnly down on this

203

precocious mite.

I tried to ignore the pair of them and, looking at Harold again, I said, 'Yes, I'm the lady who has a horse.'

'Wot ain't there, like?'

When I made no comment on this, Harold added for my information, 'You're the lady wot sees things, an' gets a barra' money for it. Are you barmy?'

I refused to look over the back of the couch. I kept my eyes fixed on this terrible infant and said, 'No, I am not barmy. What makes you think I am?'

I watched him trying to think up an answer. His fixed gaze left my face, he looked at his fingernails, then began to pick them using the thumb and the nail of the index finger of his left hand to clean the nails of his right. Then, lowering his gaze, he looked at his feet sticking out before him, and then he made another statement. 'Grandad Stodd says all the buggers around our way are barmy.'

What could I do? My head drooped; I covered my eyes as much as I could with my outstretched hand; I coughed, took a handkerchief from the pocket of my dress, and blew my nose; and, when his voice came at me, asking, 'You got the flu?' I shook my head while I continued to blow my nose.

When I uncovered my eyes and relieved my nose of rubbing it with my handkerchief, my companion asked, 'You feel better now?'

'Yes. Yes, thank you.'

'I'm goin' to school soon.'

As I saw Hamilton now cover his eyes with one

204

of his front hoofs and mutter, God help them! I said, 'That will be nice. But you must learn not to swear before you go to school.'

'Why?'

'Because ... because little boys don't swear at school.'

I almost did hear a snort coming from behind the couch as I went on, 'They'll be punished if they do.'

'You mean they'll get their ear 'oles banged?'

'Yes. Well, not exactly.' Oh dear me. I looked towards the drawing-room door and almost said aloud, Oh, Janet, hurry up! for this little fellow was getting beyond me. And when, hitching himself towards the end of the couch and placing his feet on the carpet, he poked his head forward and in a voice that was for once a tone lower, which I imagined was his type of whisper, he said, 'I know a lot of other words Grandad Stodd told me. D'yer want to hear 'em?'

'No ... not particularly. What I mean is ...' He was by the side of my chair now. His whisper still loud, he went on, 'Grandad Stodd said they were special like an' ... an' I had to keep 'em till I got to school.'

'He did? Well, I think ...' I was about to say, your Grandfather Stodd is a very nasty old man, when the small hand came up and gripped the collar of my dress, which caused me to bend my head towards him, and there he was, his face close to mine, a wicked grin on it: 'If I tell yer can I come back 'ere again?' he said.

Well, I thought, I might as well hear the worst, so I nodded slightly. Then the small mouth was close to my ear and a puff of his breath crept over my cheek before he brought out the words, 'Goal stones!'

My head swung round, our noses almost scraped in the passing, and I could see glee registered on his face at the amazement on mine. And now I whispered back at him, almost choking as I did so, 'Gall-stones?' His eyes stretched, his upper lip aimed to reach his chin, his nose poked forward, and he repeated, 'Goal stones.'

Now the imp in myself asked quietly, 'Do you know any more like that ... that Grandad Stodd said?'

He had hold of my ear now and his breath was once again fanning my cheek, and the next dreadful words which came from his small mouth were, 'Bedpan an' 'abit shirt.'

My face was screwed up tight. Whoever Grandad Stodd was, he had a sense of humour, and he was a man who realized that gall-stones and bedpans and habit shirt, whatever that was, wouldn't shock the teachers as much as bloody and bugger might.

I was saved from another confidence by Janet coming into the room carrying a tray. After placing it on the table, she came towards us and, noticing my wet face, she looked from me to her grandson, then back to me. And after a moment she said, 'Has he behaved himself, ma'am?'

'Oh, yes, yes,' I said hastily; 'he's been a very good boy. And if he remains a good boy'—I had one eye on him now—'and doesn't swear so much, you know, using those big naughty words, then you may bring him into this room when I'm away.'

'Can I, ma'am?'

Janet realizing the situation, played up, adding now, 'But I'll have to tell you if he keeps using them, won't I, ma'am?'

'Oh, yes, yes.' I nodded emphatically at her now. Then we both looked down on the subject of our exchange when it said, 'Will you tell me Uncle Max an' Uncle Greg, Gag, they got to stop an' all? And Grandad 'Arry, will you tell him an' all? 'cos he's always sayin' soddid. Is soddid a swear...?'

Janet took him swiftly from the room, the child's feet hardly touching the ground, and I dropped on to the couch and laid my head back and looked at Hamilton doing cartwheels the whole length of the room, while Begonia still stood at the end of the couch, smiling, the while she endeavoured not to. When at last Hamilton stopped and sat on his haunches in front of me, he said, Won't Nardy enjoy him? And I, nodding at him, replied, 'Oh, yes, yes, he will.'

CHAPTER THIRTEEN

It was early May when I finally brought Nardy home. The sun was shining, the trees were in their first coat of light green. The parks and window boxes were full of wallflowers, and tulips. We had come by ambulance from Newcastle. Although Nardy could now sit in a wheelchair and walk a few steps with aid, a train journey would have been out of the question. And here he was, being pushed out of the lift and into the hallway. And there was Janet waiting.

She remained still, looking at him for a moment; then swiftly coming towards him, she held out both her hands and when he gripped them and pulled her down to him and kissed her, she burst into a flood of tears, saying, 'Oh, Mr Leonard. Oh, Mr Leonard.'

*   *   *

'Would you mind?' I said to the ambulance men, and pointed to our hall door. And when they had pushed Nardy's chair through and into the drawing-room, both men stopped for a moment before pushing the chair further towards the couch. And when Nardy was seated on it, one of the men looked around him. Then bending towards Nardy, he said, 'I can see how you wanted to be back, sir.'

Nardy said nothing; he only smiled at the men, laid his head back against the couch and let his eyes roam round the room.

I thanked the ambulance men warmly. We had got to know each other on the long journey, especially the one who had sat by the bed all the way. And my heart went out to him because, not only had he read *Hamilton*, but he had been able to quote from it, in particular the bits in the doctor's surgery. Apparently his wife had already endorsed that it was exactly as I had described.

They were both surprised at and very grateful for the tip they received and they shook my hand and wished me all the luck in the world.

When I once again entered the drawing-room, Nardy extended his hand towards me, and I hurried to him. I sat down beside him; and his

208

arm about me, he laid his head on my shoulder and said simply, 'Thank God!'

I too thanked Him for having my dear one back home safe, if not sound, for now I was carrying a fresh burden.

This morning the doctor had asked to see me before we left the hospital and, after a polite exchange, he had said, 'I have written to Doctor Bell concerning your husband, Mrs Leviston, and I think you, too, should be put in the picture. You may have been wondering why we haven't continued the graftings these last few weeks. Well, we didn't think it wise owing to the condition of your husband's heart.'

At these words, a steel hammer seemed to have leapt up and hit my ribs, and the pain made me dumb. I just stared at the man, waiting for his next words. 'It will no doubt improve with time, rest, and care. The main thing in his case is rest, at least for the present. He will naturally have to have therapy to get his joints moving again. Fortunately these are all intact. Doctor Bell will no doubt arrange for a therapist to visit him.'

In a small voice I had asked now, 'Does my husband know of his condition?'

And to this the doctor had answered, 'Yes, he knows. But it was his wish that you shouldn't be informed. However, I made no promise to him one way or the other, but I felt you should know the situation, and how, in the future, he should be treated. He needs rest, but not inertia. The quicker he can walk unaided, the better, for gentle exercise will aid and strengthen his limbs.'

He then ended, 'It will be up to you whether you let him know that you are aware of this or

209

not. But my advice would be, at the moment, to pretend ignorance, for it would be of no help if he knew you were worried more than you have been.'

So here I was chatting away about the future and where we were going as soon as he was able to travel.

The door opened and Janet came in with the tea-trolley, and she stood in front of us and smiled, a warm welcoming smile, as she said, 'Oh, I'm glad to see you both sitting there again. Oh, I am. It does me heart good.'

I put my hand out towards her, asking now, 'Where is he?'

'In the kitchen. I've practically had to strap him down.'

'Fetch him in.'

'You're sure? You'd better have a cup of tea first, 'cos mind, I'm tellin' you, ma'am, he—' she pressed her lips together, and her eyelids were blinking hiding the laughter there as she ended, 'he hasn't improved.'

I wanted to say, 'Good, good,' because I had told Nardy so much about the little fellow which had made him laugh until he had begged me to stop, and the fact that the child might have improved would, I thought, have made Nardy imagine that I had created someone else to join my little menagerie.

It was Nardy now who answered for me, saying, 'I'm glad to hear that. Give us five minutes, then fetch him in.'

During the five minutes which stretched to ten we had two cups of tea each, and a sandwich, then the door opened and Janet came in leading

210

Harold by the hand, and on first sight he appeared a different child. The last time I had seen him he had been wearing patched jeans and a scruffed little jacket, over which part of a none too clean shirt collar had probed. But coming towards us now was a smart little fellow in bright blue jeans and a white tee-shirt.

When Janet relinquished his hand, he stood in front of us looking from one to the other; then he stumbled sideways as Janet's hand pushed him none too gently, saying, 'Mind what I told you. Behave yourself.'

I watched him slant his eyes up at his grandmother, then he emitted a long drawn out, 'Oo...h!' as she left the room.

'Hello, Harold.'

Harold did not answer me; he was looking at Nardy. Now Nardy said, 'Hello Harold.' And to this Harold deigned to reply, 'Hello.'

There was silence now between the three of us, and the questioning seemed to be carried on by our eyes because, first, Harold would lift his gaze from Nardy, look at me, then look back at Nardy again; and I would look at Harold, then look at Nardy, then look back at Harold once more.

'Have you been a good boy?'

There was no answer, but a definite nodding of his head. Harold wasn't acting to form. It seemed to be that Nardy's presence was stilling his tongue. Then I found I was mistaken, for what the young man now said, addressing himself directly to Nardy, was, 'You the fella as got burnt?'

I heard Nardy swallow. 'Yes,' he said, 'I'm the fella as got burnt.'

211

'All over?'

'No, no, not quite.'

'I got burnt once.'

'You did?'

'Aye, I did.'

'Where were you burnt?'

'On me arse.' He started, while at the same time I started, and Nardy started, and our joined glances went swiftly towards the door as if we expected to see his grandmother flying up the room, her hand uplifted. After a moment I heard my own voice, mock stern now, saying, 'You didn't mean that, did you, Harold? You meant your bottom?'

He looked at me, the expression on his face telling me that he definitely wasn't going to sink as low as that, for he emitted one word. 'Backside.'

Then switching his gaze to Nardy again, he said, 'You want to see?'

I daren't look at Nardy, but his voice sounded steady as he said, 'Yes. Yes, I'd like to see where you were burnt.'

I watched the small hands deftly now unbuttoning the straps that kept his jeans up and when they were dropped around his ankles, he shuffled forward, turned round, at the same time pulling down a tiny pair of clean underpants. And there, across one small bare buttock, about four inches by two, almost covering the whole pad of flesh, was a scar that proved the extent of a bad burn.

'Dear, dear! you have been burnt, haven't you?'

'Yes. An' if I sit like this'—he now bent over and pushed his bottom out—'I can see it in the glass.'

As I had once done, I saw Nardy cover his eyes with his hand; then he made a strange sound before he asked, 'How did you manage to get burnt like that?'

The small pants were being pulled up, then the jeans, and these were safely buttoned before the answer came, 'I sat on the bloody fire bar.'

There seemed to be pandemonium in the room. I was coughing hard, Nardy was bent forward, his hand still over his eyes; Hamilton was racing round the lot of us, and not alone now, but dragging Begonia with him.

When I found my voice I said, 'How on earth did you manage to get burnt by a fire bar?'

'Grandad Stodd showed me. He used to lift up his shirt at night, like this'—he now demonstrated, bending over again and holding up an imaginary shirt away from his hips—'to warm his a ... backside.'

I realized that was a good effort and, trying to keep my face straight, I said, 'And you followed suit?'

He hesitated a moment before answering, his eyes screwed up again in a manner with which, in the future, I was to become well acquainted whenever he tried to understand the meaning of some word or saying. Now, seeming to get my gist, he said, 'Well I stood on the fender, an' it was slippy an' I fell backward, an' ... an' I raised hell. Grandad Stodd said they heard me down at the fish market. An' I kept on when I was in the hospital; I raised the bloody place. An' you know what?' He now transferred his gaze from Nardy's tortured expression to mine, and he moved a step nearer to me and, poking his head forward and his face going into a smile, he said again, 'You know what?' And I shook my head as I said, 'No: what?'

I watched him press his lips tight together before he said in what to him was his whisper, 'The nurse, she kissed me when I was comin' out.'

'*Never*!' I shook my head as if in disbelief.

And now indignantly and loudly, he cried, 'She did! An' she said, if I would like to sit on any more bars she would see to me. She did. Why you holdin' hands?'

Our fingers parted as if a spring had released them; then Nardy said, 'Because we are fond of each other, we like holding hands.'

He stared at Nardy for some time, then moved from one foot to the other before he spoke again: 'Me mum went off with a bloke,' he said.

What could you say to that? We said nothing. And he went on, 'An' me dad's bit, she doesn't like me.' He shook his head vigorously now. And when I was forced to say, 'Oh, I'm sure you are mistaken, Harold,' his voice came back at me in an almost screaming bark as he yelled, 'No, I'm not mis ... mistakin'. She clouted me, not like Gag does, like that!' He used his hand to demonstrate by banging himself on the ear. 'She hit me with the dog's lead.' Then he added in almost the same breath, 'Gag says you've got a dog. Where is it?'

'A friend of ours is bringing it down by car from the north. I ... I think you'll like it. His name is Sandy.'

'Will you bring it round to Gag's?'

My eyes widened in surprise as I said, 'No, no; you'll see it here.'

'I won't, 'cos ... 'cos this is me finish.'

'Your finish?'

'Yes. I'm not comin' back any more, Gran says, 'cos ...'cos of you.' He was now nodding at Nardy. ''Cos ...'cos you bein' an old man, you want to be quiet.'

'He's not an old man.' I indignantly spoke up in Nardy's defence. But my opponent, looking my husband over from top to bottom, stated flatly, 'He is an' all.'

Nardy was nodding at him now: 'Yes, yes, of course I am, but that doesn't mean you can't come here to see me.'

'Yer mean I can? Can I?'

'Yes, of course.'

'Every day?' He was looking at me now and I nodded and said, 'Yes, except the week-ends when your grandmother doesn't come.'

He now glanced towards the door again and, his voice dropping, he emitted, 'God Almighty!'

'What's wrong?'

He was appealing to me now: 'Will ... will yer tell her that you asked me, else she'll bash me ear 'ole for me?'

'Yes, I'll tell her. And Harold ...'

He waited, and while pulling myself to the end of the couch I put out my hand and caught his and said, 'What you have just said ...'

'What?'

'The'—I stopped, looked down, and was aware of Nardy moving restlessly to the side of me—'the expression you used about ... about God.'

'Oh, God? Like on a Sunday night on the telly?'

'Yes, like on a Sunday night on the telly.'

'Gag looks at that 'cos she says it clears the house.'

Puzzled, I bent my head towards him and repeated, 'Clears the house?'

'Yes, 'cos me Uncle Greg and Rodney and me Auntie May, they go out and sit in the kitchen. But I sit with Gag ... well, 'cos, she makes me. But ... but I don't mind, I don't, 'cos I sit on her knee then an' sometimes I fall asleep.'

His eyes roaming round the room, he now made a statement: 'I'd like to live in this house,' he said.

'I'm sure you would, I'm sure you would.' My voice was brisk; and giving him now a slight pat on the bottom, I said, 'Go and tell your grandma that we'd like some more hot water.'

He didn't move, but, instead, asked, 'An' will I tell 'er I can come every day 'cos you say so?'

'Yes,' I looked at Nardy, and he endorsed this. 'Yes, yes, of course.'

With this he darted down the room, and I saw Hamilton, still holding on to Begonia, dancing after him.

'Amazing.'

I nodded at Nardy, saying, 'Yes, isn't he just.'

'How old did you say he was?'

'Five now, I think.'

'He's bright. He thinks; you can see his mind working. But what will he end up like among that lot? Poor Janet. You cannot imagine her breeding that crew, can you? I wonder whom he takes after?'

'Well, evidently not his mother, and by all Janet's accounts his father's a very ordinary

216

individual.'

'Anyway,' he laughed now, 'he's picked up a wonderful vocabulary. I don't think I've laughed so much since I first met Gran and George. Yet'—he turned and looked at me—'you know what you said when you left me the other night? It's made me think.'

'What was that?'

'Well, I imagined you were a bit tired of the constant wise-cracking of George and Gran. And, if you remember, you said, everything should be doled out in small amounts, except love and peace of mind.'

'Did I say that?'

'Of course, you did. You know you did.'

'Well, yes, I suppose it's true, because'—I started to chuckle now—'fancy having Harold for twenty-four hours of the day.'

'Oh, yes, just fancy. Still, I think I'm going to see him as a diversion in the future, during the times I get bored with you.'

As I put my arms about him and we kissed, a long, soft, tender kiss, I tried to thrust to the back of my mind the knowledge of his condition that I now carried with me.

*　　*　　*

A couple of hours later Tommy arrived with Sandy. I had become a little worried when he didn't show up about the same time as us, but as he said, he had taken it slowly because of Sandy's nerves.

Sandy's greeting of me was as if we had been parted for weeks; and he greeted Nardy the same.

217

And Tommy, looking at the dog kissing first one and then the other of us, remarked, 'What it is to be loved.'

At this I made Sandy behave.

Tommy refused tea but accepted whisky. He was drinking more of late, I noted. And as he stood sipping his drink, he looked round the room, saying, 'One can see how you wanted to be back. I'd forgotten what this room looked like.'

I noted that he had never asked Nardy how he was feeling, or how he had stood the journey. Tommy was indeed changed; he created a feeling of uneasiness in me.

I was glad when he got up to go.

I opened the door for him and crossed the hall to the lift with him, and we stood looking at each other for a moment while he said, 'This time next week I'll be on my way.'

'Really?'

'Yes, really. It's all fixed, passport, route, the lot. At least the route is until I get overseas; then who knows?'

'Have you any idea where you're actually aiming for once you arrive?'

'No, none whatever. My idea is to get lost, and perhaps in getting lost'—he paused—'I'll find myself.'

'Oh, Tommy.' I had the desire to put my hands out and take his, but I resisted, because I was afraid of what the result might be. Yet, I kept telling myself that his change of personality was not due in any way to a feeling he might have for me, because supposedly he'd felt like this before the fire, and it hadn't caused him to act in this strange way.

'Bye-bye, Maisie.'

'Bye-bye, Tommy. You will look in before you go?'

'Yes, if I can manage it.'

'Tommy!' He was inside the lift and my voice was loud now. 'You've got to say goodbye to Nardy. What's the matter with you anyway?'

He stared at me before saying again, 'Bye-bye, Maisie.' Then the lift doors closed on him and I was left standing listening to the soft hum as it descended to the ground floor. I felt angry. What was the matter with the man anyway? Nardy was his best friend and he had, in a way, put up with him for years listening to his tirades against his mother.

I actually shook my body as if throwing something off. I had enough on my plate without worrying about him. He was going, apparently out of our lives, to get lost. Well, let him get lost, and the sooner the better.

*   *   *

It was the following Thursday night when Tommy came to say goodbye. The shadow of his old self seemed to have returned and he sat with us and talked normally. He showed us two routes: one did seem to cover the world, taking in Nepal and the foothills of the Himalayas before plunging back into the crowds of Singapore and later Hong Kong. Another plan showed a less sophisticated route. Here he thought of walking through the Rockies, after realizing a childhood dream of crossing Canada via the CPR.

When we had our last drink together, he held

his glass up towards Nardy, saying, 'Here's to you taking the stairs instead of the lift.'

I helped Nardy to his feet and there they stood looking at each other. Nardy put out his hand and Tommy took it. They gripped tight while Nardy said, 'You will keep in touch, won't you? Let us know where you are.'

'Yes, I promise, if it's only by cards. Goodbye, Nardy. Thanks for everything, right back down the years.'

I saw that Nardy was too full to make any reply, and, as I looked at them, I had the most dreadful feeling of foreboding; it looked as if they were saying goodbye for ever. I turned from them and went hastily down the room and into the hall. And when, a few minutes later, Tommy joined me, I was wiping my eyes; and then, there before me, stood the old Tommy.

'Oh, Maisie, Maisie, don't please. I beg of you, don't. Look, I'm not going away forever; I'll be back in your lives before ... before you know I've gone.'

I looked up at him and said quietly, 'Nardy is in a bad way, Tommy. Before we left the hospital the doctor told me that his heart had been affected, so much so that they hadn't done any more grafting. I ... I suppose they were afraid to use the anaesthetic. And he was examined yesterday by our new doctor, a Doctor Bell, and he confirmed this. But, as he said, taking it easy and with care and attention—he's having therapy every other day—it will likely strengthen.'

I put out my hand and touched Tommy's arm, saying, 'What is it? What's the matter?' for he had put his hand to his brow, shading his eye, like I did when wanting to hide a smile from young Harold. But Tommy wasn't trying to hide a smile; his mouth was open and he was drawing in a long, shuddering breath.

'Are you all right?' I asked.

He took his hand away, blinked at me, wet his lips, then said, 'Yes, yes, Maisie,' and then he added, 'No, no; I'm not all right,' He stood with his arm outstretched and his finger on the lift button for a moment before he burst out, 'Why had you to happen to me?'

The lift door slowly closed itself across my open-mouthed gaze.

Why had you to happen to me?

It was me then that had brought about the change in him. But why had he been so affected by what I had told him about Nardy?

I walked into the hall. There was a half-moon table set between the dining-room and kitchen doors. It had a mirror above it. I leant my hands on the table for support and bowed my head and, like that, I thanked God that Tommy had gone out of our lives. When I lifted up my face, there I was looking at myself. And at this moment the image was no different to what it had been three or four years ago: the hair was brown and straight, the face was heart-shaped, the eyes were round, the nose straight, the mouth wide. Reading these features as a description, they should have made, if not a beautiful face, then a bonny face, a homely face; but their combination resulted in none of these, I was plain. That was the name for me, plain. Perhaps in my eyes I had one asset, they were kindly. Another could be my voice. But given those, what was there about me that could sever a lifetime friendship that had existed between two men? What was it about me that had attracted either of them?

The reflection in the mirror was shaking its head: it didn't know. And behind it now, the rest of the glass was taken up by Hamilton. I looked at him and he said, You'll never get the answer to that question. If you could put your finger on what creates love, you'd be Solomon's first wife. And in your case you could ask yourself, too, why that same face could create so much hate, not only from Stickle, but from your mother.

I turned away. There was a deep sickness in my stomach.

CHAPTER FOURTEEN

The weeks followed pleasantly. The therapist was getting good results: Nardy was able to walk unaided around the flat. But as I watched him I was amazed at how he could bear to move his scarred legs. At my first sight of them, I had been shocked: the left leg was burnt up to his thigh; the scars on the right leg ended just above his knee, but below the knee, down one side as far as the calf, the skin seemed to have been stuck on the bone; the other side had been built up from the skin taken from the thigh of the same leg. This had left sickly white patches here and there that appeared like burns themselves. And I was made to wonder how he had ever survived; and also how poor little Kitty had survived.

And now, according to the letters from Mary,

she was doing splendidly, still having graftings but being allowed home in between times. But even with the letters from Fellburn they all now seemed a part of another life, a dim, fast receding life. The only life I was experiencing was the daily routine in these very pleasant rooms, the companionship of Nardy, and the lighter amusing intervals provided by Harold.

Strange, but there were many days when I blessed Harold, for he relieved Nardy's growing boredom.

Nardy had work sent from the office, but the doing of it didn't seem to fill his day, not even with the time spent with the therapist, nor yet, I had to admit, his time spent with me. He missed his daily ride or walk to the office, he missed the companionship of all those who worked there. Although from Mr Houseman down, they visited him from time to time, their visits only seemed to leave him more low and depressed. Now and again he expressed the wish to go out and we hired a car and drove into the country. We would get out and walk for a little way or perhaps have dinner at an inn, but lately the journey itself seemed to tire him.

Then one day, there was presented to me a way to alleviate his periods of boredom.

The heath was only five minutes walk from the house and, at least once a day, in all weathers, I would take Sandy there to do his 'necessaries' and give him a bit of play with a ball.

On this day when I went to put on his lead, he was, as usual, in the kitchen having a game with Harold. They were wrestling on the rug, and when I said, 'Come along, up with you, you scamp,' and caught hold of Harold's arm and pulled him to his feet, he said, 'You gonna take him out?'

'Yes.'

'But him, the caretaker'—he stabbed his finger towards the floor—'he takes him round the block first thing, don't he?'

'Yes, but that's different; he doesn't get a run then.'

'Can I come along o' you?'

This was a new tactic.

Just at that moment Janet entered the room, a duster in her hand, and her grandson ran towards her, saying, 'She ... Mrs Nardy—' We were Mr and Mrs Nardy to him now; no clips along the ear could get him to call us anything else. His attempts at Leviston had resulted in verbal gymnastics, so Mr and Mrs Nardy we were. And now he was going on, 'She says I can go with her to the heath.'

Knowing her grandson better than anyone and, too, noting the expression on my face, Janet looked down on her daily cross, saying, 'She never said any such thing, did she?'

He stared back at her, silent now, and her reaction was to bring her hand across his ear as she said, 'I've told you about lies. You come out with any more of your smarties an' it won't be a clip along the ear you'll get.'

What made me say it? 'I asked him, Janet.'

'You did?' Her voice was high. I nodded and, looking to where the child was holding his ear, I said to him, 'Go and get your coat; there's a wind blowing this morning.'

He didn't run from the room but walked out

224

slowly.

Turning to Janet, I said, 'Janet, you know you shouldn't hit him across the ears like that, you'll make him deaf.'

'Oh'—she jerked her chin upwards—'it'll take a lot to make that one deaf. I wish I could, and dumb. I thought I would have been rid of him at least for part of the day. I went to the school yesterday afternoon, and what d'you think he said, the teacher? He can't take him in until September, nearly four months ahead. My God!' She ran her fingers round the hem of the duster. Then more to herself than to me, she said, 'If it was only him I had to put up with. Our house is gettin' like a menagerie. I told you about Joe comin' back, didn't I?' She was looking at me now. 'Well, last week our Bill turned up, on the dole. Couldn't pay his board, he said. No, I said to him, that would interfere with your beer money, wouldn't it? Eeh!' She shook her head. 'To think what we lived on when we were first married. They each go through that much every night at the pub, and then they grumble. Then I'm havin' trouble with the one next door 'cos of the noise, 'cos when they come in three sheets to the wind it's like hell let loose. I don't blame her in a way, but now she's threatening to go to the council, 'cos I'm takin' in lodgers, she says. You know what, ma'am, I hope she does; it'll get rid of some of them, 'cos when I tell them to scarper they look at me and say, "Mum, where else can I go, if I can't come home?' Eeh!' She glanced towards the door. 'I suppose I shouldn't take it out on that little 'un, but he's just one more sack on me back.'

'I'm sorry, Janet, I really am. And then you have all this work to do...'

'Oh, ma'am, don't pity me 'cos of that. If I hadn't this house to come to, I really would go round the bend.' And now she smiled and nodded at me as she finished, 'That's what I said to them last week: if it wasn't for Mr and Mrs Leviston, I'd take a carving knife one night an' go round and finish you all off.'

I bit on my lip and said, 'You didn't!'

'I did.' Her eyes were wide now, her lips were pursed, her head was bobbing. 'Me very words. And y'know'—her voice became serious—'you can get to such a pitch you would do anything to sort of clear your mind.'

The kitchen door opened and her grandson stood there. He was holding his hand out and he looked at me as he said, 'I've brought me new cap.'

'Oh, that is a nice one. I haven't seen that before. It matches your coat. Put it on.'

He put it on, and I held my head to one side as I said, 'Oh, you do look smart. Well, we'll be off, shall we?' Janet and I exchanged looks; then I took up Sandy's lead and we went out.

Once we reached the street, I felt my hand gripped, and there we went, like a little family across the road, down past the public garden still railed round and locked, through the suburb and on to the heath.

The wind was blowing, the air was fresh. I took off my head scarf and ran my fingers through my hair, drawing in one deep breath after another. I walked slowly, watching Harold throw the ball and Sandy scampering after it, then bring it back

226

to him.

Harold would yell, 'Sit!' and Sandy would obey. Then Harold would throw the ball again. But the procedure was interrupted: Sandy didn't run after the ball; his head went up, he sniffed, sniffed again, then turning, he looked to where, far away in the distance were the figures of a woman and a dog. They weren't coming towards us but were walking parallel with us.

One second Sandy was there, the next he was off, and I was yelling, 'Sandy! Sandy! Stay! Come back!'

Harold made an exclamation which I didn't catch; then we were both running in the direction Sandy had taken.

We were still some distance away when we saw his meeting up with what I could see now was another poodle, much smaller than he. I saw the woman stoop down and pick up her dog; and then she did what I considered a very kind thing. She came walking in our direction. My running stopped. I stood panting; then checked Harold, caught his hand and together we walked to where Sandy was alternately running round and jumping up at the woman while barking his head off.

'Oh, thank you. I'm so sorry.'

'It's all right.' The owner of the small black poodle smiled; then looking down on the culprit, she said, 'He's a fine fellow, isn't he? He just wanted to make the acquaintance of...'

Her words were cut off by a statement issuing from the mouth of a little boy who, bending down, now grabbed Sandy's collar while exclaiming loudly, 'He's not a fine fella, he's a naughty little bugger.'

227

Our new acquaintance had a refined voice; she looked a refined person altogether. Her gaze remained on the child who had coupled naughty with bugger in one breath. Her eyes met mine; then they covered me from head to foot. She likely noted that I was wearing a well-cut, seemingly expensive fine woollen two-piece. My shoes, too, were smart. I was wearing a gold wrist-watch and three rings, two of them heavily stoned. Yet, here was this person, because in the woman's mind I must have been registered as just a person, whose little boy came out with the word bugger as naturally as he had done naughty. Children, and she would know, learn by copying.

'Good-morning.'

My 'Good-morning, and thank you,' was a mere trickle of a whisper. I felt ashamed and ashamed of feeling ashamed. I wanted to run after her and say, 'He doesn't belong to me. He's the grandson of my help.' Snob. I looked down to where Harold was grinning up at me while holding on to Sandy's collar. I bent down and clipped on the lead; then, taking Harold's hand, I led him to a grassy patch and, pressing him down none too gently on to it, I sat down by his side, and as he was about to speak, I heard myself suddenly yell, 'Shut up!'

My voice even startled Sandy, and Harold's round eyes narrowed while his mouth widened.

'Do you know what you said there?' I demanded.

'What?'

'Don't you "what" me. You know what you said to the dog just a moment ago.'

I watched him think; then he said, 'I told him

228

he was naughty.'

'Yes, but you used another word.'

I could see light dawning, and his voice in his usual whisper brought out, 'Bugger?'

'Yes, that was the word, bugger. Now, you've been told before, haven't you, that these are bad words, at least for a little boy to use.' His eyes were blinking, his mouth was closed, and I went on, 'Now, I'm going to put this straight to you, Harold. I know you're just turned five, but you are not stupid. In fact, you are far from stupid. You know you've been told not to use those words, haven't you?'

Still there was no response.

'Well, now I'm going to tell you something: either you stop using these words and at once, or you don't come to my house any more. Now have you got that?'

Still no response. And now I watched his lower lip begin to tremble; then his mouth opened and he said, in a real whisper this time, 'Everybody ... everybody says 'em. They says 'em. Talks. I ... I can't help it, 'cos ... well...'

I turned my head away and looked over the heath. Of course the child couldn't help it. As I'd thought earlier, everyone learns by copying. What he needed was other words to copy. But he wouldn't be going to school until September when very likely he'd add to somebody's vocabulary while extending his own in the same direction. I looked at him again. His lip was still trembling, but I saw that he was being comforted, for there to his side, and looking not much bigger than himself, stood Begonia. Hamilton was present too, but he was some distance away, as if just acting as a spectator. Begonia was nuzzling the fair hair. Then, turning her liquid gaze on me, she said, French. Nardy speaks French like a native, doesn't he? This child, here, likes words. Haven't you noticed how he tries to repeat words, bringing in those that he's heard you or Nardy say? Didn't he only yesterday cause laughter by trying to repeat secondary? Get Nardy to take him on: half an hour or so in the mornings with, Le livre est sur la table; or, Ouvrez la porte. Fermez la fenetre. And Nardy would like that, I know he would. You were looking for something different to alleviate his boredom. He enjoys the boy as he is, but just think, if he could extract a foreign language from these small lips instead of crude swear-words, what an achievement that would be! He wouldn't feel so useless. And that's what's troubling him at present, he feels useless.

It was the only conversation I had had with Begonia, and when I nodded at her, she went on softly: And you know something more? The child is lost for love. Clips across the ears don't express affection. He has lost his mother, he has lost his father; he's in a house full of men who, to put it mildly, are rough types. What is more, and what adds to the rejection of his parents is that the woman his father has taken up with must hate him. From what you have been given to understand, the ultimatum was, either he goes or . . . So he went. Maisie, you have a piece of gold here covered in clay; it's up to you to strip it until its colour matches your room.

I smiled widely and warmly at Begonia and thanked her for opening my eyes. She said I was welcome. And as she turned away from the child,

230

there was Hamilton. He had come much closer and was waiting for her. He looked at her with pride, then nodded to me, as much as to say, You see, you can't do without one or the other of us.

The next minute they were blocked from my view. I hadn't seen the child rise from the grass, but there he was standing in front of me, his face on a level with mine. What really possessed me at that moment I don't know, perhaps it was the thought of giving Nardy a new interest, anyway; I leant forward and kissed him gently.

I wasn't prepared for what followed. The next instant his arms were about my neck, and he was kissing me in much the same way as Sandy was wont to do, but with a difference, for he was crying loudly while talking all the time: 'You let me stay in your 'ouse, Mrs Nardy. I like you, Mrs Nardy. I want to stay with you, Mrs Nardy, an' Mr Nardy. I won't swear. I won't. I love you, Mrs Nardy...'

'Sh! Sh! Quiet now.'

'Don't tell Gag on me, will you? Will you? Don't tell Gag on me.'

'Sh! Sh! now. It's all right. No, I won't tell Gag. No, I won't, my dear.' Good gracious! There I was crying myself now. 'Come on. Come on.' I groped for a handkerchief, which was difficult because Sandy, his paws resting on my shoulder, was now licking our faces alternately.

Finding the handkerchief, I wiped the child's face, then wiped mine. He was quiet now, but he didn't leave loose of me; instead he put his arms underneath mine and laid his head on my breast and curled the rest of his body into my lap. I supported him with my short arm while balancing

231

myself with my other by pressing it on to the grass because I was finding it difficult to sit upright. Then I found my body rocking slightly and, as I looked down on his face lying on my breast, I had a strange thought: I had a child ... I had a child.

CHAPTER FIFTEEN

'What! Teach Childe Harold French when his English is mostly Saxon?'

'He would hang on to strange words and forget the others, and he'd learn English and grammar as he went along.'

Nardy surveyed me through narrowed eyes. I became embarrassed in the silence, and I couldn't say to him, I'm thinking it might help you. Then, following on his first response and the look on his face that my suggestion had evoked, he surprised me now by putting his head back and laughing, as he said, 'You know something, Maisie? God is a funny fella.'

It was my turn to screw up my eyes and say, 'What?'

'I said God is a funny fella. Half consciously you appeal to Him ... well, in your thinking you say, Show me a way out. Show me how to ease this situation; and when you give up, saying, What's the good? Let things take their course, I can do nothing more, in through the back door walks the answer.'

'What are you talking about?'

'What you were talking about, teaching Childe Harold French. Anyway, tell me what brought this on. You come bursting in as if you had just drunk the elixir of life.'

So I told him what happened. And he laughed as he said, 'For once I think the word naughty was linked up with something meaningful because, you know, that word used to irritate me when in the office. Someone would say, "It's very naughty of him," when the person being spoken of had probably done something really bad, even criminal. It's like nice. That annoys me too. I've discovered if people are really jealous of a possession or of someone else, they'll say, it, or he, or she is ve...ry nice.'

The last two words were uttered in a refined squeak. And at this I dropped down to his side, laughing, put my arms about him and said 'Oh, Nardy. You know, at times you are very funny, but awfully nice.'

'I am?'

'Yes, you are.'

'Well, well.' He mockingly preened himself, then added, 'And all without the aid of a horse. But that's another word, awfully. How can anyone be awfully nice?'

I gave him a push, and as I rose I said, 'One thing I've learned about you, you're secretly conceited about your knowledge of English. Anyway, I'm off now to tell Janet you are about to take on her very small rough diamond and polish it, with the result that every one in his family will want to claim acquaintance with him, he being the only one who can speak a foreign language.'

I stopped when I reached the door and, looking back at him, I said, 'You know, there's some truth in that, isn't there? If that boy ever did turn out to be educationally superior to them all, they would be the first to claim acquaintance with him, and recall the fun they'd had with him when he was a child. Even Janet would bring back the times she had almost deafened him with her hand across his ear.'

Nardy nodded at me. 'Wise old owl,' he said. 'But I think you had better tell Janet to sit down before you give her the news.' ...

Nardy was right. Janet looked at me across the kitchen table as if she were thinking that what some people thought about me was actually true. And in a small voice, she said, 'French?'

'Yes, French.'

'Teach him French?' Her voice still small, she was thumbing to where Harold was lying on the rug, his arms around Sandy. They were facing each other and they presented an angelic picture. And I looked down on them for a moment, then I said, 'He'll pick it up, and quickly.'

'Huh! ma'am, you mean to say that Mr Leonard is for this?'

'Yes, wholeheartedly.'

She turned from the table and went to the oven; bending down, she opened the door and lifted out a casserole dish. Placing it on the table, she said, 'Well, never again will I say, nothin' surprises me. But just wait till I tell my lot about this. That'll crease them; they won't straighten up for days.'

'Well, we'll see. But whenever Harold is in this house, the notice will go up, Ici on parle francais.'

'What?' She was half smiling, her face screwed up now.

'I said, French is spoken here.'

'Oh, Mrs Leviston, ma'am.' She suddenly sat down on the chair, put her elbows on the table, cupped her face in her hands and, from the look on it, I didn't know whether she was about to laugh or cry. But the remark from her grandson tilted the balance.

Harold was now lying on his back, aiming to push away Sandy's licking tongue from his face, and our future French student said, 'Stop it! you silly sod.'

No reprimand was forthcoming from his grandmother, and I, like her now, suddenly sat down on a chair, and our heads were almost touching across the table as we groaned with our laughter.

CHAPTER SIXTEEN

One August Saturday, George and Gran paid us a flying visit. They came down on day return tickets. It was good to see them, but guilt struck me when I knew they weren't aiming to stay the week-end.

They said Kitty was getting along splendidly, but they didn't seem to have the same opinion of Nardy. They made great play of his being able to walk, but when Gran got me alone, she said, 'What's wrong with him? He looks peaked.'

'He's confined to the house too much,' I said.

One thing I found odd: they didn't laugh about Nardy's pupil. Of course, they had when I had first described how he interspersed his speech with swear-words—this they could recognize and

235

so understand—but when I told them Nardy spoke French to him for an hour every morning and that it was amazing how the child had taken to it, they both stared at me, then looked at each other. And Gran said a strange thing: 'You adopting him?' she asked.

'Adopting Harold?' I laughed out loud. 'Of course not! He's got a family, seven uncles and aunts, a mother and a stepmother, sort of, and his own father. Adopt him? No, of course not!'

'Doesn't he go to school?' Gran asked.

'He starts next month.'

'What about the French then?' said George.

'Oh, Nardy is going to take him at the weekends and whenever he can come around at night.'

'My, My!' Gran shook her head. 'Some people are lucky.'

Yes, I had to admit I was glad when they left; only to lie awake far into the night trying to work out the change in pattern of the emotions that life cut out for you and apparently without your consent. And Gran had been right, Nardy did look peaked.

And it wasn't for the want of fresh air. Nardy was changing. In some subtle way he was changing right before my eyes. He was more quiet. I would find him sitting staring at me, and if I asked, 'What is it, dear?' he'd come out with some little compliment, such as, 'I love you.'

One day he said that he wished he didn't.

'What is it, dear?' I had said, and he had taken my face between his hands and replied, 'Sometimes I feel sick at heart because I love you and I wish I didn't.'...

236

Then there was Tommy. As promised he had sent us cards from various places across Canada. And when on one of them was written, 'Still looking,' Nardy had said, 'What does he mean, still looking?' And I said, 'I think he's looking for himself,' to which Nardy had replied, 'Well, there's one thing I know for sure, he won't find it out there.' . . .

So life went on. We had visitors. The Freemans called regularly. They were always very nice to me, but I never seemed to get close to Alice. Although she accepted me, kissed me warmly, I felt that, like all Nardy's friends, she, at bottom, couldn't understand what it was about me that had attracted their charming friend to this small plain girl . . . or woman.

Bernard Houseman and his wife came. Now, I knew where I stood with Mrs Sarah Houseman, for her manner towards me had always indicated that I was of an inferior class.

But one week-end we had a visitor who did warm my heart. Mike came and he brought with him all the warmth, understanding, and kindness that I needed. Until we had a quiet talk I hadn't realized the effort it was taking for me to keep up the easy-going normal attitude that indicated everything in the garden was lovely. I said to him, 'Tell me, is he in a really bad way?'

He had answered, 'I haven't examined him myself, but I can only go on what two highly experienced men have said. His heart's in a poor condition. And apparently it wasn't caused by the fire, only exacerbated by it. What has come to light is that his father died from a heart attack when he was fifty-two and an uncle in the same way. So Nardy's condition could be partly congenital, which obviously wouldn't have mattered so much if it hadn't been for the fire and the physical strain the burns have put on his system. But,' he had ended cheerfully, 'there's no need for you to despair, nor to worry yourself more skinny than you are. Given a quiet life, a bit of exercise, no undue worries, and he could be attending your funeral in your eighties.'

I think the highlight of Mike's visit was his introduction to Harold.

'So this is our little linguistic genius,' he had said, bending over the minute but wide-eyed figure.

When Harold made no reply, Mike went on, 'I hear you can speak three languages: English, French, and your own.'

Still no reply.

A little push from Nardy's hand brought Harold's face towards him, and when Nardy said, 'Well, what have you to say to the doctor?'

Harold waited some further seconds before he replied, 'He's hairy...like Flannagan's dog. It's got long hair.' And he made a dramatic gesture with his hand from his small shoulder down his body and outwards to describe the length of the hair on Flannagan's dog.

Nardy and I both cried together, 'Harold!' And Harold looked at Mike who had straightened up, turned about and was walking towards the window. An elbow was sticking out, indicating that he had his hand across the lower part of his face, and his shoulders were slightly hunched.

'Now you see what you've done,' Nardy's voice was stern. 'You've upset the doctor.'

238

'Haven't.'

'Oh, yes you have.'

'No, I haven't; he's too big.'

Nardy's puzzled glance was on me. There were times when he couldn't follow his pupil's thinking; but it was plain to me that anybody as big as Mike could not possibly be upset by anyone as small as himself. Get angry with him, swear at him, box his ears, kick his backside, as his uncles did, but not get upset by him.

This line of thought brought Hamilton on the scene. It seemed that it was he who swung Mike round to face his opponent again and then walked by his side until Mike was once more towering over Childe Harold.

'So, I'm like Flannagan's dog, am I? What kind of a dog is it?'

Harold appeared slightly puzzled for a moment, then answered, 'He's a dog.'

'You said that, but what type? Is he like Sandy there, a poodle? or a...?'

'No, silly, he's not like Sandy, he's a scruffy bug...he's a scruffy dog.'

'Oh, my goodness.' I hung my head.

'So, I'm like a long-haired scruffy dog, am I?'

'Well—' Harold looked from Nardy to me and, noting that we weren't pleased with him and the latent diplomat coming to the fore, he now said, 'Bumps is all right. He once caught some burglars at night. They was takin' the wheels off me Uncle Rod's banger. 'Twas outside the front door.'

Nardy, Mike, and I kept our faces straight but our eyelids were blinking rapidly. 'So they call the dog, Bumps,' Mike said. 'Why give it a name like that?'

'Eh?'

'I said, why do they call Flannagan's dog, Bumps?'

Harold thought, then said, 'Cos of "Bumps-A-Daisy".' And without further prompting he went on to explain: ''Cos he's big, I s'pose, an' gets in the way of Mrs Flannagan's feet, and she says she'll make a mat of him after she's cut him up, and so the lads bump him out of her way.'

I could imagine how the lads bumped the poor dog out of the way, likely with their feet. Anyway, that session ended with Mike lifting Harold high in the air and shaking him while Harold laughed a high glee-filled laugh.

And I held the picture in my mind for a long time afterwards.

CHAPTER SEVENTEEN

I remember the day when I first registered the fact that Nardy was fading away before my eyes. Harold was in the picture that day too.

It was a Saturday morning in November. Harold had been at school since September, so he came only on a Saturday morning for his 'is he on' lesson, as he called it. But during the half-term holiday he came every morning with Janet.

It was amazing how the child had progressed with this new language, while still dropping his aitches in the English one and occasionally falling back on his flowery one.

Nardy had not dressed this morning, but remained in his dressing-gown, which was unusual because he was meticulous about his attire. So much so, that I laughingly put it to him one day: 'You feel undressed, don't you, when you are not wearing a collar and tie?' And good-humouredly he had come back at me with, 'Yes; especially at night in bed.' But this morning he said, 'I feel a bit lazy today, dear; I hope our young genius doesn't object to my dressing-gown.'

'Our young genius wouldn't object to your being stark naked as long as he was with you,' I assured him, to which he answered, 'Tut-tut!'

After depositing her grandson, Janet usually did some odd shopping for me while I went to my study and left the tutor and his pupil together. But I'd been in the room only about twenty minutes when the door opened and in rushed Harold, gabbling, 'Mr Nardy, 'e's got a pain. 'E's 'oldin'...'

I didn't hear the rest of what he had to say for I had scrambled out of the room and into the dining-room where the lessons usually took place, and there was Nardy, bent over the table, one arm tight around his chest.

'What is it, dear?' Even as I said the words I was chiding myself for asking the road I knew.

He couldn't answer for a moment; then he said, 'A...a bit of a pain.'

'Sit quiet. Don't move.' I rushed out of the room again and grabbed up the phone and dialled the doctor...

Doctor Bell lived a five minutes car ride from us. He arrived in less than ten minutes. Luckily he

241

had just finished surgery.

He did not examine Nardy, but said brightly, 'We'll have to get you into hospital, laddie.'

Nardy, making a great effort to speak, said, 'No ...no hospital...bed.'

When the doctor began to speak again, saying, 'Well now,' Nardy slowly raised his hand from his chest and, looking up and after a pause, he managed to repeat, 'Bed.'

'Stay still for a moment then.'

As the doctor hurried out of the room I followed him, and in the hallway he said, 'I've got something in the car that might help, but the place for him is hospital. He's in a very bad way. You understand that, don't you?'

'Yes, yes, doctor, I understand that. And he knows he is, too, but he wants to stay at home.'

He made an impatient movement with his head, then hurried out. A few minutes later he was back and, after getting Nardy to swallow some pills, he gave him an injection, saying, 'This'll help.'

Between us, we got him into the bedroom and into bed, and all the while I'd been conscious of a spectator in the form of Harold.

Just as the doctor left Janet returned, and she became so distressed that I had to plead with her, saying, 'Janet! Janet! I need help. Don't, please, don't give way like that.'

'Oh, I'm sorry, I'm sorry, ma'am. I really am. I'll be all right. But ... but I've seen it comin', the change in him. You see, he, I've got to say it, he's been like me own because I've pushed him along since he was a bairn. I love him, I do, I do.'

'I know you do. I know you do, Janet, but

you've got to help me. He...he should be in hospital...' I didn't finish and voice my thoughts, but said, 'Do you think you could spare me a few hours this afternoon if the family...?'

'Blast the family. They can look after themselves, today and tomorrow and as long as I'm needed here. It'll do them good.'

A sniff and a choking sound, coming from the side of us, caused us both to look at the boy. The tears were running, down his face. Then, coming to me, he clutched my hand and said, ''E'll get better, Mr Nardy, won't 'e?'

'Yes, yes, of course he'll get better.' I put my hand on his hair. 'Of course he will. Of course he will. Be a good boy now;' then hurried out and into the bedroom.

Standing near the bed I looked down on my dear one. His face had taken on a blue tinge but his breathing was easy. He was asleep; the injection had done its work.

Sometime later Janet said, 'I'll take this one home'—she thumbed towards Harold—'and tell my lot what they can get on with.' And Harold said, 'Don't want to go, Gag.'

'It doesn't matter what you want, young man, it's what you're goin' to get. Come on, get your coat on.'

'But I want to stay, Gag. I want to stay with Mrs...'

'You heard me.'

'Janet.' She looked at me. 'Let him stay.'

'You've got enough on your plate without...'

'Please, Janet, let him stay.'

'Well, if you say so, ma'am; but mind'—she had turned to her grandson again, her fingers

243

wagging—'you make a noise an' open your mouth when you shouldn't an' I'll put me foot in it when I come back, because I'll know, I'll know.'

The door had hardly closed on her when the child came to me and I almost wailed aloud my misery and foreboding when he held out his arms and I lifted him up and he cuddled my neck tightly while his face was pressed close to mine and he never uttered a word. It was then that my two friends appeared, one on each side of us: Hamilton's whole demeanour was grave; Begonia's eyes were large and soft and full of understanding, and it was she who said, It is strange—isn't it?—from where you derive comfort in times of need.

*　　*　　*

The doctor called every day for a week. Nardy took his pills three times a day. If he felt further pain he didn't show it. He lay relaxed and quiet but ever ready to hold my hand when I neared the bed.

Janet had slept in one of the spare rooms for six nights, but I had insisted she went home on the Friday, because I am sure, in spite of her protestations, she had been worrying about how they were getting on at home. But when she arrived on the Saturday she wasn't accompanied by Harold, and I felt a keen sense of disappointment. And so, apparently, did Nardy, for although there was no possibility of a lesson taking place, I felt he was disappointed at not seeing the boy. And he voiced this when I was sitting by the bedside and we were having a coffee: 'Saturday mornings don't seem the same without Childe Harold, do they?' he said.

'No.' I smiled. 'He always made us aware that it was Saturday morning, if nothing else.'

'You like the boy, don't you?'

'Yes.' My reply was quiet and I nodded at him, saying, 'And you do too, don't you?'

'Oh, yes, yes, I like him. I'd like to think he'd be given a chance to be something later on. He's got it up top, you know, that child. It's amazing how he picks things up. He's learnt more French in two months than I did in a year when I began. And his pronunciation is amazing, seeing that sometimes he's as broad in all ways as a Billingsgate porter.'

I was sipping at my coffee when he said, quietly, 'Would you like to adopt him?'

'*What*?'

He chuckled now as he said, 'That's how you must have sounded in the surgery to Mike with your Wh-at! every Monday morning. You know, you do sound funny when you say it like that.'

'I'm not the only one that sounds funny. You did say would I like to adopt him?'

'Yes, that's what I said.'

I was silent for a moment before I answered in the same way as I had done Gran, 'And him with a father, a mother and a half, a grandmother, and, as far as I can count, seven uncles and aunts. And you saying, adopt him.'

'Well,' his voice was sober now, 'as far as I can see it, dear, between his father and his mother and a half, and his seven uncles and aunts, his future is going to stand a very thin chance. He'll end up either driving a lorry, or working in a

245

warehouse, or some such. And he'll become popular because of his quick mind, colourful vocabulary. And that will be about the limit of his career.'

'But...but, my dear, they'd never agree to that.'

'You don't know what they would agree to until you put the question to them.'

I remained quiet for a moment, and then I said, 'I don't think I could stand him running around this flat seven days a week; and he would upset you; it would be too much of a good thing.'

He put down his cup and his hand came out and sought mine. 'My dear, let's face facts. Now, now, don't get agitated.' He shook my hand. 'There's bound to come a time when he won't irritate me, let's put it like that.'

'*Nardy, Nardy, please*, I won't listen to you.'

'All right, my dear, don't listen to me, only think about it.' His blue lips stretched into a broad smile as he ended, 'Consult Hamilton. Yes, that's what to do, consult Hamilton, and, of course, his good lady.'

'Oh, Nardy.' I pulled my hand away from his, picked up the coffee cups and put them on to the tray, shaking visibly as I did so while I said, 'I don't need to consult anyone. And, I am not going in for adoption. So get that out of your head, Mr Leviston.' And on that I left the room, and I arrived in the kitchen at a run where, dropping the tray on to the table, I flopped into a chair and held my face in my hands. But I daren't cry, because I knew that once I gave way to the despair that was in me there would be a deluge that I should be unable to control.

246

At about half-past three the following day I heard the ring from the downstairs hall, and as I went to open the door I was thinking it could be Bernard Houseman and his wife or the Freemans, or someone else from the office. But to my utter amazement, there, stepping out of the lift was the tiny form of Harold.

'What on earth!' I looked beyond him, then asked, 'Where is your...?'

'I came meself.' He had walked past me and, after closing the door quickly, I grabbed at his collar, swung him round and said, 'You came on your own? It's nearly dark. Do ... do they know?'

'No. They were asleep.'

Asleep. Of course, after a Sunday dinner and likely their usual swig of beer, the men, like those in the north, would be taking their Sunday afternoon nap. But surely not Janet.

'Your...your grandmother?'

His brief reply gave me the picture.

'It's all right,' he assured me airily now; 'I know me way. I get on the bus for school, but comin' this way I didn't get off at Gag's corner, I come all the way. I have enough money.' He put his hand in his anorak pocket now and held out his palm upwards towards me and on which lay three ten pence pieces and one penny piece.

I looked around me as if searching for someone to tell me what to do with this child, and then, my eye catching the telephone, I said, 'I must phone your grandmother,' or at least, I thought, the shop on the corner who would get in touch with her.

247

She had given me the number in case I should want her in an emergency. I rushed to the telephone table, but he was there by my side, his hand on my waist, pleading now, 'Please, Mrs Nardy, don't get Gag to come. She'll only belt me. She belted me yesterday 'cos I followed 'er to the bus.'

'But Harold'—I leant over him—'they'll be worried to death when they find you're gone.'

'They won't 'cos I was out to play.'

'But they would expect you in—well...for your tea.'

'Mrs Nardy.' His voice was quiet, unusually quiet for him, its tone a deep plea. 'I ... I want to stay 'ere 'side of you an' ... an' Mr Nardy. I ... I won't make any noise. I'll sit quiet in the kitchen with Sandy, an' I can wash up.' He nodded his head. 'I wash up for Gag, an' I take the ashes out.' He looked around and, seeming to remember there were no ashes here to be taken out, he ended lamely, 'I can do things.'

I straightened up, closed my eyes tightly, bit on my lip, then said, 'Go in the kitchen. Keep quiet; I'll be there in a minute.'

I got on the phone to the shop. I asked if they could please get a message to Mrs Flood, and to ask her to phone me. They weren't very enthusiastic, it being Sunday, but they said they would. I went into Nardy and, standing by the bed, I said, 'We've got a visitor.'

'Yes, who?'

'Childe Harold. He's come on his own.'

'No.'

'But yes. What am I to do?'

His smile slowly widened and he said, 'I
248

suppose you've phoned Janet?'

'Yes. Well, I mean when the shop people get to her.'

'If they do and she phones, tell her he's going to stay here tonight and there's no need for her to worry.'

'*Oh, Nardy.*'

'*Oh, Maisie,*' he mimicked. 'Funny isn't it; the adoption's on the other foot now so to speak.'

Adoption. Adoption.

The phone rang and I went to the side table. I could hear Janet's voice but she talked so quickly I couldn't understand what she was saying. And so I put in, 'Janet, it's all right, he's quite safe, he's here, and he's going to stay the night.'

'What! What did you say, ma'am?'

'I said, Harold's here. He was very naughty to leave as he did, but it's perfectly all right. He's going to stay the night.'

'Oh, my God! ma'am. You mean, Harold, he's...he's come all the way there himself?'

'Well, what did you think I was saying?'

She said something now to which I could not refer: she had thought that Nardy must be worse or dead. And then she cried, 'He just went out to play down at the Flannagans. I saw him running round mad, with their dog. Then I just sat down and looked at the telly. Oh, God in heaven! what's to be done with that boy? I'm so sorry. I'll come...'

'You won't, Janet, you just won't. Now, do as I say, stop worrying. He won't be a nuisance. He's as good as gold. I'll get him up in the morning and if you get here a little earlier with his school things, you'll get him there in time.'

'Oh, ma'am.' There was a long sigh; then, 'I won't be able to keep me hands off him.'

'You will, Janet, you will, or I'll never forgive you. I'm going to say it now, but I've said it before, you must stop hitting him, especially across the ears. And another thing I can tell you, Mr Leonard is very pleased that he is here. When the doorbell rang, he thought it was some boring individual from the office, but he brightened up considerably when he knew it was his Saturday morning friend. Now I'll see you in the morning. Don't worry. Bye-bye.'

As I put the phone down, Nardy said, 'You can't only write tales, you can tell them. Well, go and bring him in. And you're right, I shall be pleased to see him.' And he was.

The boy sat quietly by the bedside for the next hour, regaling Nardy with stories of the exploits of Flannagan's dog, and of Mr Flannagan who apparently went to confession on a Saturday night and then got drunk but was always steady enough on a Sunday morning to go to Mass. And apparently Harold's Uncle Max could do Mr Flannagan, as Harold said, like as if he was on the telly, like. And when he ended solemnly, "'E makes game 'e's in church, 'e does, an' says,

"Please Father I want to say me prayers
'Cos I kicked me wife up the apples and
    pears."'"

It was too much. Choking, I almost hauled him out of the room because I was afraid of the result of Nardy's laughter, for he was holding himself as if in pain.

In the kitchen, the entertainer said to me, 'I never said nothin', well, not swears or anythin'. I just said about Mr Flannagan...'

'It's all right. It's all right.' My eyes were blinking back the water. 'But you see, Mr Nardy isn't very well, as you know, and if he laughs too much it might bring on a pain.'

'Oh...you're not vexed then?'

'No, I'm not vexed.'

I made the mistake again of bending down and kissing him; and once more I was enveloped in a choking hug.

Adoption! Adoption!

*   *   *

I shall pass over the Monday morning and the meeting between Janet and her grandson, because I knew how difficult it was for her to keep her hands off him, when he greeted her with, 'I didn't cause an uproar, Gag. Ask Mrs Nardy.'

It was on the Wednesday morning that we got a surprise, an actual letter from Tommy. We'd had a few cards but this was the first real correspondence. Nardy said, 'You open it. Read it out.'

The letter was short; it didn't even cover a full page. It told us that he had been laid up with a bug, but a couple he had met, a Mr and Mrs Atkins, had been kind enough to let him stay with them. The letter finished by saying, he just wanted to wish us a happy Christmas, and he didn't know where his next stop of call would be but that he intended to go to the Rockies.

After reading the letter I remarked sarcastically,

251

'Brief and to the point, very unlike Tommy,' then handed it over to Nardy; and, he scanning it, said, 'It's his new friends' private notepaper. There's an address on the envelope.'

When I said, 'Well, I don't think I'll be writing back,' he made no comment.

I felt bitter against Tommy these days: of all Nardy's friends and acquaintances, it was he that Nardy would like to see pop in each day. But no, he had to go off to find himself. Well, I hoped when he did find himself, he wouldn't be disappointed with what he saw.

Either Gran, or Mary, or George phoned every day; and it was strange, but when Gran asked if she should come down and, to use her own words, give me a hand, I had replied quickly, no, there was no need for that; everything was under control. Why was it that I couldn't bear the thought of either her, George, or Mary living with me day in, day out? I knew I still loved George and Gran and that at one time I should have been pleased to spend any hour of the day with either of them.

The thought conjured up Hamilton and Begonia. I was surprised to see them for they hadn't put in an appearance for some time now. Hamilton looked at me while pursing his great lips, and he said, Well, don't let that worry you. You've grown up, you've moved away, not only to another place, but inside your head. You know that piece in the Bible about, When you are a child you act as a child, but when you are a man . . .

I waved him to a stop. I knew all about the piece from the Bible, but I couldn't see that when one matured one's feelings towards those one loved could change, or should change. Yet, I wondered if my estranged feelings had started with the refusal by Mary and George to take up my offer of a new house; they said they had already made arrangements to go into a council house. And Gran had backed them up. It was she who with her non-tact said they thought that none of what had happened would have taken place, at least not to them, if they'd had a place of their own.

* * *

It was on the Saturday night when I was lying by Nardy's side that he said, 'Maisie, let's talk.'

I did not say what about, because his words had heightened the dread that seemed to be gathering speed these last few days.

And then my feelings became almost unbearable when reaching out my hand to turn out the light, he said, 'Leave it. I want to look at you.'

Over the great lump in my throat I brought out the words, 'Nardy, please, don't tire yourself. Go to sleep.'

'I'm past being tired, dear, and I'm not going to sleep until I have to.'

What did he mean by that? 'Oh, God!' I said to myself. 'Don't let him talk to me about when...'

'You know, dear, you've given me the happiest period of my life. It's been short compared to the rest of it, but I'd give up the whole just to experience one day with you. Please, please, dear, don't cry. Now Maisie'—he was patting my

253

cheek—'don't, I beg of you, give way like that, because I have things to say.'

He went on talking, but I hardly heard his words because even my ears seemed to be blocked by my emotions and withheld tears. Yet they were alive to the cry in my head: Don't leave me, Nardy! Don't leave me! What would I do without him? He was my way of life, this new wonderful way of life. I couldn't go back, not even to those days between the freedom from Stickle and my marriage. I was still in limbo then, not believing anything good could happen to me. I now visualized the years stretching ahead with only Hamilton, and he getting larger and larger in my consciousness, because inside, I was a lonely creature; my real being wandered in arid places to where I had been thrust as a child by my mother. As any other normal human being, I needed hands to hold mine; I needed kind words; I needed friendship; but above all, I needed love and the feel of a body close to mine.

He had hold of my chin, shaking it, 'You're not listening.'

'I am.'

'What did I say last?'

When I was silent, he said, 'There you are. Maisie! Maisie! Maisie!' He again shook my face. 'You must listen. Don't close your mind to facts, it isn't like you. And it is a fact that I won't be much longer with you ...'

'*Oh. Nardy. Nardy.*'

'No, no. Now stop it. Listen.'

'I won't listen.' I pulled my face away from his hand. 'People with bad hearts can go on living for years and years, if they want to. That's the point,

254

if they *want* to. You're not putting up a fight; you're letting go. I've seen you, you're letting go. Yes you are. Yes you are.' I heard my voice getting higher and higher.

'My dear, be quiet. Now be quiet. I know people with bad hearts can live for years, but mine isn't only a bad heart. I've never gone over my medical history with you. I had scarlet fever as a child; it left me with a weakness then. I thought I had outgrown it.'

'But they can do anything today, they can give people new hearts.'

'Yes, I know that. But in this case ... my case, there is the complication that is no use going into, and ... and the fire didn't help.'

I half buried my face in the pillow as I muttered, 'Stickle, and through him, me. If it hadn't been for me ...'

'Don't be silly, woman. You could say, if you hadn't been born, or if I hadn't been born, we wouldn't have met. These things happen. But, look at me.'

Through a thick mist I looked into his dear, dear face and those kindly eyes, and I listened to him as he said, 'There are one or two things I want you to promise me that you'll do. First of all, try to adopt the child. If it had been possible I myself would have taken this matter up, because I should like to see that boy make something of himself. The second thing is, you must keep on writing. Not about Hamilton, no; write about people; you have a very good insight into people. And, lastly, and this to my mind is the most important, you must not let yourself be lonely, you must marry again.'

255

I actually did spring away from him almost out of the bed, and I said one word: '*Nardy.*'

'Yes, my dear?' His tone was gentle, even had a thread of amusement in it.

'You can say that to me?'

'Yes, yes, I can say that to you.'

'Well, Mr Leviston, which of the line of suitors would you suggest I take? Because there's dozens of men out there breaking their necks to ... to ...'

He caught my hand and gently drew me towards him again. 'You know, my dear, that's your fault. It's been practically inbred in you, you undervalue yourself. Oh'—he made an impatient movement—'forget about looks. You can't live with looks, they fade, it's the personality that counts, it never fades, it grows, it deepens.'

'Nardy'—my voice was low now—'are you thinking of Tommy?'

He made a sound in his throat like a choked cough; then he said, 'Well, I won't say he wasn't in my mind.'

'Well, I think you'll have to scratch him off the list, dear, because all Tommy wanted, if he only knew it, was another mother.'

'Don't we all. That's why I took you.'

'Please, please be serious.'

'I was never more, my darling, never more. But apart from Tommy, you will find that your horizon won't be devoid of males, for one reason, you are a name now.'

'And they'll want me only for my money, which they would find is surprisingly little.'

'Not with my not so small estate attached to it.'

I knew that Nardy owned this part of the house. I also knew that his mother had left him another property further into the city. I had seen it. It wasn't a very prepossessing place, a tallish house let off into four offices. And as if picking my thoughts, he said, 'That little city block is worth a small fortune at today's prices. So you'll be quite a warm lady. Then there will be the pension.'

'*Nardy. Please.* I beg of you. I've never had any money, not real money, so it doesn't really matter what...'

'Don't be silly. And don't say money doesn't matter. You only say money doesn't matter when you have plenty of it. If you were left alone without money it would matter, and very much.'

He was right; as usual he was right.

As I went to put my arms around him my toe accidentally rubbed against a bad part of his leg, and when he winced I said, 'Oh my dear, have I hurt you?'

'You've never hurt me, or anybody in your life,' he said. And at this and with tears running down my face, I spluttered, 'You've forgotten I went to jail once for trying to knock somebody off.' And at this, he too, laughed gently. Then we lay close and quiet and I died and died again until we went to sleep. Who went first I don't know. I only know that the next morning I woke with a start, fearing at what I should find on the pillow beside me. But he was asleep and still with me.

CHAPTER EIGHTEEN

Nardy died at the beginning of the second week before Christmas.

I awoke this morning and he was no longer with me; he had gone. How long I lay beside him with my arms holding him, I don't know; I only know that Janet came in and found me like that and pulled me from the bed. Strangely, I hadn't cried, and all that day, and the next, and the next, I didn't cry. When I phoned Mike that morning, he said, 'Keep your pecker up, girl. I'll be with you shortly. Just remember this: You've had love and happiness not known to many. Like everything precious, such things are either small or short.'

When I phoned George, his response was characteristic. 'God, no!' he said. 'I'll bring Gran down.'

He brought Gran down the following day, and it was from the moment she entered the flat, or rather the kitchen, that the feeling of harmony left the place, because she became violently jealous of Janet, and Janet had never taken to her. But I took little notice of it at the time, although when she said openly, while looking down on Harold, 'That child shouldn't be in the house,' I had to say openly to her, 'Nardy would want him here to be with me, Gran. In fact, it was his wish.' She took real umbrage, hardly speaking for the rest of the day.

Nardy was cremated. Although the weather was really awful, there was an amazing number of people in the chapel. It is strange, but immediately after Janet had pulled me from him until his coffin had disappeared I had felt I had lost him, he had gone forever; but when I came out of the chapel, it was as if he were near me, his spirit was almost tangible. At one point, when someone was shaking my hand and offering their

258

condolences, I saw him standing with Hamilton and Begonia and, strangely, my mother. Their faces looked bright, even happy, as they looked towards me, seemingly over the shoulder of the man who would keep talking until George took me by the elbow and led me to the car, in which Janet and Gran were already seated.

Much to Gran's chagrin, I had insisted on Janet riding with us. As I had explained to Gran, Janet had practically brought Nardy up; she had been with him since he was born. Gran, I recall, had said nothing, only given me a very odd look. Her feelings were to be expressed to me later.

Mike had been unable to get to the funeral. One of his partners was off sick and there was an epidemic of colds and flu keeping him busy most of the day and quite a part of the night. But he arrived at eight o'clock that night, having flown down.

All the friends and sympathizers had left. There were only Janet, Gran, and I in the house, and, of course, Harold. When I look back, the sense of that boy at that time amazes me even now, for he did exactly what he was told. He remained quiet, but whenever he was near me he took my hand and held it firmly, and never uttered a word.

However, it wasn't until I saw Mike's hairy face that the built-up emotions in me were set free and, held in his arms, I went into a paroxysm of weeping as I had once done when I had lost Bill. But now, I hadn't only lost a dog, this time I had lost my love, my stay, that wonderful man who had told a small plain partially deformed woman that he loved her.

Mike let me cry for a while; and then, in that

259

voice of his I remembered from the surgery days, he said, 'Now that's enough. Come on. That's enough. Life's out there; it's got to be seen to. Now, you either stop or I give you the needle, and that'll put you to sleep for the next twenty-four hours. What about it?'

Presently I choked to a standstill and, sitting on the couch, my head on his shoulder, I whimpered, 'What am I going to do, Mike?' and he answered practically, 'What all women in your position have to do, or go under: face up to the fact that your life has changed, the pattern has altered; you've got to start, as it were, cutting out a different frock.'

It was later that evening when I was sitting, dull and slumped, that he said, 'I like that little fellow. Nardy wanted you to adopt him, didn't he?'

I was brought from my lethargy and my eyes widened as I said, 'He told you?'

'Oh, yes; I had a letter from him a few weeks ago.'

'You did?' The surprise in my voice made him repeat, 'Yes, I did. Is there anything strange about that?'

Yes, there was, because Nardy hadn't told me he had written. I couldn't remember posting a letter in Nardy's handwriting to Mike. I would have remarked on it at the time had I done so.

'So, what about it? There's little chance of you having any of your own, you know, after that bad do you had. You must think about it.'

'Oh.' I shook my head. 'It's impossible. I told Nardy. He's got a houseful of uncles and aunts, and a mix-up of his parents, and a grandmother...'

260

'And the whole bunch would likely jump at the chance of your taking him on.'

'I can't see it that way, not...not at the moment.'

'Well, leave it. But it's a good idea. And don't forget, it was Nardy's wish.' Then he said, 'What's up with Gran? She's not her usual breezy self.'

'She's jealous of Janet, I think.'

'Oh. Oh, I see.' Mike nodded. 'Of course, she would be. She looks upon you as her own bit of property, and she's too old to let go. Women are queer cattle. Do you intend to go on living here?'

'Oh, yes, yes.'

'You wouldn't think about coming back to Fellburn?'

'No, no. Never.'

'What will you do with yourself then? Have you made any really close friends?'

I hadn't to think for an answer, but again said, 'No. No, I haven't.'

'Then, you're going to find life very bare, my dear.'

'I'll get through.'

After a moment's pause he put his arm round my shoulder, saying, 'Yes, yes, of course you will.'

Mike's departure the following day left the house empty of male influence, except for the boy in the kitchen. And it was to be deprived still further, before very long, of female influence this time.

At about eleven o'clock of the morning of the day before Christmas Eve I was sitting in the drawing-room staring at the fire, thinking of our first Christmas together, and the house all decorated. And my tears were about to spring from my eyes again when the door opened and Janet came in. She had a cup of coffee on a tray, and after placing it on a side table, she looked down at me and said, 'Ma'am, I'm sorry to say this, but that kitchen isn't big enough for the two of us, I mean for Mrs Carter and me. I'm upset as it is. I'm missin' Mr Nardy, you know that, ma'am, but somehow, she just won't fit in. She keeps going for the lad. Oh, I know I go for him, but there's different ways of goin' for a child. And he understands me. Anyway, ma'am, until she's gone I'll cut me hours down to two in the morn...'

'Well! you won't have long to wait if that's the case. I know when I'm not wanted.'

Neither of us had heard Gran come into the room. In full war cry, she now approached us, and when I held up my hand, pleading, 'Gran, this is not the time ...' she interrupted, 'There'll never be a better! Who does some people think they are any road? Here's me, knowin' you all your life.'

'Gran!' I actually screamed the name, at the same time getting to my feet. 'I can't stand this,' I said; 'I can't. I can't.'

I watched Janet bow her head, then turn and hurry from the room. And there we were, Gran and I, facing each other. And now, my voice calmer, I said, 'What's the matter with you, Gran? Here I am, in this state of not knowing what I'm going to do without Nardy, and you acting like ... like ...'

'Like what, lass? Like what?' Her voice was harsh.

And mine was equally harsh now as I replied, 'Well, not like yourself, the understanding woman that I've always known.'

'Well, when we're gettin' down to home truths, you're not like yourself either, an' haven't been since you came to live up in this quarter. You've grown away from us.'

'That's not fair; I've done no such thing. But...but we've all changed since the fire.'

Quite suddenly I saw the stiffness go out of her body, and she let out a deep sigh, saying, 'Aye, since the fire. Perhaps you're right, nothin's been the same.' Then her voice taking on the edge of its former tone, she said, 'But there I was, dashing up here to look after you an' see to things, an' what do I find? Her runnin' the place; an' that lad. He's a cheeky little bugger and wants puttin' in his place. And that's all I've tried to do. What there's about him you can take to, God alone knows.'

At a different time I could have laughed and replied, Because he's a male replica of yourself, Gran. Instead, I said, 'I've already explained to you that Janet has been in this house since Nardy was a baby, and she's been very good and helped to look after him ... and ... and obliging me...'

'Oh yes, that's her favourite word; I'm obligin'. That maddens me; you would think she was doin' it for nothin'. She gets a good enough screw I bet, besides rollin' in it, I would say, with eight of 'em.'

'She isn't rolling in it, Gran. The eight of them, I think, are without exception all hanging on to her ... You've never tried to get to know her.'

'An' I don't want to. She's a different kind from

263

me. All them down here are.'

'That's prejudice, Gran.'

'Aye, well, you can put what name you like to it. It's always been the same an' it always will, the north and the south are like two different countries. As somebody said in the club the other night, we're nearer to the Germans than we are to the southerners. An' I think he was right.'

I had a retort to make to this, but I stilled my tongue as I thought, Yes, perhaps, she's right, for, as long as there were people with closed minds like herself, the north and the south would be at variance. And which side was at fault? More so us, I thought, we northerners, for we were insular, we were afraid to move away from the known. And there was a thread of bumptiousness running through our genes to cover up our feelings of inadequacy. The result was, I'm as good as thee, lad. And everybody who tried to rise above the norm, was an upstart.

But yet Gran was right in one way, I had changed. My outlook and opinions now weren't those I held three years ago, even apart from the tyranny I'd undergone under Stickle.

I looked at Gran now. Her head was bowed and the tears were oozing from under her lashes. Quickly I went to her and put my arms about her, saying, 'Don't...don't cry, please.'

She sniffed, wiped her eyes, then said, 'I feel ashamed of meself, lass. I shouldn't have gone on like this. But to tell you the truth, I'm missin' the bairns an' one thing an' another.'

Again I thought, how odd human nature was. Gone from her was the idea that the bairns just belonged to Mary and had no connection with her

264

son: they were her bairns now, she was their gran. And the one thing and another that she referred to was her bingo, and her club nights. She had been told how sorely she had been missed at the club during her illness, and I could well imagine it: she was a voice there; she could be amusing; she was the one who could start up a sing-song; she was the one to get things going. I had never thought up to this moment about the contrast between her life in Fellburn and that which she was experiencing in this house. If I had, I should have imagined that she would have looked upon the sojourn with me as a holiday, even under the present circumstances. But no, she had been bred in the north. She had lived there all her life; she was a woman of the north, and of her particular class, let's face it, of her particular class, in which she was happy. Take her, and any other like her, out of it, and what happened? Conflict, unhappiness. To put it in her own words, A fish out of water.

'Would you like to go home, Gran? Now, now'—I patted her cheek—'I'm all right here. You haven't got to worry about me. I've got to face up to my kind of life, and it's to be lived in this house where all the memories of Nardy are. I've got to get used to being on my own some time or other; and ... and I'll have my work...'

What was I talking about, having my work? I didn't think I'd ever put pencil to paper again; there was no incentive. As for my imaginary friends? They had vanished as surely as Nardy had done. My mind had, as it were, become merely a receptacle for pain and a new kind of loneliness. While I was married to Stickle, I

265

longed to be alone; only when I was alone did I have any peace. But after my life was joined to Nardy's, I was alone when I wasn't with him: there was always the fact that he would be in for tea, that we would lie side by side through the night, that we'd have the week-ends together. Now what stretched before me? I didn't know. I couldn't visualize how time would be filled.

'What did you say, Gran?'

'I said, lass, are you sure you wouldn't mind if I went home?'

'No, of course not. And you would like to be there for the holidays, wouldn't you?'

'Aw, lass, I couldn't leave you by yourself here on Christmas Day.'

'Now look, don't you worry. Alice Freeman is determined to yank me off for Christmas, and for as long as I'd like to stay afterwards. I've had invitations, too, from here and there. So I've got a choice. Now look, I'll send a telegram off, and I'll put you on the afternoon train.'

'Oh, no, lass, I couldn't leave you like that, not at a minute's notice.'

'Well, if you don't go today, you won't be able to get on a seat on the train tomorrow.'

'I feel I'm desertin' you, lass.'

'Don't be silly. I'll feel more content myself if I know that you're back with the family.'

I watched her face lighten and she put her hand out and gripped my arm, saying, 'You wouldn't come back with me, would you? You needn't fear anything now, and...'

'No, Gran, no. I know I needn't fear anything, but it will be a long time before I can face up to going north again. The house business has been completed. As you know I'm not having it rebuilt, and those on either side have been compensated for what damage was done to their property ...' My voice trailed off, and she said, 'I understand, I understand.' She now put her arms around me and we kissed. And when she muttered brokenly, 'I'm sorry. I'm sorry,' I pressed her away from me, saying, 'Now, now stop it, and go and get your things packed, and I'll see about that telegram.'

When she left the room I sat down and after letting out a long, long, drawn breath I almost said, 'Thank God!' only to chastise myself: How could I feel so relieved that she was going; I was fond of Mary and the children, but I loved her and George, they were woven into my life. She was right, I had changed. Indeed, indeed, I had changed. I had changed because I had met a man like Nardy, and he had shown me another side to living.

Oh, Nardy, Nardy. How am I going to bear life without you?

CHAPTER NINETEEN

It was Christmas Day and I was alone. I couldn't take in the fact that I was alone. I had been awake since five o'clock. I got out of bed at seven and made myself a cup of coffee, and I switched on the radio, to hear a sanctimonious voice saying, 'All over the country, and in many parts of the world, children are excitedly examining their Christmas presents. Fathers are testing model trains they've given to their sons; mothers are oohing and aahing over dolls they've presented to their daughters; some so-called lucky wives are examining diamond pendants, their husbands exclaiming over hand-made silk shirts, the cuffs linked with ruby studs. At the other end of the spectrum, a man is saying, "Ta," for a pair of nylon socks, while his wife is trying on a fancy apron. But on this morning, even if only for a short time, there is, in the main, giving and taking and love...'

I switched off, went and had a hot bath, got dressed, then asked myself what I was going to do? I would not allow myself to dwell on the happenings of that first Christmas morning together because, had I done so, I was afraid that I would throw myself on the floor and beat the carpet with my clenched fists whilst demanding of God why He had recompensed me for my life of torture only, with the taste still full in my mouth, to cry, 'Enough! You were never made for happiness.'

Having walked from the drawing-room into the dining-room, from there into my study, then into the spare bedrooms, one after another, I found myself back in the drawing-room. I did not sit down, I looked out of the window. The day was grey and cold. But what did the weather matter? I would go out. I would go for a walk, perhaps go into a church and hear a service...No, no; because, there, I would likely break down. No, I would just walk, walk, with Sandy who, with the intelligence of the poodle breed, sensed sorrow in me and was as lost as I was.

We went out and we walked. By lunchtime I

was home again. I was used to London by now. I was used to the streets around this district, but I'd hardly encountered a dozen people in all the time I had been out. I had shut my eyes to the Christmas trees in windows and my ears to the sound of laughter coming from behind doors. And now, still fully dressed, I stood in the hallway and asked myself what I was going to do. I could phone Alice Freeman. Hadn't she pressed me to spend Christmas with them. But I had said that Gran was with me and I'd be all right. Bernard Houseman, too, had invited me to their place, but I had refused. As I stood there the phone rang, and I ran towards it. I don't know whom I was expecting, but when I heard Mike's voice I couldn't answer for a moment. He hadn't said, 'A Happy Christmas,' he had just said, 'How are you?'

His voice came again, saying, 'Are you there, Maisie? Are you there?'

'Yes, Mike, yes, I'm here.'

'What's this I hear?' he said. 'That Gran's come back? I was in the hospital this morning. I looked in on Kitty; they were all there.'

The lump in my throat threatened to choke me.

'Are you all right?'

'Yes, yes. Mike, I'm all right.'

'Is anyone with you?'

I looked first to the right then to the left, then said, 'Yes, yes, Janet and the boy.'

'Well, I suppose that's enough; you wouldn't want company at this time. But look, Jane and I are going to slip down early in the New Year. We'll stay over the week-end if you'll have us.'

'Of course, of course, Mike. I'd ... I'd love to

269

see you.'

'Well, I must be off now. I'll phone again later. Take care of yourself.'

'I will, Mike. I will. Thanks for phoning.'

They were all there. His words had conjured up Kitty's bed and the whole family around her. I closed my eyes tight while exclaiming aloud, 'I should have been with them. I should have gone with Gran. I can't stand this.' But I didn't want Gran's company, did I? nor George's, nor Mary's, nor the children's. Then what did I want? Who did I want?

I wanted Nardy.

Nardy's gone. Face up to it, Nardy's gone.

He's not; he's here, all about me. I spread my arms wide. Then, suddenly gritting my teeth, I said, 'Stop it! Stop it!'

I turned to the phone again. Now I was dialling the shop at the corner of Janet's street. I knew they wouldn't be open, but they would go and ask Janet to get on the phone.

It was almost twenty minutes later and I was still sitting in the hall in my hat and coat when the phone rang again, and Janet's voice came over, saying, 'Ma'am, are you all right? What is it?'

'Janet.'

'Yes, yes, ma'am, I'm here. What is it?'

'Janet. I'm on my own.'

'Oh God! What! On your own? I thought you were going to Mrs Freeman's?'

I had told Janet this, because she said that she would come in on Christmas Day if I was alone.

'I . . . I didn't go, Janet. Janet, do you think that Harold would like to come along this afternoon?'

'Yes. Why yes, of course. He'd come this

minute if I let him.'

'I ... I don't want to disturb your day, or the child's.'

'You certainly won't be disturbing his day. But look, I'll tell you what. I'm in the middle now of gettin' their dinner, but I'll get one of the lads to bring him along. Do ... do you want him to stay the night?'

'Yes, please, Janet. As long as he would like to. Perhaps over the holidays.'

'You're lettin' yourself in for something mind 'cos he'll want to bring some of his toys.'

'Oh, of course, I understand that, about his toys. And as for letting myself in for something, Janet. Oh, Janet, I'm so lonely.'

'Oh my God! I shouldn't have taken any notice of you. I should have come along. This lot could have fended for themselves.'

'No, no, please; if one of your sons would bring him, that would be wonderful, lovely.'

'Are you cookin' your dinner?'

'I ... I'm not hungry, Janet.'

'Oh, God in heaven! Christmas Day and no dinner!'

'Oh, there's plenty in the fridge, you know there is, and there are the pies and things you made the other morning.'

'Well, get somethin' into you. And there's soup in the freezer. Now see you get somethin'. I'll send him along right away.'

'Thank you, Janet. Thank you.'

I took my hat and coat off now and went into the kitchen. Harold was always hungry. I ... I would have to prepare something, cold or otherwise ...

271

It was an hour later when the bell from the hall rang. I went out and I met the lift. As soon as it came to a stop, he was there, wearing a very nice new cap and coat; but in contrast he had on his feet, a pair of black and white sneakers, also new, something like you would have seen one of the gangsters wearing in an old film. I guessed these had come from one of his uncles, the one with the sense of humour. His arms were full of parcels, as were those of the young man who was standing awkwardly behind him. Before I had time to say hello, Harold made the introduction. 'This is—er Uncle Rod, Mrs Nardy.'

I smiled at the broad-shouldered, square-faced young man, and he smiled at me, saying, 'How do?'

'Come in. Come in.' I marshalled them across the inner hall and into the drawing-room; and there, Harold, dropping his parcels on to a chair, again turned to his uncle, saying, 'This is it, like what I told yer.'

'Nice. Nice.' The young man's head was nodding as he turned it from one shoulder to the other, and he now added, 'Yes, nice, very nice.' Then, his tone changing, he looked down on his nephew and, in a voice very like his mother's, he said, 'You're lucky, son. You know that? You're lucky.'

'Would...would you like a drink?'

'No, thank you, ma'am. If it's all the same to you, I'll be makin' me way back. It's Mum, you see...loses her hair if we're not all in for the dinner.'

'Yer goin' to the pub?'

The young man looked sideways down on Harold now, saying almost under his breath, 'You watch it. Mind your tongue.'

'Well, are yer?'

I couldn't find words to save the young man further embarrassment, when Harold, turning to me, said, 'Gag says they're never out of the pub an' they've all got bellies like poisoned pups ... D'yer want to see what I got for Christmas?'

'In a minute. In a minute. Take your coat and hat off and go into the kitchen and put your slippers on.'

I could see from the young man's face that he had great difficulty, not only in restraining his tongue, but his hand. And when his nephew, looking now at me, and then at his feet, said, 'I'm not gonna take these off; me Uncle Max give 'em me,' Janet was reincarnated in her son when he almost bawled, 'Do what the lady says, an' get 'em off! Go on, or else.'

Harold went, but with a backward glance and a grin at his uncle, who now turned to me, saying in a tone that spelt his bewilderment, 'You sure you want him to stay, missis?'

'Yes, I'm sure.'

'Huh!' His head was shaking again. 'It's funny. It's as Mum says, you can manage him, but you're about the only one that can. He's a holy terror. An' him learnin' to speak French. That nearly killed the lot of us.' His voice trailed off now, his head drooped and he said, 'I'm sorry, missis, about...about your loss. All me life I've heard me mum talk about Mr Leonard. He was a

273

fine man. Well, missis.' He moved from one foot to the other, and I said, 'Yes, he was a fine man, and your mother was very fond of him.'

He nodded, then muttered, 'Well, I'll be off now. You're sure you'll be all right?'

'Yes, I'll be all right. Thank you. And thank you for bringing the boy.'

'It was a pleasure, missis, it was a pleasure. And as the youngster's always said, this room's like a queen's palace.'

'He says that?'

'Oh aye; he's always talkin' about Mrs Nardy's queen's palace.'

He had reached the lift when he said, 'I forgot to tell you, Mum'll be along later.'

'Thank you. Goodbye.'

'Goodbye, Mrs Nard … Leviston. It's been a pleasure meetin' you. Goodbye.'…

I now went into the kitchen, but Harold wasn't there. I went into the drawing-room, and there he was sitting on the rug before the fire with his slippers on, his Christmas parcels spread around him and Sandy lying amidst them. He was in the process of winding up an object that looked half animal and half human. But he got to his feet when I entered the room, and when I sat down in the chair he came and stood by my side and, looking up into my face, he said, quietly, 'Yer were all on your tod, weren't yer?'

I pressed my lips together to try to stop their trembling. I widened my eyes. I sniffed audibly and when, his voice still low, he said, 'I liked Mr Nardy. I liked him a lot,' it was too much. My head drooped, the tears blinded me, and when I felt him climbing onto my knee and his arms go

274

tightly around my neck, I knew that here was the answer, Nardy's answer, to my lonely cry. This child had to be mine.

CHAPTER TWENTY

The weeks passed into months. It was May again. I looked back and asked myself how I had come through this time. But since taking on the care of Harold, which included making arrangements for him to attend a small private school, my days had been pretty well occupied; but my nights had remained, for the most part, wide-eyed and sleepless ... and lonely. I did not now have even the comfort of Hamilton and his Begonia. It would have been as puzzling to a psychiatrist, as it was to myself, that bereft of what the psychiatrist would have termed hallucination, I was dull, I lacked initiative, and was apparently very normal, whereas, generally whenever these two appeared on the screen of my mind I was happy and full of quirky humour, or at least alive to life.

Definitely, I think that Harold could be given credit for saving me from a breakdown. Not that my new change had been an amenable subject. My main trouble had been and still was getting him to understand that it wasn't always funny to repeat the sayings of his uncles. And this matter had come to a climax today.

Harold had dutifully brought me a letter from Miss Casey, the lady who had turned her private house into a school for middle-class children between the ages of five and eight. I had explained my situation to Miss Casey when I first proposed sending Harold into her care. And she smilingly said she understood. Her first report of him had come at the end of a month, when she proudly stated that she had only twice heard him use a swear-word. And she was very pleased to inform me that he was above average intelligence for his age. And his grasp of elementary French was amazing in one so young and from his background. That was the first month.

The second month his report was not so glowing. It seemed it was difficult to get him to concentrate on any subject for very long.

Now here I was reading her letter, and the third month hadn't expired yet, there being another week still to go, and the gist of the letter was that Miss Casey thought it would be better if my charge could attend a more ordinary school where his language would not be so noticeable. It was distressing to state, she went on, but she'd had complaints from three parents whose children had surprised them with their knowledge of other than standard English. She had to admit that all the words didn't come under the heading of swearing but were, nevertheless, words that the parents did not approve of their children repeating.

I took Harold into my study. I had found it was a better place to talk to him. The drawing-room somehow altered my attitude towards him and his towards me, for there, he would curl up on the couch and beguile me with a smile or some funny remark, mostly about Miss Casey, or Miss Dawn, a wizened lady to whom you could only apply the word spinster, for she seemed to have dropped out of the middle of the last century. She was, I understood, a poor relation of Miss Casey. But in the study, which I have said was also a sitting-room, I kept him from the couch and made him stand to the side of the desk while I sat in the leather chair behind it.

'Well, now, what's all this about?' I wagged the letter in the air.

'That?' He pointed. 'It's a letter.'

'I know it's a letter, and it's from Miss Casey, and it's about you.'

''Bout me?'

'Yes, about you, and your language.'

'What lang-gage?'

'Your swearing.'

'I never. Well'—he turned his head to the side—'just a little bit, 'cos Piggy Caplin said I didn't know no more.'

I sighed. 'And of course you did know some more?'

'Just them bits Grandad Stodd said.'

'Gall-stones?'

He shook his head.

'What then?'

'Anty . . . mackassas.'

'What?' I screwed up my face, and he repeated loudly and slowly, 'Anty . . . mackassas. Gag used to put 'em on chairs like.'

'Oh, antimacassars.' I didn't smile, not outwardly. 'Is that all you said?'

Again he looked away.

'Come on,' I said. 'Come on; let's have it.'

He pursed his lips, then brought out, 'Sylvia Watson said that was nothin'; she knew a bigger one. Her mother had it in hospital.'

'Well, what did she get in hospital? What word

was that?'

'Histry.' I saw him thinking, then he added, 'Rectory. Histry-rectory.'

At this I closed my eyes as if I was shocked. I put my elbow on the table, and leant my head on my hand. Hysterectomy. I kept my hand tight against my cheek as he went on now, 'Nigel Broadhurst, he said it was nothin' an' all, an' that you wouldn't have to go to a hospital to get it, you would have to go to a church. And he should know 'cos his grandad's a parson like, an' wears a collar backside front, not like the Salvation Army crew.'

I took my hand away from my face and said, solemnly, 'And you didn't swear, not real swearing?'

'No, no, Mrs Nardy, I didn't, not...not today.'

'Oh. Did you yesterday, then? Or the day before?'

I watched him thinking again, and he said, 'I don't know, but Sylvia did. She swore today, she did, Sylvia Watson.'

'What did she say?'

'Well'—his head wagged—'she pushed me an' said I was always swankin' 'bout me words, an' she didn't believe there was an antymackassa. And when I said there was, she said, "Oh, you an' your anty ... bloody ... mack ... assa." So, she said it, not me. And Miss Dawn came out and put her hands over her ears. She didn't say anythin' to Sylvia, but she slapped my hands.' He held out his hands now; then brightly, he added, 'But it didn't hurt, not like when Gag wallops me ... But it was her not me wot said it ... Sylvia. An' she didn't belt her.'

278

Anty...bloody...mack...assar. Children learn quickly. And Miss Sylvia Watson was apparently another one of the bright ones.

What was I to do with him? The children at Primary school really did seem to proclaim the truth of all the good things that I had heard went on there. But I was worried that he would have to follow that by going to the nearest Comprehensive. I'd heard some of the boys as they scampered along the road, and their language was akin to that which Stickle had used on me. And as yet, Harold's had not got beyond damn, bloody, bugger, and that word I couldn't stand, which was sod.

I said, 'Go and wash your hands and have your tea.'

He didn't move. 'You mad at me or summit?'

His English hadn't improved either under Miss Casey's tuition.

'Something, not summit.'

'You still gonna 'dopt me then?'

'It all depends on what your father says and on how you yourself improve.'

He moved nearer to me, put his hand gently on my knee now, looked up into my face and said, 'I ... I don't want to go back to Gag's, I don't ... I won't. I won't go...I won't, Mrs Nardy.'

Now his lips were trembling, and I took his hand and said, 'Don't worry, you're not going back to your gran's. But don't forget what I've told you before, your gran's a fine woman, it is only that she has that large family hanging round the house that makes her impatient.'

He blinked his eyes, moved one lip over the other, then said brightly, 'Will I bring you a sup

279

tea?'

'A cup of tea. Where did you get sup tea from?'

'Your gran says sup tea.'

And Gran was here for only a day or two.

I was about to say, 'Yes, I'll have a cup of tea,' when the bell rang.

Rising to my feet, I said, 'Go on, have your tea, and take Sandy with you. I'll see who that is....

I opened the door into the outer hall just as the lift stopped. The door gates swung open and out stepped a tall man. He was very thin; his skin was tanned to a dark brown; only his eyes and voice were recognizable. He moved into the hall and stared at me, and I caught my breath and said softly, 'Tommy.'

'Hello, Maisie.'

Even his voice seemed to have changed. It had a rusty sound like that of someone unused to speaking.

I backed from him, pushed open the door into the inner hall, closed it after him, then held my hands out for his hat and the light coat he was wearing.

We exchanged no words as we went towards the drawing-room, but I saw him smooth his hair back and noted that it must have been cut recently.

In the drawing-room he did not pause as I might have expected and make a remark about the room as he had done once before, but he followed me to the middle of the room, and when I pointed to the armchair, he sat down. And I sat on the couch, but towards the edge of it. He was the first to open the conversation, and he did so by saying, 'You all alone?'

'No ... well, not really. I have Harold with me. You know, the little fellow. And there's Sandy. They're in the kitchen.'

'How've you been?'

'Oh ... well, you know.' I spread out my hands. Then I asked, 'When did you hear about Nardy?'

I watched him ease himself further back into the chair, then cross his long legs before looking from one hand to the other where they were resting on the arms of the chair; then he said, 'I think I knew about it the day I received his letter. Although, I didn't get confirmation of it until I got yours about six weeks later.'

'Nardy ... Nardy had written to you?'

'Yes, yes, he wrote to me.'

Nardy had never said anything about writing to him either.

'You were travelling then?'

'In a way, yes. I'd come down from the Rockies and was in Calgary. Then I went back again.'

The old bitterness against him returned. He went back up again without writing a note of condolence after hearing that his one and only real friend had died. I asked with not a little sarcasm in my tone, 'Did you find yourself up there? That's what you were looking for, wasn't it?'

He didn't answer for some seconds, but kept his eyes on me; then, his lips going into a twisted smile, he said, 'Yes, Maisie, you could say I found myself, but I didn't much like the look of me. Maisie'—he brought his body forward towards me—'don't hold bitterness against me; Nardy didn't, and he should have.'

'Yes, he should have.' I was nodding at him

now. 'You, his so-called...life-long friend, could walk out on him when he most needed you. Oh, yes, he had me, but you were in his life long before I came, and you walked out of it with never a care towards...'

'Don't say that!' His manner changed abruptly, and I saw him now as I had seen him the night he had stood in this room and told us of his mother's duplicity. 'Who are you to condemn? You know nothing about it. While being the centre of it and the cause of it, you still know nothing about it.'

This new tone and manner was like a physical onslaught: I sat back in the couch pressing my back tight against it as he went on, 'I loved Nardy like a brother, but that love turned into an intense hate. I became eaten up with it. I ... I ...' Suddenly his back straightened, his eyes closed and his teeth clamping down onto his lower lip drained the blood from it.

The drawing-room door opened abruptly and Harold came running in, and stopped half-way up the room when he caught sight of the visitor. Then, his steps slow, he approached us, and I, at this moment thankful for his presence, was about to say, 'You remember Mr Balfour?' when Harold said, 'Hello.'

But it was with an effort I saw Tommy reply with, 'Hello.'

Scrutinizing the visitor, Harold said, 'By! your face is brown.'

'Yes, yes, I've been in the sun quite ... quite a lot.'

Harold now turned from Tommy and, coming to me, held out his hand, saying, 'Yer'd better come, 'e's done it on the mat again, all that

282

yellow stuff. I told him yer'd scud his backside.'

He had picked up the word scud from Gran: during her short stay here she'd often said in his presence that such a punishment should be meted out to him.

I rose, saying to Tommy, 'Would you excuse me a minute?' And Harold ran before me out of the room, crying loudly, ''E's had fish. Yer told me yer weren't goin' to giv 'im any more fish, the little bug ... beggar.' We were in the hall now and this imp of a boy turned his head up to me and smiled his impish smile as much as to say, 'There, you see, I didn't say it.'

Sandy greeted me with wagging tail and lolling tongue, but I demanded sternly, 'What have you been up to now, you naughty boy?' And his friend answered for him, ''Tisn't 'is fault if yer stuff 'im with fish. Uncle Max can't take fish, 'cos it's oily, he spews...'

'He's sick.'

'Who?'

'Your Uncle Max.'

As I wiped up the bile with a wet disinfectant soaked cloth, my charge stood by my shoulder as I knelt on the floor, his head level with mine; and his eyes looking into mine, he said, 'Sick, not spewed.'

'That's right.'

'Sandy was sick.'

'Yes, Sandy was sick.' As I rose from my knees I saw that look on his face which meant he was trying to work out why the same word should not be applied to a man vomiting as to a dog. And being unable to do this, he dismissed it and asked, 'Is 'e goin' to stay?'

'Who?'

'Im, Mr Wotsisname.' He thumbed towards the door.

'Mr Balfour?'

'Yes, 'im. Is 'e goin' to stay?'

'No. He's just calling.'

''E's big.'

'Yes, he's big.'

'Can I come back in with yer?'

'No, you can't. What I want you to do now is to put those things away off the table, and then get out your books, and I'll be with you shortly.'

'Can I take 'em into yer study?'

'No, you can't. You stay here with Sandy until I come back.'

'Tripe.'

'*Harold.*'

'I only said, tripe. Gag gets it from the butchers an' she puts taters on it.'

This was no time to go into the culinary effects created by Janet with tripe and the effect of the word on the ear when used to take the place of yet an even more telling adjective.

In the drawing-room once more, I said to Tommy, 'He's a bit of a handful, but very lovable.'

'Yes, I can imagine that. You couldn't be lonely where he was.'

I confirmed this point by saying, 'He's been a comfort to me of late, and before Nardy went we discussed adopting him.'

'Adopting him?'

'Yes.' I nodded. 'It was Nardy's wish, and mine too. The matter is under discussion at the moment.'

284

He sat back in his chair, his head drooping once again. Then, as if coming to a decision, he muttered, 'I've got to talk to you, Maisie. I ... I mean really talk, not just this polite jargon. I ... I must tell you why I acted as I did.' His head jerked up now as he said, 'May I sit beside you? I...I won't need to look at your face then.'

In a small voice I answered, 'Yes. Yes, of course, Tommy.'

He pulled himself up, then sat down on the couch my short arm's length from me, and, leaning forward once again, he put his elbows on his knees and joined his hands together before he began to talk. And his first words startled me. 'I am a potential murderer, at least in my mind. You see, Maisie, just shortly after I met you, I fell in love with you. I could never understand when in the office why anyone should question the reason Nardy would want to marry you. To me, at first, you were the antithesis of my mother: you were kind; you were loving; you had a sense of humour. One forgot, when in your presence, that you were small, or that you had a deformed arm, and, as you have so often stated yourself, had no claim to beauty. I thought then the feeling I had for you was bound up with that which I held for Nardy. But later, I realized that I was kidding myself. You will remember I made this house almost a second home for a time, presumably to get out of my mother's presence, but really it was to be in yours. But—' His whole body now seemed to heave as he drew in a long breath; then as it subsided, he went on. 'But my feelings for you weren't the reason I went away. It was because I was consumed with guilt. The fire did it. That fire didn't burn me physically, but it did mentally and spiritually. It ripped the skin off my hidden thoughts. In that smoked-filled attic, when I felt I was going to die, I thought, well, it was the best way out; it would save me being a traitor to my friend. This mightn't have been conscious thinking but I know now it was there. Then when I came out alive and heard that Nardy was in a bad way, one thought filled my mind...'

His head drooped further now towards his joined hands, and when he spoke, although his words were weighed with pain, they shocked me, for they were: 'I waited for him to die. I wanted him to die. I willed him to die ... Don't move away from me, Maisie, please, because I moved away from myself so much at that time I became a different human being, and the remorse will remain with me forever.'

I hadn't moved away from him. Although I was shocked by his words, there had erupted in me a feeling of pity for him. Yet at the same time there was also the feeling of amazement that I, who was exactly as he had described me a few minutes earlier and who knew myself to be unprepossessing, could have in me something that had the power to drive a man such as Tommy to such lengths. It wasn't real; it didn't seem possible. In a way, it was like *Beauty And The Beast* in reverse.

He went on talking: 'The feeling became strongest when I visited him in hospital. Each time after seeing him I got in that car and drove hell for leather, looking for an accident to happen. One day, I remember, after almost crashing into a car I stopped and got out and upbraided the fellow for his careless driving. I remember the man being almost speechless because I had come straight out of a side road and almost into him broadside on. And there were three children in his car. I think the man was in shock or he might have felled me for the things I said to him. The police sorted it out. After that I went to a psychiatrist. I remember he smiled and said I was still in shock from the fire; that this would pass, and to carry on my work as normally as possible. He said the love for this woman that I had which was driving me to act as I was doing towards my life-long friend was equivalent to a teenage crush. He ended by saying I was suffering a breakdown. I only paid him the visit. Then—' he turned his head now and looked at me, and after a second's pause he said, 'my thinking took another twist. I began to hate you for being the cause of breaking up my life-long friendship with Nardy and for this dreadful desire to see him dead that was eating me up. I had to get away. So I went, but still refusing to believe I was in a breakdown which had the seeds of its beginnings in Mother's death.'

He was looking at his hands again. His voice slow now, he said, 'I kept a diary for a time about the places I stopped at or passed through, and then I let it go. What did it matter? It was after arriving in Calgary that things changed. I was feeling ropey. Then I met this couple. They invited me to their home. I stayed for a week. It wasn't that they had taken a liking to me, I think it was simply because I was British; they were that sort of people. It was just before I left them that I sent you the note on their headed paper. I wouldn't face up to the fact that I wanted to hear how things were at this end. Anyway, I started on my travels again and came across a family in a place they called a home and in which I'm sure you would hesitate to leave Sandy. There were seven of them and all in one room including a father and mother, grandmother, and great-grandfather, the son, and his wife, and their child. And we all slept on wooden boards. But what was in that room beside all those people was peace, a kind of peace that I cannot explain. It was through talking with the son that I came to myself. I worked with my hands for the first time in my life, really worked, grubbing the earth. I've promised to go back, and I will sometime. One day he asked me a question: 'Are you better now?' he said, and I answered simply, 'Almost.' It was odd, for I'd never mentioned that I was ill, physically or in my mind. Anyway, the following week I picked up your letter. But still I did not hurry back. I purposely made my way slowly. The feeling of guilt had gone but the remorse still choked my step.'

He now turned and looked at me again. I knew this, but I wasn't looking at him, I was looking at Nardy's photograph that stood on a side table. He was smiling at me. And now at each side of the table, I saw my two friends standing, but as in a mist. Lately, since Harold had come, if I saw them at all, it was through a mist. Yet, even as I looked at them, Hamilton's form took on a more defined outline, and slowly he came towards me. And as he passed me, his eyes still on me, I turned my head and saw him put his front hoof on Tommy's shoulder. And there was Tommy now holding a letter out to me. 'Would you like to read that?' he said.

I took it and opened it, and saw Nardy's handwriting. It began:

'My dear friend,

   We won't go into the why's and wherefore's but time is running out. So let me say that, although I don't understand your attitude over the past weeks, I do understand the reason that lies at the bottom of it. When I am gone, Tommy, Maisie is going to be lost. I loved her dearly and she loved me in return. But death is death and life without companionship or love, I should imagine, is worse than death. I don't think she will fall into your arms right away, she is not that kind, but give her your friendship and company, and time will tell. My affection for you has never lessened, Tommy. You were my friend. You will always be my friend. Until we meet wherever the Gods direct.

Yours,
Nardy.'

It was like the day I lost Bill. A cry tore its way through my throat, the tears sprang from my eyes, nose, and mouth. Tommy's arms were around me, his voice was pleading, 'Oh, Maisie, Maisie, don't, don't. Please. I'm sorry. I shouldn't have shown you that, but I wanted you to know. Oh, please, please, dear. Maisie, I wouldn't upset you for the world.'

Then I knew there were other arms about me and claws pawing at me, for Harold was standing on the couch and Sandy was jumping up at my side, and Harold's voice penetrated my crying as he yelled, 'Yer done this, mister! I'll bloody well get my Uncle Max at yer.'

Slowly, but forcibly, I disentangled myself from the hands and the paws. Pushing both Tommy and Harold away, I leant back on the couch and when Tommy handed me his handkerchief, I dried my face. And as I did so, my champion demanded, 'Did 'e 'it yer?'

I told myself not to laugh for I would become hysterical. But I shook my head, then glanced at Tommy and said, 'No, he didn't hit me.' Then I added, 'He is Mr Nardy's friend.' But I had to turn my head away because I could not bear to see the look in Tommy's eyes, for I saw that he, too, at any moment might burst into tears.

When I handed Tommy his handkerchief back, he took my hand and held it firmly. Then, as if not to be outdone, Childe Harold caught my other hand. And there we sat linked for a moment in silence, and in it I saw Hamilton and Begonia emerge from the mist once again, their coats shining brightly, their manes flying, their tails outstretched. Slowly, they came towards me, stopped for a second and looked at me, then walked through me and were gone.

I closed my eyes.

One life had ended. Another was to begin.